ALSO BY CATHRYN GRANT

ALEXANDRA MALLORY PSYCHOLOGICAL SUSPENSE SERIES

The Woman In the Mirror ◆ The Woman In the Water

The Woman In the Painting ◆ The Woman In the Window

The Woman In the Bar ◆ The Woman In the Bedroom

The Woman In the Dark ◆ The Woman In the Cellar

The Woman In the Photograph ◆ The Woman In the Storm

The Woman In the Taxi ◆ The Woman In the Church

The Woman In the Shadows

SUBURBAN NOIR NOVELS

Buried by Debt ◆ The Suburban Abyss ◆ The Hallelujah Horror Show

She's Listening ◆ Faceless ◆ An Affair With God

THE HAUNTED SHIP TRILOGY

Alone On the Beach ◆ Slipping Away From the Beach ◆ Haunting the Beach

NOVELLAS

Madison Keith Ghost Story Series ◆ Chances Are ◆ Jealousy Junction

SHORT FICTION

Reduction in Force ◆ Maternal Instinct

Flash Fiction For the Cocktail Hour ◆ The 12 Days of Xmas

NONFICTION

Writing is Murder: Motive, Means, and Opportunity

PSYCHOLOGICAL & DOMESTIC THRILLERS

The Good Neighbor ◆The Good Mother ◆ The Guest ◆ The Assistant

The Other Couple ◆ Only You ◆ Always Remember ◆ Best Friends Forever

The Favorite Child ◆The Secret She Kept

THE WOMAN IN THE SHADOWS

A PSYCHOLOGICAL SUSPENSE NOVEL

ALEXANDRA MALLORY
BOOK THIRTEEN

CATHRYN GRANT

ISBN : 978-1-943142-71-2

This book is a work of fiction. References to real people, events, establishments, organizations, or locales are intended only to provide a sense of authenticity, and are used fictitiously. All other characters, and incidents and dialogue, are drawn from the author's imagination and are not to be construed as real.

Visit Cathryn online at CathrynGrant.com

Cover design by Lydia Mullins Copyright © 2022

CHAPTER 1

 ew York City

* * *

With Stephanie gone from my life, I had expected a rush of freedom. Instead, I was now sharing an apartment with her daughter, which was turning out to present its own, slightly different type of claustrophobia.

Knowing someone was interested in when I was coming home made me wonder if I'd made a deal with that mythical horned creature who had loomed in the shadows of my childhood, blamed by my parents for holding too much sway in my heart. I had exchanged my privacy and freedom for a larger, more luxurious apartment and the promise of upscale furniture. I'd traded psychological comfort for physical comfort.

For the most part, I was still content, but I was constantly aware of Eileen's presence. Before my race to escape from the curious eyes of Kent, to escape roaches and damp and stifling heat, I should have considered how different it would be from my previous shared living arrangements. Those relationships had been transactional, but now I was sharing space with someone who viewed me as a friend. We were *sharing our lives*, as she liked to say, sending chills down my spine, conjuring images of shackles around my ankles and cuffs around my wrists.

Within two weeks of moving in together, it became clear that we needed a more detailed discussion of boundaries. But when I suggested a meeting to hammer out the details of our agreement, she turned it into a party. She held up her laptop and showed me several open windows, telling me we could spend part of our *roomie meeting* viewing furniture and discussing our tastes and vision for the apartment. Then she told me she would make lasagna and salad. She asked me, but it sounded like a directive, to pick up a fresh baguette and a nice bottle of red wine. I smiled and lied—*no problem*.

The dinner sounded delicious. The furniture selection would be fun, but I wondered how I was going to weave in my boundary conversation while we sipped wine and drooled over creamy leather sofas and sleek, well-constructed dining tables and chairs.

She'd assured me it was her intention and *pleasure* to cover the cost of the furniture. I'd told her I didn't know how long I'd be staying in New York, which was true but also not entirely true because it implied I had definite plans to leave at some point, which I did not. Still, I was happy not to weigh myself down with a bunch of enormous objects. So we were in agreement. Except for the constant togetherness. And the expectations.

Eileen had assumed that when we were both home in the evenings, we would watch TV together or eat ice cream and talk. Our weekends would include pre-planned visits to museums and galleries and spontaneous shopping trips. When she suggested we should go running together, I felt as if someone had thrown a plastic bag over my head, shutting off my oxygen supply.

CHAPTER 2

*A*s I entered the apartment after work, the seductive aroma of tomato sauce, cheese, and meatballs consumed me. Eileen had put two gray tapers in glass candlesticks on the table. The flames swayed gently as I passed by, making the empty wine glasses glisten. Music was playing from the tiny speaker connected to her phone, and there was a vase of fresh flowers on the coffee table that she'd brought from her mother's house. I did not like having Stephanie's furniture in my apartment, so I was very eager to begin shopping for new things.

It would be best to have the boundaries conversation first, and then we could get to the fun part.

I asked if she needed help with the salad.

"Sit down." She poured a splash of wine into both our glasses and clicked hers against mine the moment I picked it up. "Cheers. To our new life together. Friends and roommates. Aren't we lucky." It wasn't a question.

She took a sip of wine. "How was your first day in the new manifestation of your consulting business?" Her voice softened, struggling to remain steady as she silently stepped around the fact that the changes in my job were the result of her mother's cold-blooded murder of Trystan and the wiping out of her own life.

"Surreal."

She took another sip of wine, fortifying herself in case the awful thing her mother had done crept into the conversation. "I kept expecting Trystan to walk down the hallway or step into my office. Seeing Diana sitting at his desk was ... it really was surreal. But even stranger, by afternoon, it seemed normal."

She nodded. Her eyes turned glassy with tears, but she didn't say anything about her mother or about her mother's brutal shooting of an incredible, fascinating man who deserved to live much longer than he had.

"We came up with a business name," I said.

"I never thought it made sense that Trystan refused to give the company a name."

"He thought it was too confining."

"But not having one was confusing." She opened the oven and pulled out the lasagna pan, setting it on the stovetop.

"That smells divine."

"Thanks. Melted cheese always does." She laughed. "I'll let it set for a few minutes." She put a wooden board with a sliced baguette on the table, refilled our glasses, and dribbled dressing onto the salad. "What's the name?"

"Fly Higher."

"Huh."

"It's a little clunky, but Diana's in love with it."

"I guess it gives an impression of what you offer, which is the important part. It gives a hint, although it's not really clear without some explanation."

I took a sip of wine. I put a slice of bread on my plate and smeared butter across it. I took a bite. While I chewed, she told me about her photoshoot that day—a layout for a department store's fall lineup of boots and designer jeans. "I got to choose a pair of boots as a bonus. I picked camel ankle boots with a little heel and square toes."

"They sound classic."

She served the lasagna and sat across from me. "I was thinking we could look at some decorating sites to get ideas of what environment we want to create before we just start scrolling through stores."

"I need to talk to you about something first."

She looked at me, her face bland and unconcerned.

"I'm feeling a little ... strangled."

She laughed. "What are you talking about?"

"Maybe that wasn't the best word." I cut a tiny meatball in half and watched the steam curl out from the center. "I like sharing an apartment, and it's great hanging out with you. But I need space and time to myself."

"You already told me that." She took a long swallow of wine. "I feel the same way."

"I don't think it's quite the same." Now, it was clear what the issue was. She assumed our desires had a similar intensity. She assumed that what she wanted was what I wanted, that what she felt, I felt. It was the same as someone mentioning their desire for *nice* clothes, referring to clothing from a nice department store, and the other person agrees but is picturing clothing purchased on Rue St Honoré in Paris.

"I like to spend time alone," I said. "I don't want to eat every meal together. Some weekends, probably most, I want to do my own thing."

Her eyes filled with tears so fast I wanted to hand her my napkin.

"It's me, not you," I said, plucking out of the air one of the most over-used clichés, although it didn't usually pop up in a conversation between women in a platonic relationship.

"I get that we both need space. I definitely need time by myself, but I thought ..." She swallowed a large slug of wine. "I thought we were friends. I thought you wanted to share our lives and have some of the same experiences. If you don't, why are we living together?"

Clearly, I couldn't tell her about my desire for a more spacious, attractive home, one that I couldn't afford or didn't *want* to afford on my own. That's what had shoved me too fast into casually shifting my priorities. At the same time, I did like doing things with her. Just not all the time, and I didn't like her asking for explanations.

The situation made me wonder if I would ever have people around me who were permanent facets of my life or if I would ever find a man I could live with. From what I'd observed, people wanted too much from each other. I wondered how they could breathe, how they could think freely, and make choices if they were constantly required to compromise and soothe the wounded feelings of others. "I do want to share our lives." The words sounded stiff and utterly fake. My usual skill at creating an effect that echoed the feelings shared by most others, concealing the essence of myself, had failed me. Maybe this living together thing meant exposing more of myself than I'd realized.

"It doesn't sound like you do." She finished eating her bread and stared morosely at the wine left in her glass.

I took a bite of lasagna. The music seemed louder than necessary as if we were playing it to cover up the awkward spaces in our conversation. I cut another section of noodles and cheese but left it on my fork. "It's great hanging out. I just don't like to plan every minute of my life. I like to spend a lot of time doing whatever pops into my head. Sometimes I want to go out to eat alone after work. I like to run alone—"

"You went hiking with Diana."

"One time." This was getting worse by the minute, and I had no idea how I was going to fix it. All I could think about was the furniture we were supposed to be drooling over. Why did relationships have to be so complicated? Why did I have to explain

THE WOMAN IN THE SHADOWS

anything at all? Maybe I shouldn't have tried to clear things up. I should have simply declined the next time she suggested another night of ice cream and chit-chat, or a movie, or plans for the weekend.

Never explain, never complain, suggests another well-used cliché.

Maybe the best plan was to get up at four in the morning and slip out for a run. She wouldn't know until it was too late. To simply not show up for dinner when I didn't feel like it. But that would probably create more complications. I wasn't going to start sneaking around so she wouldn't feel bad. Why did people have to be so sensitive?

"Are you here only because you can't afford rent on your own?" she asked.

"No."

"It's okay if you are, it would just be nice to know that upfront. *Would* have been nice to know that ..."

"Of course, I want to save money. Don't you? Paying rent in New York is impossible."

"I like it when people are straight with me," she said.

"So do I, and that's what I'm trying to be."

"So I'm smothering you."

I refilled our wine glasses. I glanced toward the living room, taking in the twenty-year-old furniture that had migrated from Stephanie's apartment to mine. I'd only been inside her apartment once, but that disastrous Thanksgiving was etched in my memory— too many tired pieces of furniture in a very tiny space. I turned back toward Eileen and awkwardly clicked my glass against hers that sat on the table. "I can't wait to get settled, and I know we're going to have lots of good times together." Maybe what I'd said was enough. She would walk on eggshells, knowing I felt crowded. I didn't need her to see what I meant or force her to acknowledge what I wanted. All I needed was space and freedom.

But killing people requires a whole lot more space and freedom than she could begin to imagine. She really had no idea what I was asking of her.

Looking at the wounded expression on her face, an expression she was trying to hide, gave me an unfamiliar sense of longing—I wanted a person in my life who experienced the world as I did. There had been a few over the years, but at that moment, I was reminded that I was a freak of nature. A shark in a pod of dolphins.

CHAPTER 3

During our first formal meeting, Diana showed a set of slides outlining our short-term plans. The first slide had a flow chart illustrating our hiring process and the positions we needed to fill, as well as the dates by which she wanted them filled. I had to give it to her that she was more organized than Trystan. I wondered what else I was going to learn about her over the next few weeks and months. I had a feeling she might have kept a lot of her thoughts, and any exposure of them through micro-expressions, well hidden. When we'd gone hiking, she'd said she would do things *differently* if she were in charge. She hadn't said what would be different, and neither of us imagined she would ever be in charge. Now, it seemed as if she'd been prophetic.

Meeting in the conference room with slides was slightly pretentious since there were only two of us, but she wanted to *set the right tone*. I wasn't sure what that meant, but I didn't ask. I was too busy staring at the roles outlined on the slide:

Micro Expression Expert

Photographer

Office Manager

Was she baiting me? Maybe she wanted to see if I was truly

committed to making Fly Higher a success. She'd been quite clear that success meant teamwork. The conflict that had gone on between Stephanie and me would *not be tolerated* under her leadership. I'd managed not to roll my eyes, even though she'd sounded like every spoof and cliché of office work and management-speak ever.

I turned my attention from the slide to her face but said nothing. I folded my hands and placed them on the conference table, waiting for her to say something about the photographer position. She let the silence stretch and lengthen and change shape before she finally spoke in a low, clear voice. "It might seem counter-intuitive, but the Office Manager is the most critical position at this point. We need someone to get in touch with existing clients. I've already contacted them, of course, but we need to set up meetings to introduce our new structure and to get them back on track quickly before they lose momentum and interest."

I nodded.

"I have a list of candidates from a recruiter I know. Please look them over and choose four to come in for interviews."

"Sure." I was stunned by her demeanor. She'd definitely stepped into the CEO role with both feet. In fact, she'd even changed her appearance slightly. She no longer wore stacks of bangles covering her wrists, jangling every time she gestured. She wore a delicate gold watch on her left wrist and a thin gold chain on her right. Her makeup seemed lighter, and she wore a suit that was nothing like the fun, comfy, slightly quirky clothes I'd admired every day since I'd started working with her.

"Do you have any thoughts about what kind of personality type we want in that role?" she asked.

"Someone who isn't mentally unbalanced and doesn't plan to wage a religious war in the office."

She laughed.

I was relieved. I smiled and decided to put forth some effort to show my own enthusiasm. "I think we need someone who just likes people. Someone who's energized by the details and the logistical aspects of life. There are people who look at scheduling as if it's a puzzle. Not someone with dreams of moving up."

"How would we identify those qualities?"

"I'll come up with some questions," I said.

"If we can manage to figure that out, your profile is right along the lines of what I was thinking."

From there, she told me about the two people, both men, that were coming in for interviews the following day for the micro-expression position.

"I know them from industry conferences. Both are really good and would be perfect for this role, so I've asked them to come in for interviews. If, for some reason, neither one of them works out, I'll get in touch with the recruiter for that role as well. I'm hoping they do because that won't be an easy skillset to find." She smiled. "In fact, I'm confident both of them would be an asset."

It was interesting that she hadn't asked me to look at their resumés before setting up the interviews, but I supposed since it was her area of expertise and not mine, she had a better sense. Still, you can tell a lot from a digital sheet of paper. You can pick up on arrogance and qualification inflation as well as vague accomplishment descriptions that suggest they might be obscuring problems. You can get a sense of the person before they're sitting across from you. "Did you already do phone interviews?"

"I didn't have to." She tapped the trackpad to advance the slide, then glanced up and clicked back. "I've talked to them many times. I have relationships with them. They're both qualified."

"Okay."

"So the only other role, obviously, is for a second photographer."

I said nothing.

"I know this was an issue for you with Stephanie—"

"It wasn't an issue. It—"

"Yes, it was. You want to be the star of the show."

"That's not true. You're misreading me."

She narrowed her eyes, and I knew she was thinking she'd read my micro-expressions, and they were shouting out my thoughts more clearly than I realized. What she didn't know was that my area of expertise was letting people think one thing when something entirely different was going on, micro-expressions or not.

I didn't want to share the photography, not because I wanted to shine or get attention or any nonsense like that. It was because I liked to be in control. And I liked knowing that if I ran across more misogynists among our clients, I had the freedom to remove them from the picture. A second photographer would make that difficult, if not impossible.

"If that's the truth, then why all the conflict with Stephanie?"

"First, the issue with her was that she wasn't qualified. That's it."

"It seemed more intense and more personal than that."

I spread my fingers in front of me and studied my new manicure —turquoise with silver glitter. "I'm not sure where you got that idea."

"Things Stephanie said … and your antagonism."

"I can get along with just about anyone if that's what you're worried about."

"In my experience, you can't."

"She was one person. In the end, I was right. She was unbalanced."

"True," she said.

"And did you pick up on all of that in her micro expressions?"

"To be honest, no."

I liked that she was bluntly honest. I'd liked that about her from the first time we spoke. It was the reason we got along, and it was the reason I thought I wouldn't mind knowing her outside of work. "I don't like it when people force their beliefs on others. I told you that, ages ago."

"I just have concerns."

"You don't need to. It was a religious war."

"I think she just wanted your respect."

"If she did, she had a bizarre way of trying to get it.

"Still, I think you were invested beyond just being sure we met our quality standards."

Obviously, I couldn't tell her about the second thing, the thing about removing misogynists. And I didn't want to tell her about the first—my need to control things. Half the fun of this job was manipulating the client. If I had to share how much I liked that, I wouldn't be able to direct the encounters the way I wanted. I always got the photographs we needed, but I would miss out on the fun of leading a person into thinking differently about themselves, of unwittingly exposing themselves to the camera and to me.

"So what is it?"

"I like to be in charge."

"This isn't a joint role. You're the lead. So you are in charge."

"I like flying solo."

She laughed. "Then why are you even here?"

I stared at her. She stared at me.

As she advanced to the next slide, her attention on the screen, she said, "Let me know if you have a source for photographer candidates or if you want me to talk to the recruiter about that as well. I need the resumés for anyone you might want to consider or recommend by the end of the week."

I turned toward the slide displaying our mission statement and wondered—Why *was* I here?

CHAPTER 4

$\mathcal{M}$y optimistic belief that I'd solved the personal freedom issue with Eileen was premature.

She greeted me that evening dressed to go out—wearing very high-heeled ankle boots, pink leggings, a top that hung off one shoulder, her hair twisted into a messy updo, and a lot of makeup, even for a model.

"I should have texted you," she said.

"Are you and Ned going to a club?"

"He's working. I thought we could go out to dinner and then look at furniture."

Her outfit didn't seem to fit that agenda, but I put that aside. "I was ... I was going to meet ..." The lie refused to take shape as quickly as I was used to. Partially because I'd sliced Kent, my most convenient excuse, out of my life as cleanly as the amputation of a hand.

"Do you have a date?" she asked.

"No." I hadn't even planned what I wanted to do that evening. I didn't want to plan anything. I needed to think about my job. At the same time, I wanted to not think at all. I'd known I wanted to come home. I'd known the evening might involve a martini and most likely, takeout food. It might have also involved a trip to the gym where I could burn off my concerns about the job I loved turning into another prison, with regulations and constant harassment from another photographer. It did not involve hanging out with Eileen for a second night in a row.

"Change into something fun, and let's go."

The ghost of Stephanie, embodied in her furniture, was keeping me from settling in, so it made sense to get busy choosing new things. It wasn't as if the new stuff would be delivered in two days like an Amazon package, so I decided I didn't want to fight it after all. I went into my room and stripped off my work clothes. I wanted a shower, but there didn't seem to be time, so I shoved my legs into jeans and my feet into boots. I put on a cool, silky top. I brushed my hair and left my makeup alone.

We walked to a sushi place a few blocks from our apartment. After dinner, we would Uber to Lazzoni. It was the place Eileen was most drawn to, even though it was too popular for my taste. Buying from that store meant the chance of seeing one of your possessions in someone else's apartment. But the furniture would belong to her, not me, so I followed along.

As we lifted the last pieces of sashimi and rice off the shared plates, Eileen looked at me and held my gaze. "You never talk about your love life," she said.

I laughed. I splashed sake into my cup. "Do you want any more?"

She shook her head.

I filled my cup, ending up with a perfect pour from what was left in the bottle. I took a sip.

"Weren't you with some guy who lived down the hall at your old apartment? Kent, right?"

"We split up."

"Why?"

I shrugged and sipped my sake.

"Are you okay?"

"Yes."

"Who ended it?"

I considered this. If I said it was me, she would return to the question of why. "It was mutual."

"I had the impression you really liked him."

"We weren't right for each other."

"What does that mean? You seem a little cold about it."

"I don't want to talk about it."

"You know I'm a good listener."

I signaled the server and asked for our check.

"Don't shut me out. You were there for me with my mom, you still are." Her eyes filled. "I want to be the same for you."

I stared, fascinated, studying all that precise, elegant eyeliner, its precision threatened by the tears ready to spill out. "I'm not shutting you out. I just don't have anything to say."

"You're so cold about it. He must have hurt you a lot."

I shook my head. The check came, and I slid my credit card out of my purse and placed it on the tray.

"Let's split the bill," she said.

"Nope. Not when we're getting ready to drop more than a few grand on furniture."

"I said I wanted to do it. You don't owe me."

"But some balance is required."

She shrugged. "I'm not keeping score, but okay. Thanks."

"Should we go?" I slid toward the end of the bench.

"We have to wait for your card. Is that how anxious you are to avoid talking about your heartbreak?"

"I'm not suffering from heartbreak. It's fine."

"You're a hard person to figure out."

"I know."

She laughed. "You could help me out a little."

I was starting to realize how much of our relationship had centered around our careers and her mother. With Stephanie gone, it seemed she'd left a void that Eileen was planning to fill, at least partially, with me.

"I tell you a lot of things about my relationship with Ned."

"You don't need to."

She stared at me. Finally, it seemed that she'd run out of things to say.

I smiled so she wouldn't feel hurt, so she wouldn't think I was rejecting her, so she would know we still could have a good time choosing classy furniture. The server brought my card, and we walked toward the entrance. I could feel her staring at my back, I could feel her questions boiling up, ready to spill out once we were seated in an Uber.

The minute we closed the car doors, barely settled in the seat, my safety belt still undone, I unlocked my phone and opened my notes app. Before Eileen could ask about my love life or our friendship or tell me things I might not want to know about her own love life, I said, "We need to make a plan. What are the key pieces we should start with? Don't they say you should have one important piece and build around that?"

"Yes, but you're still shutting me out. Why are you so afraid to talk to me about your breakup? Is it that painful?"

"I'm not afraid."

"It feels like you've built a wall between us. When I close my eyes, it seems as if I can actually touch the bricks and sense you on the other side."

"I don't want to gossip."

She laughed. "It's not gossip when it's your own experience. You need to talk about it, otherwise, you hold it inside, and it does real damage. The wounds keep going deeper until you can't handle it."

"I don't think that will happen." I tapped the couch displayed on my phone and reached around to grab the seatbelt, stabbing the metal tab into the lock. "Starting with a couch makes sense to me unless you'd rather do the dining table and chairs as the focal point."

"I'm a little worried about you," Eileen said.

"Don't be."

"It's not good to bottle up your feelings."

"I'm not bottling up anything. We're here to focus on furniture. This is supposed to be fun. Who wants to talk about a guy who's no longer in my life? We should be planning the future."

"You don't ever want to talk about him? You *never* think about him? Have you returned the things he left at your place?"

"He didn't leave anything."

"That's strange."

The Uber took a sharp corner, forcing my shoulder into Eileen's upper arm. My phone slid out of my hand and fell to the floor. I stuck out my foot, nudged it toward me with my toe, and leaned over to pick it up. "I'm really excited to choose our furniture together. Even though it won't be mine, I'll get to enjoy it for a while."

"You aren't thinking of moving already, are you?"

I laughed. "I just did. Why would I want to go through that again?"

"Maybe I'm only a bridge to something better."

"You're not. So we'll start with the couch and then the dining table. Those are the two main pieces."

She nodded. She pulled her purse to her side, hugging it close. She turned and looked out the window at the buildings sliding past.

It was clear she was upset, but I wasn't going to ask her and start the whole conversation over again. I supposed she felt we needed to share our stories before we could choose furniture together. Maybe she wanted to know more about me so she could understand what style fits me and what kind of life I wanted to create in our new place. Was I romantic, hoping to get back with Kent or fall in love with someone new? Was I the kind of person who would help her with any problems that might come up between her and Ned? Maybe she was worried I was too detached, suggesting I might be suicidal over the breakup. Maybe she was worried about not doing enough to help me, then blaming herself if I ended my life. Maybe she even had a bit of a cold streak herself and was worried she

18

would be left with a mess or left with the outrageous rent on a two-bedroom apartment and no one to step into my shoes.

I stared at the back of her shoulder. She didn't seem interested in the list I was trying to compile. I wondered if she might start crying. I suppose most women would have placed their hand on her back to soothe her, but that seemed a bit too much.

I sighed. "There's nothing to say because I was ready for it to be over. We didn't go out for that long, and to be honest, a lot of it was about sex, so I'm honestly fine."

She half-turned. "People say that, but it's not true. They delude themselves when they say it's just about sex."

She was wrong, but I'd done enough explaining. "We're almost there."

"I'm not sure I feel like shopping."

"You will once we get inside. Come on, we're all dressed up and ready to go."

She turned to face the window again. A moment later, the car pulled to the curb. I tapped the app to pay the driver, gave him a tip and a good rating, and we climbed out.

As we wandered through the spaces decorated to look like the rooms of a home, right down to books and reading glasses left oh-so-casually on a coffee table and wine glasses placed on end tables, Eileen began to relax. She laughed at a couch that was upholstered with the white and black spotted faux hide of a cow. We snapped photos of pieces we liked and checked prices. We talked about our favorite colors and the kind of mood we wanted to create—I wanted tranquil, she wanted cozy. I told her I would be good with cozy as long as that didn't mean claustrophobic.

In the end, we ordered a large gray leather sectional, a sleek, dark-stained, almost black coffee table, and an ash dining table with eight chairs. The table opened with a leaf that popped up in the center and fit seamlessly to the other sides. In its open state, it comfortably accommodated all eight chairs.

I couldn't imagine ever inviting six people to join us for dinner, but I had no doubt that Eileen had other plans.

CHAPTER 5

*D*iana met me in the hallway before I reached my office door. It was clear she was eager to tell me something she considered important, possibly exciting. She gave me a triumphant smile. "I realized the best way to differentiate Fly Higher will be to only take on female clients."

"That sounds like the opposite of flying higher." It immediately struck me that the pool of people I could remove from abusing the other half would now be out of reach.

"Focus is a powerful force."

"We're focused on helping people achieve success. Cutting out half the people who want that seems like a mistake."

"I've thought about it a lot."

"But—"

"It's my decision to make," she said.

"Trystan was really good about getting everyone's input. Even if he didn't always follow it, I think that helped make us successful."

She smiled calmly as if she were explaining to a child. "A woman-owned firm, women clients. It's clean. It's easy to sell. I think more women will be interested when they know we have deep, exclusive experience with female clients because anyone in the business world, any career, really, knows that things are different for women."

"They don't have to be. And the principles of success shouldn't matter for men versus women. That's what you've always said."

"The application of those principles is different. That's reality."

I shrugged. "If you say so."

"I need you to be enthusiastic, Alex."

"I'm enthusiastic about photography."

"Please don't throw attitude all over the place."

I sighed. She had definitely changed. If I was putting a positive spin on it, I might assume she was feeling the pressure of wooing and selling our services to new clients settling on her shoulders. Still, I felt her quiet, somewhat detached style in the past had been hiding a fierce businesswoman that I was only now recognizing, and possibly, a rather inflexible boss.

It wasn't that she was trying to exert power over me or forcing me into something I didn't like, not yet. But she definitely wanted me to follow agreeably and only offer my ideas or point of view when she asked. I was pretty sure there would be no more hikes with easy conversations about life and work. I wanted to get along with her. I didn't want to lose those interesting conversations, even though there had only been a handful. I wanted to look forward to coming into the office. I wanted to experience the synergy of seeing what our clients needed and working together to help them remove barriers to their limitless ambition.

"Why are the candidates for micro-expression analysis male?" I asked.

"They're the best in the field."

"Wouldn't a woman be better at reading other women's expressions?"

"Maybe. But the two I know who have the best credentials are men."

I stared at her, waiting to see if she realized her opinions about men and women had an arbitrary quality. If she recognized that, she wasn't saying. Clearly, her decision had been made. Maybe she realized sales and persuasion weren't her top strengths, so an easy concept to sell mattered more than consistency.

I regretted the loss, at least for now, of male clients. Our male clients had always been fun to flirt with and tease. It had also been incredibly satisfying to do a bit of house cleaning in the high-rises of New York City. Not that I couldn't or hadn't removed women who mistreated their own so-called sisters, but men who marginalized and abused the other half of the human race were far more prevalent. I hadn't taken the photography job for that purpose, but it had worked out that way once, and I was curious to see where things might go.

"Let's plan to meet in the conference room at ten to go over the profile for Pauline, and then we can prep for tomorrow's interviews."

"Sure."

She turned and swept down the hall to her office, where she quietly but firmly closed the door.

At ten, I was already seated in the conference room. She came in, turned on the projector, and displayed the career vision essay that Pauline Herrera had written.

Pauline ran one of New York's top modeling agencies. I'd been tempted to ask Eileen if she knew her but had decided that might get me into trouble.

I'd already read her essay, her answers to our probing questions, and her personality test results. She claimed she didn't know what she wanted at this point in her career, but during my brief time working in this field, I'd learned that wasn't always accurate. Often, clients claimed not to know, they were simply too embarrassed to admit it to themselves. If they truly didn't know, it was usually a shocking lack of self-insight into their deeper desires.

Diana began speaking. "She isn't sure what she wants, which we've seen often enough. The agency is incredibly successful, without a lot of room to go much higher, and she makes a phenomenal profit. She believes the margin is higher than her competitors, and her models continue to win awards."

I nodded. I knew all this. Maybe Diana's newfound urge to explain the obvious had something to do with becoming the person in charge—there was a natural desire to communicate things as if she was the only one privy to the information, to take ownership by talking about the business as if she was the one who would single-handedly determine our client's future. Maybe she saw herself as a savior.

"It seems as if a lot of people at these levels just get bored," I said. "They're so used to climbing the ladder that once they arrive, what they really miss is the adrenaline. They don't realize that's what was keeping them energized. Not the work itself."

"Good insight." Diana smiled. "Do you have any insights specific to Pauline?"

"I think it would be good to push her to figure out why she wanted to start her own agency. Did she realize she was going to age out as a model, or was there something else? She didn't mention that in her essay."

"I noticed that too." She clicked slowly through the other slides, and we talked about Pauline's personality type, her relationships with her employees, her feelings about success, her relationship to money, and all the other details revealed in the standardized tests that helped us dig into our clients' heads.

When we'd settled on our approach for the initial meeting with Pauline, Diana turned off the projector. "Regarding the candidates for the micro expression analysis role—the main thing I want you to focus on is putting them on their back foot, which should be easy for you to do."

I laughed.

"Do you disagree?"

"No."

She gave me a curious look as if she wasn't sure why I'd laughed.

I wondered if she was going to love running the show as much as she'd thought she would. If you can't have fun with work, if everything is so serious and so critically important, then what's the point? But maybe I was alone in that view.

"I want to stress them as much as we can. I want to do our best to see if any self-control issues surface, or—"

"Or any issues with women being in charge."

She seemed to freeze for half a second, then gave a single nod. "I suppose that's a good point. I hadn't thought of that. But I'm more interested in finding out if there are ego problems or any tendency to not be a team player. That's really important to me."

"So I've noticed."

"As I mentioned, they're both highly qualified, but if our team can't function smoothly, we'll have challenges with clients. I think Trystan made some critical mistakes, allowing that conflict between you and Stephanie to turn into the mess it became at the end."

"As much as it bothered him, and you, I don't think it affected our clients," I said.

"It absolutely did. Look at Matt Shera. Flirting with him just to get under Stephanie's skin made him very uncomfortable."

I held her gaze but said nothing. I thought the opposite. It had worked out well—Matt was given some food for thought. And he wasn't all *that* uncomfortable because he hadn't ended his relationship with us. We'd had to put him on pause because of Trystan's death, but he'd understood. He hadn't seemed bothered by how I'd exposed his weaknesses by flirting with him. "Now that we're women-only, what are you going to tell him?"

"I haven't made a final decision, but I'm looking to see if we can refer him to someone else who does similar work."

Late that afternoon, when we arrived at the sleek offices on the twenty-fourth floor of a Park Avenue skyscraper where the Herrera Modeling Agency was located, we were shown to a small conference room. Unlike most of its type, the oak conference table was oval. Enormous potted plants stood in the corners, and smaller plants hung from the ceiling, making it feel like an indoor garden. The sound of gently moving water came from a stone fountain on a low rectangular table in front of a wall painted dark green.

Pauline wasn't there. Instead, a guy sat at the table with an iPad open in front of him and the latest model iPhone resting beside it. He had wavy blond hair that hung to the base of his neck, tangled in that messy way that's enticing, not bedhead. His eyes were dark brown, and he had a faint shadow of blond and light brown hair that hadn't been shaved for two or three days. I had a gut feeling it wasn't planned for effect but that he might not have bothered to shave because he had other things to do. A complete and utter fantasy since I had no way of knowing his thoughts regarding shaving, but it was my impression, and who knows where these assessments of people come from. They feel utterly real, even though they've been fabricated in your own mind. Maybe it's animal instinct, or maybe it's a projection of your own thoughts because something activates a memory that can't be identified.

He wore a turquoise T-shirt and black slacks. He was sitting about a foot and a half from the edge of the table. His eyes were locked on the doorway, suggesting he'd known we were being ushered into the room. He smiled, but it didn't appear to spread to his eyes—a smile calculated to offer a wary welcome.

The receptionist asked us to take a seat, then inquired whether we wanted coffee, tea, water, soda, or fruit juice. Diana asked for tea, I asked for water, and she wanted to know if that would be sparkling or still. I chose sparkling, and since they seemed to be one step shy of a bar, I also asked for a wedge of lime. The receptionist assured me that was no problem.

The guy didn't stand to shake our hands or offer more than a brief smile. "I'm Hunter," he said.

Neither of us spoke, waiting for a title or a last name, but none was offered.

"Pauline will be here in a few minutes," he said.

"Perfect," Diana said. "I'm Diana Clarke with Fly Higher, and this is Alexandra Mallory."

She sounded chirpy, almost nervous, which startled me. I supposed her first time introducing herself as the head of our company had twisted itself inside her head, and she'd made too much of it, just as staring at this single-named guy was twisting inside of me. He was as thin as a stereotypical seventies rock star, not the kind of guy who usually grabbed my attention. There was something about him that made me want to watch him do whatever came into his head—anything from cooking dinner to dancing to sweeping the floor—for the sheer pleasure of seeing him move.

Hunter nodded once to acknowledge our names, shocking me out of the scenes unfolding inside my head. He stared at us, and we stared back. Finally, he spoke. "Anything you want to know about Pauline?"

"I think we'll let her speak for herself," Diana said.

"In that case, I'll give you a short history of the agency."

I could hardly make out the words he was speaking. All I could do was keep my gaze focused on those luscious brown eyes, those soft lips, that delicious hair the color of morning sunlight, and a tenor voice that made my ribs throb. I couldn't understand why he was having this effect on me. When I blinked and studied his features again, there was nothing picture-perfect hot about him. Many women would pass him on the street without looking twice.

I felt him looking back at me, noticing me on a layer beneath the words coming out of his mouth, aware of my presence but not letting his attention linger on my face for a moment longer than it paused on Diana's. He talked about the agency, giving background information I already knew from reading Pauline's material and the agency website. That was a good thing because I didn't absorb a single word he said.

Already my mind was circling the situation, wondering if he might be there for my photography sessions with Pauline, wondering if he would ask about me, curious about his role, trying to figure out how I might talk to him outside of a conference room and beyond earshot of Diana or Pauline. I wanted to outline the shape of his lips with my index finger and comb all my fingers through his hair.

He kept talking, drawing me closer, luring me into his orbit with that voice.

CHAPTER 6

 ortland, Oregon

* * *

There are people who pass through your life that leave such a mark, it's difficult to talk about them. Often, it's hard to even *think* about them. All your words and thoughts, even your dreams, are utterly inadequate for capturing their essence, giving shape to their place and importance in your life. Words can't embody even a single molecule of who they are.

This is how it has been for the woman in the shadows of my life. A person who would be diminished if I breathed a word about her existence or tried to describe her in a way that did her justice.

This woman was stunning. She had dark, almost black hair. Her equally dark eyes often appeared bold and solid as onyx stones when her pupils dilated with wonder. The milky white surrounding them made them blacker still. Her hair was like silk, long and wavy. Her skin was perfect—smooth and fresh and vibrant, never touched by a single drop of makeup, never marred by teenage inflammation or adult whispers of aging. Her lashes were never clogged with mascara, and the tender skin beneath her eyes never smudged with the remnants of shadow and liner.

Her movements were lithe, her body flooded with energy. She moved like a creature from another world. Even when she walked up and down stairs, she seemed to dance—a songbird darting through the sky, spinning and dipping, reversing direction, full of delicate poise and perfect balance. Each step and every gesture were works of art, there for a moment, then gone.

The sound of her laughter was musical. That's been said a hundred times, a thousand times, of women around the world in every era, but this girl had a laugh that truly echoed the tones of a flute. Everyone smiled when they heard those notes rising from her lips. It was impossible not to laugh alongside her, adding your voice to the chorus, even when it wasn't clear what had caused her amusement.

She was smart. Witty. Curious. She was kind and too good to live on this earth.

The course of her life wasn't perfect. No one's is.

* * *

* * *

* * *

But in my dream of her, that life had a clear direction, a purpose that consumed her. She did well in school and studied seriously in college, her eyes on a horizon that was always sharply visible in her mind.

When she graduated from college with accolades, she became a brilliant scientist. The natural world had intrigued her from the start, and everyone who knew her was unsurprised that she was drawn to science. As a child, she collected everything—sticks and leaves, the carcasses of insects, feathers, shells, and pebbles. She displayed them in tiny boxes and on shelves built for that purpose.

At the library, when other children were looking for stories, she gathered armloads of books about animals and sea life, geology, and astronomy. She wanted to know everything. She worshipped the natural world.

Her work uncovered new cures for diseases that afflicted children, bringing hope and health to thousands of kids. She was applauded and honored, and financially rewarded. She started a foundation that spread more goodness throughout the world—with programs that addressed hunger and clean water challenges, improved agriculture and literacy.

She was a goddess, with compassion and altruism flowing from her fingertips, like strands of magic wrapping around the planet, bringing peace of mind and comfort and a better quality of life to countless people. If there ever was a god, she was that spirit. The walls of her home were covered with photographs of her, always smiling, her arms around people she'd met and befriended in nearly every country in the world.

Filled with energy and light, and endless stamina, she was a magnificent cook. She threw glorious dinner parties that gave birth to fascinating conversation, adding even more flavor to the delicious food she'd prepared that melted in the mouths of her guests. The home she'd created was designed to bring in natural light during every hour of the day until the sun disappeared at night. It was filled with music and provocative art, and exquisitely made rapturously comfortable furniture.

Others were in awe of her talent, in awe of all she was willing and capable of doing for other human beings.

Everyone wanted to know her. Everyone wanted to be near her. Everyone was captivated by her presence, knowing they truly stood in the presence of a goddess.

Her name was Alexandra, and all of this was a dream that had never happened.

CHAPTER 7

$\mathcal{N}$*ew York*

* * *

James Lipman was seated across from me, his gaze locked onto mine, his shoulders back. "Taking photos is something you either know how to do, or you don't. There's not much to it if you have the natural instinct."

How could he be so right and so wrong at the same time?

Without acknowledging I'd heard him speak, I asked, "What's your biggest fear?"

"Right out of interviewing 101, am I right?" He laughed as if to assure me he was teasing, and he and I were both in on the joke.

The guy was reasonably good-looking. He was tall, with dark hair standing in sharp contrast to his pale skin, and very light eyes of a color I couldn't quite name. Those eyes drew attention to themselves because of his dark hair and brows. He had a nice smile—charming and seemingly genuine. His fingers, which were an odd thing to focus upon, but were attention-grabbing, were extraordinarily long. His hands rested on the arms of the chair, and his fingers looked like large worms, writhing around the padding of the arms as he moved his hands, almost stroking the dark blue pad and the metal bar that connected the arms to the seat.

I couldn't stop watching those constantly moving fingers. They behaved as if they were separate from his body. It appeared to be an unconscious tic, and I couldn't figure out the source of it because he didn't seem nervous. Unless he was, and that was his unique but obvious tell.

I shifted my attention back to his face.

"Oh, you expected me to answer that." He laughed. "Let's see, my biggest fear is being locked in a room with no light."

"That's specific."

He shrugged. "All fears are specific."

"Are they?"

"How do you like working here?" he asked.

"I love it." I'd learned people liked to hear that word. Love. Telling someone you simply *liked* or appreciated a particular item or an aspect of life opened the door to questions about what your hesitation was. If a claim to enjoy something wasn't exuberant—outstanding, fantastic, or otherwise worthy of gushing adoration—people were suspicious. At least in my experience.

"Why?"

"We're here to talk about you," I said. "How did you get into the field of microexpression analysis?"

"It's in my resumé."

He seemed quite confident of getting this job. I wondered if Diana had hinted he was the top candidate of only two or if he was simply confident to the point of arrogance. "Not the details of your education. I want to hear how you discovered the field, why it interested you, and what made you decide to make it a career."

"You just asked three questions."

"I'm sure you can handle them. One at a time."

His fingers writhed on the chair arms. I decided he must be nervous but had practiced controlling other giveaways as a result of what he'd learned about micro-expressions. Perhaps if people try to subdue the expressions on their faces, those feelings need to find a way out.

"I read a blog about micro-expressions when I was in high school, believe it or not."

"I believe it."

"It seemed as if learning how to recognize and interpret them would be like having a superpower."

I laughed.

"I'm serious."

"I'm sure you are. I'm not laughing at you, I'm laughing because you were an astute kid if you saw the power in that skill."

He looked pleased that I'd called him intelligent and didn't seem to realize I was focused on the person he'd been over fifteen years ago, not the man sitting in front of me who didn't seem any more intelligent than most.

"I liked the idea of getting insight into what people are thinking."

"But of course, you can't know that with certainty. That's part of the finesse this role requires. You make educated guesses about general emotions, but you can't get too imaginative, or you'll mislead us and sabotage our work."

His fingers moved forward on the chair arms, then he pulled his hands back as if he were afraid they might run away from him. "You'd be surprised."

I waited for him to elaborate. He didn't. Anything about his credentials or his approach to his work would be handled in his interview with Diana. I wouldn't push him to answer the other question. My assignment was to put him on the back foot, and it was time to get to it. "Tell me about your worst manager."

He laughed. He curled his fingers around the arms of the chair until his knuckles were white, then released them, wiggling them as if he were a concert pianist, preparing to place his fingers on the keys. "That sounds like a setup."

"How?"

"If the characteristics match Diana's, I'll be digging my grave."

I smiled. "Don't overthink it."

His brow furrowed ever-so-slightly. It was a crease that most wouldn't notice, a spasm of his facial muscles that he corrected so quickly, I wondered for half a second if I'd imagined it.

"This isn't a conventional interview," he said.

"I'm not a conventional person, and this isn't a conventional consulting firm."

"Fair enough." He crossed his legs and leaned to the side, resting his elbow on the chair arm. "My worst boss was a woman. The only woman I've ever worked for. Until now." He gave me a confident smile.

I waited. The smile remained in place. I waited another beat or two. "Please elaborate."

"She had low standards."

"Please tell me more about the experience."

"This feels like a negative approach to interviewing."

I'd never interviewed a candidate who was so eager to correct and argue. Mostly, candidates were eager to comply, some even rushed to make themselves subservient. The other candidate had been agreeable. In fact, it had been difficult to get him on the back foot as Diana had asked because he rolled with everything that came up and never seemed uncomfortable. I thought it was a good trait, and I'd told Diana that.

Did James have a streak of the same stuff I was made of? Or was he just supremely confident he was getting an offer? It wasn't as if microexpression experts were surfing the web, looking for work. Diana had already spoken to him on the phone. I wondered what she'd said. But then, she'd asked me to push him off balance, so I couldn't believe she would have hinted that the job was already his.

"We show who we are when we're under stress," I said. "I'd like to hear an example of her low standards and how you handled it."

"I have to think for a minute. I certainly wasn't prepared for this question." He winked, then shifted his gaze to the window, staring at the light as if he expected a message from god. Finally, he spoke. "As you can see on my resumé, if you read it carefully, my role at GH Tech was to sit in on meetings where someone had been accused of workplace misconduct and assess whether they were lying. My manager was the head of HR, which you can also see on my resumé."

As he talked, I kept my expression neutral. Despite his expertise, I knew this was possible, with a bit of focus. Micro-expressions are created by stray thoughts, and keeping those to a whisper reigns in your face before it betrays you. It was clear James was annoyed that he had to relate this incident to me, and that he wanted to suggest I hadn't prepared for the interview. It was also quickly becoming clear that there was something in him that might make him difficult to work with. I wondered if it was severe enough that I should flag it to Diana.

"I sat through hours of meetings for a guy accused of smacking a female co-worker's ass." He narrowed his eyes, checking for my reaction. I gave none.

"I was having a hard time reading the guy, and the gal, for that matter. I was starting to think, although the odds were against it, that they were both sociopaths." He laughed. "It's hard to read sociopaths, you know."

I smiled and let the corner of my mouth twitch as if I was ready to urge him to get on with his story. He rushed forward.

"I was pretty sure the gal was lying. Every time she was asked a direct question about the things she claimed he'd said to her before the alleged smack, she had a spasm at the edge of one nostril. But the guy was overly nervous. His face was twitching like a jar full of crickets. My boss saw this, and since she knew next to nothing about the micro-expression discipline, she was certain he was lying. I wanted to meet with them one more time, individually, but she said we were done. It was taking too long. People were suspicious of the practice anyway. We needed to get closure, submit a report, and move on. Nice string of corporate-speak lingo, right?"

I smiled.

"I argued with her. An argument that turned to shouting, but I lost. Then, she gave me a virtual kick a month later just to let me know she was the boss. My bonus was a percentage point lower than I'd been promised. It was at the bottom of the scale for my position. So yeah, I didn't get along well with her."

"Why did you feel the need to shout at her?"

He stared at me. He cleared his throat. "*Why?*"

I nodded.

"Isn't it obvious? Sometimes passion for what you do gets the best of you. She was sloppy. There were careers at stake. It was an outrage."

"I can imagine."

"Yeah. So do you want to hear about the good managers I've had? There were two. The first was—"

"No."

"No?"

"Why did you shout at her? It's unprofessional. It suggests a lack of self-control."

"I already told you."

"You told me how you felt, that you had passion, that she was sloppy, that you were worried about the guy's career, although maybe not the woman's."

He glared at me.

"None of that justifies shouting in the workplace."

"I think we're getting off into irrelevant details here ... with all due respect," he said.

"A calm environment and good team coordination are really important to Diana."

"I'm an excellent team player. You'll find out when you check my references."

"Shouting is out of line."

"I probably shouldn't have used that word. I get wound up just thinking about the situation. And I think at home I was probably shouting while I told my girlfriend about it, but I wasn't full-on yelling in the office."

"It sounded like you were."

"You had to be there."

"Your boss seemed pretty upset by it ... lowering your bonus."

"It was vindictive. Can I be straight with you? I get the impression you're not one of those women who is all about the feminist sisterhood. We're all professionals, right?"

"That's true. Or at least we pretend to be." I laughed as I said this because I was thinking about myself.

He laughed cautiously. "Anyway, I'm passionate about getting it right. I think that matters, especially in a very delicate field like microexpressions. You need to be careful, you need to study, you need to make sure you aren't reading into something or jumping to conclusions. It's a delicate and sometimes tricky science."

"Yes."

"Yeah, well ... I still know I was right. And I stand up for my opinions. I think that's an admirable trait. It's an asset to any workplace."

I pushed my chair away from my desk. "It's past two, and you were scheduled with Diana at two."

"Good discussion," he said.

I smiled and held out my hand. He stood and took it carefully, shaking it once.

There was a knock on the door.

"Come in, we're all finished." I moved from behind my desk as the door opened, and Diana stepped into the room. "We were just heading your way."

"Did you have a good conversation?" Diana asked.

"Absolutely," James said. "She held my feet to the fire."

"Good." Diana smiled and stepped back into the doorway. "Alexandra is very forthright. You always know where you stand with her."

I laughed. "Do you?"

Diana rolled her eyes.

"She's one sassy lady," James said.

Diana turned away from the door. "Do you want a water or coffee before we talk, James?"

"Nope. I'm good." He followed her out.

I crossed the office and closed the door behind them. I was confident I'd done what Diana had asked. I also knew I did not want to work with anyone, male or female, who called me sassy.

CHAPTER 8

The minute I saw Diana's face, I knew we were not going to agree. Again. We sat across from each other at the conference table for our interview post-mortem. We sipped lattes that I'd gone out for, mostly because I craved fresh air and needed to escape my small office and our narrow hallway and tiny break room to move my body with a fast-paced walk to the coffee shop.

Diana's expression was composed. Her posture and laid-back look suggested the meeting was perfunctory. There wasn't really anything to discuss. Her decision had been made. She didn't even have the candidates' resumés on the table in front of her. She wasn't looking at her phone to check notes from her interviews. She simply sat with her hands folded, resting on the edge of the table. The face of her wristwatch caught the overhead light, gleaming like a beacon.

"I have to confess," she said. "I knew James was the best candidate, but I didn't want to bias you, so I didn't mention it. I still wanted to give you a chance to recognize that for yourself."

"I think Dave is the better candidate."

She laughed. "Are you serious? He's smart, of course. But he is not a go-getter. He lacks passion. He—"

"I can't work with a man who calls me sassy."

Her laughter stopped abruptly. "It's a bit archaic, yes. But, seriously?"

"It's demeaning."

"Don't be ridiculous."

"I'm not. I don't like it. He shouldn't have said it, especially in a professional context. It's disrespectful and demeaning."

"It's not *demeaning*." She shifted her hips and pulled her phone out of her pocket. She tapped it a few times. "In fact, it's a compliment. It means lively and bold, full of spirit and cheeky."

"*Cheeky*. Maybe you should look that up."

"You don't know how he intended it, so you have to take the primary meaning."

"He strikes me as somewhat misogynistic."

She laughed. "That's a little much. Using an old-fashioned word makes him a misogynist?"

"Sassy is a word men use to put women in a category. A word that suggests they like *their women* with fire in their bones. They respect the sweet little thing for speaking her mind."

She placed her phone face down on the table and studied me, not smiling. "I can't tell if you're playing games, trying to undermine me, or genuinely concerned."

"Words matter."

"I agree. And it wasn't the best choice on his part, but he's brilliant. Surely you recognized that. He's driven. Outspoken. Which is so important. It aligns with what we're about. I don't want someone who's intimidated by our style." She gave me a charming smile, suggesting she and I were a team, the insiders, a smile that tried to imply she was doing this for me. "He's willing to take risks."

"Obviously, you've made up your mind."

"I don't think there's even a choice, but I wanted you to observe that for yourself. I'm a little shocked that you don't recognize that he'd be a huge asset, that he's superior to Dave in every way."

"I'm sure Dave would work out fine."

"I don't want *fine*. I want the *best*." There was a gleam in her eyes that made me understand she was very serious, that she was more ambitious than I'd realized. It seemed as if Trystan had held her back in some way, as if she'd bided her time, waiting for … for what? Trystan had been in his early forties. It wasn't as if she'd been waiting for him to die. His death was a freak occurrence that no one could have predicted. Maybe she'd assumed he was going to tire of what he was doing or make a few serious errors and be forced to hand control over to someone else.

"You understand the ins and outs of micro-expressions, and I don't, so it's probably better that you make the decision without me."

"It sounds like you're sulking," she said.

"I'm not. Are you going to require him to take harassment training?"

"No."

"I thought we were all about empowering women."

"We are."

"It makes me wonder about having a guy on our team who seems to view women as a different species to be patronized and coddled and put on display."

"That's a lot to infer from an off-hand comment, from a single word. Women are held back when they expect the world to evolve to their specifications."

"Are they?"

"Sure, we want society to evolve, but if you wait for that, your career will be over. You need to work with what you're given and try to make those changes in areas where you have influence. But you can't force people, men or women, into viewing the world differently. Those ideas are baked into our personalities, and it can take years, sometimes decades, or a lifetime for individuals to change their mindset."

I was both surprised and not surprised by her beliefs. I knew that her way of dealing with racism was to meditate and remain detached, that she didn't see herself as a force for societal change. She left that to others. I should have realized she would feel the same way about the obstacles women face. I had no doubt it would give a unique angle to what Fly Higher had to offer.

"Look, Alex. You and I have a good relationship. I think you're funny and you're definitely interesting. You do a stunning job capturing people without their masks and pretenses. I want to get along, and I want a collegial working environment. I hated all that animosity and conflict between you and Stephanie. It was exhausting and distracting. It was—"

"This isn't like that."

"It is, in a lot of ways. You have strong opinions, and I like that. I also have strong opinions. You're not afraid to say what you think. But I don't want conflict over seeming slights and general quirkiness and the variations in human behavior that are absolutely normal. In fact, diversity is welcomed. No one wants to live in a world where we're all the same, where we all think the same way. How boring would that be?"

I agreed it would be boring, within reason. But I didn't say that to her, I let her finish lecturing me.

She took a sip of her latte. "Do you think you can dial it down? Not turn everything into an epic battle?"

I was pretty sure I could not *dial it down*. For me, there are epic battles. She didn't seem to understand that calling me sassy wasn't about me feeling personally insulted or ridiculed. It was about the kind of man who used that word and the tone with which he'd spoken. It was about the kind of man who viewed women as entertainment, as precious creatures, and a remarkable sub-species that warmed his heart. That kind of man was now part of our consulting service. It felt as if she were inviting a snake into the garden.

She was right—his views weren't going to change. He probably wouldn't even recognize why that word would offend me. There would be issues down the road, but I didn't need to predict that. She would see for herself, eventually.

CHAPTER 9

*T*he hiring wasn't over. Next up was our office manager. Even though Diana had wanted that role filled first, she didn't have acquaintances that were easy to tap with a text or a call inviting them to an interview without a screening. By the time we finished our interviews and found someone we agreed would be a good match for our driven clients, James was already settled into Diana's former office, already making the coffee every morning—excellent coffee that was strong and smooth—and already creeping down the hall at the end of every day, fishing for a private chat with Diana.

He was so obvious and eager about it, I wondered if he wanted to hook up with her. He didn't seem like he needed the reassurance of personal attention from the owner of the company. At the same time, he wasn't flirting with her either. But he couldn't seem to stop himself from ending his day with a casual, hands-in-his-pockets stroll to her door, where he knocked firmly, unwilling to accept a rejection.

Our new office manager, Fallon Gregory, was only twenty years old, but she had chutzpah, her most admirable attribute, according to Diana. Fallon was charming and friendly. She was smart, very well organized, and knew how to get things done. We knew all this because, despite her age, she had a hefty resumé. She'd been working since she was seventeen—first for a bookstore, then a boutique clothing shop, then managing the staff at the clothing store, then as a PA for a guy who sold custom yachts.

She was short with light brown hair, blunt cut to her chin with a streak of copper running through it. She wore hardly any makeup except bright red lipstick that most women could never pull off. Her arms looked like she worked out with weights. She had a very loud laugh and gave the impression she was ready to interrupt whoever was talking, but she never did.

I liked her, and I thought we could get along, but she was a little dismissive of me. She had all her attention on Diana, looking for every opportunity to impress.

James pointed out that Fallon was sassy. I managed not to laugh when he said this. I figured there might be some fireworks between him and Fallon I could look forward to. It was a little funny that Diana seemed to think she could find the perfect personality types to ensure a harmonious office at all times. It's unlikely that a group of people who are valued for speaking their minds freely will never object to others doing the same or hold back from fighting to the death for their points of view.

Although I was wary of how James was going to fit in with our objectives or get along with me, it was clear we had a decent group of people, and I was almost certain I was going to be able to do as I pleased and continue to have fun with my camera. It was actually kind of exciting. Diana hadn't said another word about the second photographer, but I wasn't fooling myself that it wouldn't come up again at some point. For now, she wanted to make sure we booked as many new clients as we could, as well as bring along those who had been left hanging when Trystan was murdered.

Only a few days after she started, Fallon and I found ourselves alone in the break room. She was pouring a cup of James' delicious coffee. She held up the carafe as I walked in the door. "Want some?"

"Sure, thanks."

She filled a mug and handed it to me. "You seem to have an inside track with the boss," she said.

"Not really." I placed my other hand on the mug to steady it as I turned toward the door.

She laughed. "Don't bullshit me. It's obvious. But I guess maybe it's because you're the same generation."

I stopped and turned back. "We've worked together for a while."

"Tell me what she's about."

"She selected you. She's confident you can do your job. You don't need to put on a show for her if that's what you're thinking."

"The boss always wants a show, if that's what you want to call it. C'mon. You must know a few secrets."

"There aren't any secrets. She's passionate about doing the best for our clients. She's easy-going but has very high standards."

"That sounds like a resumé."

"It's the truth."

"I guess you want to keep the secrets to yourself. To make sure you're the top dog."

I shrugged.

"Do you like taking pictures?'

"Yes."

She leaned against the counter. She picked up her mug of coffee and took a long swallow.

I started toward the door again.

"Why are you in such a rush to get away from me?"

"I'm not."

"You keep making for the door."

"I have stuff to do."

"Like what?"

"Like my job. I assume you do too."

"I'm all caught up."

"Good. Things are going to get hectic."

She stared at me. "Isn't that the point?"

I supposed it was.

"James is a piece of work." She followed this with a loud slurp of her coffee.

"Why do you say that?"

"Full of himself."

"He's confident."

"*I'm* confident. He's full of himself. I hope he's not going to start ordering me around. I work for Diana."

"You sort of work for all of us."

"That's not how she explained it."

"You shouldn't worry about it. She wants us to work as a team. There's not really a hierarchy."

She laughed. "There's *always* a hierarchy. Especially when people insist there's no hierarchy."

"If you have trouble with him, you should tell Diana."

"I don't think so. She thinks he's awesome, and I'd be stepping in a pile of it."

"What did he say?"

She shrugged. "Nothing too much. He just acts like he's all that."

I wondered if she realized the same about herself, about quite a few of us really, some just show it more than others. "You'll mostly be working with clients, so don't let him bother you."

"He's everywhere. Holding the elevator for me. Asking if the AC is the right temp for me. Making *coffee*." She laughed. "I guess he wants everyone to know he's *evolved*."

"Could be."

"But he's not."

I nodded. I took a sip of coffee, watching her over the rim of my mug. I really did not want to form some sort of alliance with her against James. For one thing, if Diana saw that, she would be pissed. For another thing, Fallon didn't seem like someone I could trust.

What I really wanted most days was to escape our small cluster of offices where we were constantly tripping over each other. I wanted to be in the glamorous offices of our clients, following them to restaurants and, occasionally, their palatial homes and five-star hotel conference rooms, taking photographs. I already spent too much time staring at a computer, reading all the things our clients wrote about themselves, half of which were probably lies, and the other half mistaken and distorted delusions.

"It's weird what he does," Fallon said.

"What's that?"

"Reading expressions. Sounds like bullshit." She laughed.

"It's not."

"You're awfully gullible. I wonder if Diana is too?"

I studied her expression as she eagerly waited for my reaction. "She's not."

She shook her head as if she were a wizened elderly woman, saddened to tell me that I would learn the hard way. Someday.

Microexpression analysis was not bullshit. Not any more than expecting someone to hold up one hand, place another on the holy book of their choosing, and swear to tell the truth. I would put my money on the former providing much greater access to the truth.

CHAPTER 10

*T*he first photo session with Pauline Herrera was scheduled for a Tuesday evening at her office.

Usually, with a female client, I would be dressing to look not quite as good as I expected her to. It was part of my effort to minimize my presence and put her at ease. With male clients, of course, it was a different story. This time, I found myself dressing for Hunter. When I closed my eyes to pull on a flimsy top that I might wear dancing, I saw his golden hair and his slim, wiry body. I opened my eyes and thought of the dark brown irises that held my gaze and told me nothing. I thought about the sound of his voice and how he'd made it impossible for me to concentrate. Each time I tried to divert my thoughts, they returned to him.

I took a cab, which was one of the client-meeting protocols Trystan had insisted upon. I was glad Diana hadn't gutted every single aspect of what he'd relied upon to manage the perception our clients had of us. Although there was no doubt she was dedicated to helping people reach their potential, I suppose the things that had changed were mostly superficial, except for cutting half the population out of our target client base.

The receptionist at HMA was still on duty at six-thirty in the evening. I wondered what they paid her to elicit that kind of dedication. She asked me to take a seat in the lobby, where I was surrounded by larger-than-life photographs of the ultra-slender, superbly well-dressed women represented by HMA. I studied their faces and poses, deciding that Eileen was more stunning than many of them. I'd never seen her perform for a camera, so maybe these women had something indefinable that she didn't. Eileen did very well in her career, but she wasn't in the league where the public knows your name.

At six-forty, I was still sitting there. The receptionist seemed to have forgotten about me because her voice had grown increasingly louder as she gossiped with a friend. Her hair was carefully arranged over her earbuds so that no one passing through the lobby knew she was equipped for taking personal calls.

I stood and walked to the ridiculously long desk, devoid of anything decorative, just a long plane of expensive-looking wood in a flattened S-curve.

"Is Ms. Herrera almost ready for our session?"

"Oh. Yes. She said to tell you, just five more minutes."

"Is her chief of staff around to take me to her office so I can get set up?"

"Her chief of staff?"

"Hunter."

"Oh. He's not her chief of staff. He's the head of PR." She laughed, showing me a pierced tongue.

"It would be great to get my camera set up, so we can make the most of her time."

She smiled and shrugged, then turned slightly, lowering her gaze to the computer keyboard and her cell phone sitting beside it.

I returned to my seat. My eagerness for the photo session had dimmed. I'd allowed myself to imagine Hunter joining us for the first few minutes, but I hadn't realized I'd expected it. Now, it seemed as if half the fun had gone out of the evening.

I sat down and scrolled through my new emails, sent a message

THE WOMAN IN THE SHADOWS

to Tess since we hadn't talked in a while, and when I looked up, Pauline was standing in front of me.

"Hi, Alexandra. Sorry to keep you waiting."

I followed her down the hallway to the literal corner office. Two sides were floor-to-ceiling glass, allowing me a spectacular view of the lights spread out around us, the sky still light as we neared the summer solstice.

I placed my camera and bag on one of the couches in a sitting area near the windows. I set up my tripod facing a glass desk that was easily eight feet long and five feet wide. Like the counter in the lobby, it was bare except for a computer monitor.

"So what do we do?" Pauline asked.

"Is Hunter joining us?"

"Hunter? No. Why—"

"I thought he sat in on all your meetings."

"Diana was very clear that the only people here would be myself and you. This is personal."

"Is he the agency attorney, or ...?"

"He's the head of our PR department."

I nodded.

"But this is all about me, right?" She laughed. "Not my employ- ees. It's time to be self-centered."

"Yes." I took the camera out of its case, removed the lens cap, and attached it to the tripod. "Let's start with you behind your desk."

"That seems stiff."

"We're looking for lots of different moods. Did you know you behave and even think differently depending on what part of a room you're occupying and what piece of furniture you're sitting on?"

"Really?"

"Yes, look it up." There was not a shred of doubt in my mind that somewhere on the internet, someone would have written an article or a blog that stated this was a verified fact, with or without the verification, it didn't matter. She believed me right now.

She walked slowly around behind her desk and pulled out the pale gray chair. She sat down and arranged herself, moving easily despite her fitted white skirt and equally tight jacket over a light pink shell. I framed her face and began taking pictures.

She laughed nervously. "Diana told me it would be like this. You'd think, for someone who was a model in her former life, that I'd be used to being stalked by a camera."

"Is that what you think photographers do? Stalk their subjects?" I snapped three photos as she considered the question.

She laughed softly. "I'm not sure why I said that. But now that I think about it, being photographed can feel like that."

"This is a little different. Maybe because you're aware my objective is to capture you unposed."

"Same with our photographers."

"That's not what the photos in the lobby look like."

"Those are captivating because the models were caught in a moment of unawareness. They look posed, but they're not. Trust me, those are the best photographs."

It shouldn't have surprised me that she knew this.

"What made you choose modeling?" I asked.

"My mother was addicted to fashion magazines. I grew up on them. When other kids were reading fairy tales and *Where The Wild Things Are*, I was looking at Vogue and Elle. I was lucky enough to have the height and a face that photographs well, and from the time I was fifteen, there was nothing else that seemed even vaguely interesting to me. Maybe our bodies are our destiny, right?"

"It's fascinating you knew what you wanted when you were so young and that you actually achieved it. That's rare."

She lifted her hair off the sides of her face, and her eyes glazed over as she sank into mental images of the past. "It's not that I made a conscious decision, I literally could not think of anything else."

"Why don't you stand and walk to the windows."

I removed the camera from the tripod and took a continuous stream of photos as she pushed out her chair, stood, adjusted her skirt, patted her fingertips against her exquisitely made-up face, and walked to one of the glass walls. As she gazed out at the city, I took about ten photos, moving ever closer to the side of her face. "Now, take off your jacket. Slowly, so I can capture you in the various stages."

She turned toward me. Her cheeks glowed pink, showing through the thick layer of foundation covering her face. "What is this, a strip tease?"

"Is that what it feels like?"

"I'm not sure. I just—"

I snapped her picture.

"Wait, don't."

I smiled. "It's okay. That's why I'm here. No one but our small team will ever see them." I snapped two more.

She tugged her jacket off, exposing nicely toned shoulders. I took as many pictures as I could, keeping the lens locked tightly on her face so that I didn't get a single shot of her removing the jacket, but she didn't know that.

I asked questions about how long she'd been running the agency, whether she'd signed on her former colleagues or searched for new talent, and what had made her decide she wanted to own an agency. All the while, I was taking her photograph. After about fifteen minutes, I was aware that, like all clients before her, she'd forgotten about the camera.

"A modeling career is short. You're on the decline by thirty or so, done by the age of thirty-five, at least for the lucrative jobs. I was ambitious financially. So, it was the next logical step."

"Do you have kids?"

"No."

"Did you ever want any?"

She shook her head. "No. My younger sister was born when I was sixteen. Nothing about it looked enjoyable. And I saw what giving birth did to my mother's body." She laughed. "Superficial me."

"That doesn't matter if it's the truth, right?"

"I agree. I wanted a beautiful home and beautiful clothes. I wanted parties and financial security. I have it all."

"But something's not right."

"It's frustrating," she said. "To arrive at where you were headed and look around and realize something isn't quite right."

"Do you think it's biological? Wanting kids or anything?"

"I've asked myself that. It's not. It's just this vague feeling of uneasiness and, to be honest, a little bit of boredom."

"We see that fairly often."

"What is it?"

"That's Diana's role ... to work that out with you. I'm just here to find out what your subconscious might be trying to say. I don't figure it out, I just try to make it show itself."

"Has it?"

"Oh, I think so."

She laughed. "You make it sound like there's some dark spirit inside me that you're luring into the open."

I smiled.

We talked for a while about our favorite restaurants and photography while I captured a few more images.

As I was packing up, I turned my back to her, thinking I might appear more casual that way. "Why did Hunter join our first meeting if this is a personal venture?"

"I expected to be late and wanted someone there to introduce you to the agency. I didn't want you to feel abandoned." When I turned, she gave me a curious look as if she'd known I was going to ask more about him and that more questions might still be coming. I restrained myself, although it wasn't easy. I wanted to see him, and I wished our photo session had started earlier. Now, he was likely gone for the day, as the entire floor had that hollow quality you sense in a nearly empty space.

"You're interested in him."

"No. I just had a different expectation because he was there. I assumed he was an assistant and would always be around."

"Or, you're interested in him."

I laughed. I closed my camera case and folded up the tripod, talking somewhat aggressively about the next steps, hoping to keep her from saying more. I was there to get inside her psyche, not the other way around.

CHAPTER 11

 ortland, Oregon

* * *

The woman in the shadows of my life is my sister.

A woman I never talk about, but she is always there, in the shadows of my thoughts, in the shadows of my dreams.

My sister was born one year and three days after I was. We shared a bedroom from the very start. We did absolutely everything together. It seemed as if she was the other half of me. Maybe ... she was my heart.

Our connection was almost like that of twins. It seemed as if a few stray cells from my body had lingered inside my mother's womb. Later, those same cells clung to the cells that formed the person who was my fabulous sister. This is actually true. A mother's cells slip into the child's body, and her cells circle back into the mother. It's called fetal-maternal microchimerism. This means some of those cells may migrate into the bodies of siblings.

No one *really* knows who or what we are.

When my sister was three, and I was four, we were told we

would be getting bunkbeds to make better use of the space that was our shared bedroom. Until then, she'd slept in a crib that was squashed between the foot of my bed and the wall.

On a Saturday morning, just as the sun was rising, my mother came into our room. She opened the blinds and pushed the window up, letting the breeze flow inside. She lifted my sister out of her crib and placed her on the floor while she went to the dresser to choose an outfit for the day. My sister rushed to the side of my bed and shoved her face close to mine. "Wake up!"

I grinned at her. She kissed my nose, and I smelled her sweet breath. "I'm awake."

"You had closed eyes."

I laughed, and she clawed at the bed, starting to climb up beside me so she could crawl under the blankets.

"There's no time for that," my mother said. "Remember what today is."

"Our new beds." I sat up and threw the blankets off.

My sister pouted. "I like mine own bed."

"You're too big for it," I said. "I can hear your head thumping against the end at night."

She giggled.

My mother dressed my sister and directed me to hurry up with my clothes. We followed my mother down the stairs for breakfast like a short string of baby ducklings.

After we ate and cleaned up the dishes, my father drove my mother, sister, and me to a discount furniture store. He pulled into a parking spot, shut off the engine, and turned to face the back seat. "No touching anything in the store. We're not here to run around or look at everything we see. You'll follow your mother and me to the children's section. There are two bunk beds in our price range, and you can choose the set you like. You can thank your mother for that —letting you choose."

We climbed out of the car and walked toward the store, my sister and I holding hands, my parents behind us to make sure we didn't wander off where we didn't belong. Inside, I stopped to stare at the display of a magnificent pool table surrounded by leather couches. My parents nudged us forward until we reached the escalator, where we rode to the second floor.

Everywhere we looked were displays of furniture designed for children. Until that moment, I hadn't known there were so many kid-sized things. My current bed and dresser were about forty years old, passed on to us when a man at our church died. Now, I saw pink desks and small white bookcases. I saw blue child-sized armchairs with footstools. I saw beds and dressers with tiny drawers for collected treasures. I gulped it all in as my father pushed us forward.

Finally, we reached the section my father had already scoped out. Fake rooms with three partial walls featured bunk beds, dressers, small desks, prints of children flying kites and riding bikes on the walls, knick-knacks on the dresser tops, and toys on the floor. Kid-sized chairs were placed in the corners, and kid-sized shelves held books and more toys.

My sister darted into the first alcove, sat on the bottom bed of two that were painted white with a pink ladder to the top bed. They were covered with fluffy pink comforters and enormous pink and white pillows. She bounced once, then tumbled to the floor and began taking the clothes off the baby doll that was lying in a wooden cradle.

"Put the doll down," my mother said.

"I want to play," my sister said.

"It's just to look at."

"Why?" My sister hugged the doll to her chest. The dress it had been wearing was already pulled down to the doll's waist.

"It's not yours, and it's not meant to play with. It's to give you the feeling of a child's bedroom."

"I want a doll."

"You have a doll."

"I want this one."

My mother shook her head. She went to my sister and pulled the doll out of her arms.

"I want it. I want it. I want it …" my sister chanted.

"Stop that," my father said. "If you don't stop right now, I'll choose the beds."

I went to my sister, took her hand, and tugged her toward the bed where she'd bounced. Her cheeks were bright red with frustration.

"You'll get to sleep right under me," I said.

She gave me a loopy smile.

"We'll have matching comforters. But not pink." I glanced at my mother, hoping she would make sure we also got to choose our bedding. I couldn't imagine sleeping in a bed of pink. It looked like that awful stuff they gave us when our stomachs were upset.

"Red," my sister said. "I want a red blanket."

"We'll see," my mother said.

"Not red." My father shoved his hands in his pockets and stepped back, walking toward the next display area. "Come look at this one."

We followed and saw another set of beds. These had dark brown wood and bedding that was obviously targeted at parents who wanted their boys to be boys—red and yellow trucks on a blue background.

"I like the pink room," my sister said.

"Well, that was easy." My father turned, scanning the space behind us for a salesman.

My sister pouted again when we chose our bedding, which was not red. Red was not an appropriate color for little girls, according to my father. We settled on pale green with flowers and bumblebees printed on it. The new sheets were yellow to match the bees.

There was a brief, mild storm of tears when my sister learned we were not going to simply shove bunkbeds into the back of our minivan and drive them home that day. My father had placed the order and paid, but the beds wouldn't be delivered for three weeks.

All the way home, my sister whimpered that she wanted her new bed.

Every night between the day we'd gone shopping and the day the beds arrived, she talked to me in the darkness of our room. "I love our beds," she whispered.

"Me too."

"I'm getting big," she said.

I smiled in the darkness. "So am I."

"Can I sleep in your bed up on top sometimes?"

"Yes. But we have to be quiet. Mommy and Daddy won't want us to do that."

"Why?" she said.

"I don't know why. I just know."

"Why do you get the top?"

"Because you're still little. You might fall out. I'm used to a bed that doesn't have sides."

"I want the top," she said.

"Maybe when you're older, we can switch."

"Can we?"

"I think so. If Mommy and Daddy let us."

"They will," she said.

"Go to sleep. They'll be mad if we're talking in bed."

"Why?"

"Go to sleep. Sweet dreams." I didn't know what sweet dreams were, but my mother always said it, so I said it to my sister and after that, she didn't ask any more questions. I liked her questions. A lot of her questions were the same as mine.

CHAPTER 12

 ew York

* * *

James had looked through all the photos I'd taken of Pauline. As I was refilling my mug from yet another fresh pot of coffee he'd brewed, he came into the break room to tell me this and to let me know I was a *damn good photographer, which shouldn't have surprised him, but it did.*

I said nothing and started toward the doorway so quickly coffee sloshed out of the mug and stung my fingers.

"Don't run off."

"I have things to do."

"Like what?"

I took a sip of steaming coffee.

"Hey, when you're done with the coffee, how about you and I grab lunch?"

I took several more sips of coffee. The last thing I wanted to do was eat lunch with James. Over that thought, Diana's voice sang in my head as if it were a choral group with a hundred voices—*I advise you to make an effort to get along with the rest of the staff. Petty conflicts are not something I have time to deal with.*

"Okay."

"Don't sound so thrilled."

"I'm trying to drink my coffee and thinking about what else needs to be done today."

"We all have stuff to do, but we need to eat."

"We do," I agreed.

Diana was out of the office. She was conducting her final consulting session with Eliza, the painter who had wanted Trystan to help her understand why, just as she was starting to explore building an international audience for her whimsical paintings, she found herself bored with her own work.

"What kind of food do you like?"

"Pretty much everything," I said.

He laughed. "All women say that until you're in the restaurant, and then they whip out a list of offensive foods, most of which are listed on the menu."

"Not me," I said.

He laughed again.

"That's really annoying."

"What is?"

"Laughing when you don't know what you're talking about."

"Prove me wrong."

"I will. You choose the place, and I'll eat whatever is offered. I can always find something I like."

"Always?"

"Always. Let's go at twelve-thirty." I walked out of the break room, into my office, and closed the door. I leaned against it and sipped more coffee. It suddenly tasted weak, nothing but darkened water that had nothing to offer aside from a shot of caffeine. I could feel it coursing through my veins already as if I were mainlining a thrilling drug. I placed the coffee mug on the corner of my desk, settled in the chair, and pressed my back against the mesh that provided such firm but breathable support for my spine. I loved that chair. Trystan had chosen the chairs, telling us that the most important part of functioning well in front of a computer was physical comfort, paying hundreds of dollars for chairs that looked average but felt divine.

I wondered what restaurant James would choose for lunch. I wondered if we'd take a cab or Uber or the subway. I wondered if I would be able to keep my tongue under control for an entire hour, possibly longer.

He ended up choosing Indian food. I wondered if he really wanted Indian food or if he was trying to test me, forcing me to assert my pickiness. I love Indian food. The hotter, the better. Maybe I would force him to reveal some pickiness of his own.

The restaurant was only six blocks from our office building, so we walked. I wasn't thrilled about walking with him because it extended the amount of time we'd be together, but so did the back seat of a car or a subway. He made my skin crawl, and it didn't matter where we were, that sensation was not going away.

Seated across from each other in elaborately carved and sublimely comfortable wooden chairs, we opened our menus.

"We'll order family style," he said. "Do you agree?"

"Yes."

I told him the two items I wanted.

"Is that all?"

"Yes, with rice and naan, that's a lot."

We closed our menus, and the server came. James ordered Aloo Gobi and Tandoori chicken. I added my choices.

"Good variety and we didn't even plan it," he said. "We must be simpatico."

I gave him a hard smile. We were not at all simpatico. Did he truly believe we were?

As the server took our menus and turned away from the table, I said, "Oh, I'd like to order one more dish." I asked for the pork vindaloo.

"Of course," the server said.

I tried not to smile. The dishes James had ordered were savory but not particularly spicy. My last-minute addition, when he didn't have time to re-check the menu to see the spiciness indicator, was the hottest thing I'd ever eaten at an Indian restaurant. There were hotter items to be had, but pork vindaloo could set your body on fire. I wasn't sure if I was being malicious or just having fun. It seemed fun to me, so I would go with that mood. He was the one making assumptions about women being picky, he deserved whatever discomfort the pork delivered to his mouth and throat.

"Tell me a little bit about yourself, Ms. Mallory."

I took a sip of water to keep myself from reacting to his mocking tone of voice. "I've lived in New York for about a year and a half. Before that, I was in Australia for six months, and before that, California. Before that ..."

The server brought a pot of tea and placed it between us. I reached for the handle, pouring a splash into the small cups that sat beside it on the tray.

"Shouldn't that steep first?" James asked.

"They usually do that before they bring it." I wondered if he'd ever eaten in an Indian restaurant or had chosen it only in the hopes of proving me picky.

He leaned forward, raising his voice ever so slightly. "So, tell me about yourself."

"I did."

"You told me where you've lived."

I shrugged. "Where have you lived?"

He glared at me over the top of his cup. "I'm trying to build a team here, and you're actively sabotaging that. You can be difficult to talk to. Did you know that about yourself?"

"Yes."

Before he could speak, our server returned with a plate of naan. She was young, no more than twenty, with long dark hair, dark eyes, and skin the color of walnuts. She wore a short skirt, sandals, and a white tank top. A gold chain hung around her neck, the gold unicorn on the end settled between the tops of her breasts.

James smiled with too much effort, straining to get into her line of sight that was directed away from him, trying to will her into making eye contact. She flashed him a smile and turned away. As she turned, her skirt swung across the backs of her thighs, which grabbed his attention. I waited for him to notice me watching, curious if he would tone down his gawking when he remembered I was sitting there.

Finally, he turned back and gave me a rubbery smile. "How did you get into photography?"

"Trystan hired me to photograph clients."

"That's how you got into it? What about before you started working for him?"

"That was my first experience as a photographer."

"That's …" He let his eyes rove across my face and down my upper body.

"Remember, you said you either know how to take good photographs or you don't."

"Well, yes, but … you didn't study photography?"

"No."

"Did you go to college at all?"

"Yes."

"Is your degree in art?"

"No." I figured he didn't need to know there was no degree.

"What did you study?"

"A lot of things."

"If you didn't want to have lunch and get to know each other, you should have said so."

"Maybe you're asking the wrong questions."

He sighed. He picked up a piece of naan. Instead of tearing it into smaller pieces as most people do, he took a large bite, ripping it with his teeth as if he were an animal tearing into a chunk of flesh. It was both disturbing and kind of fascinating.

I smiled.

"What's so funny?"

"Nothing."

"You're grinning."

"Just being friendly. I don't like to talk about the past."

"How can you get to know someone if you don't know their history?"

"By how they behave. Ripping a piece of bread with your teeth as if you haven't eaten for weeks is more interesting than what college classes someone took ten years ago."

He slapped the bread down on the plate beside his teacup. He settled back, leaving a large space between himself and the table, trying to push himself as far away from me as he could get.

I was aware I should probably change my tactic because he was likely to report back to Diana on the details of our lunch. Even if he told the truth, it would irritate her, and from what I'd seen of him so far, it wouldn't surprise me if he embellished our interaction to make himself look charming and me look like I was not fitting her ideal of a *team player*.

"I probably shouldn't have said that. About the bread."

"I don't need a critique," he said. "I'm trying to enjoy my meal."

"And we will. You were challenging whether I was qualified to be a photographer." This made me sound insecure, but I figured if he believed he had a bit of power over me, he would settle down.

"It's unusual to walk into a job like this without any qualifications."

"Trystan was looking for a certain personality type, and he figured photography could be learned, personal style cannot."

"True."

I was surprised we agreed.

He smiled, clearly as surprised as I was.

The server returned with a tray and a rack that she popped open before placing the tray on it. The tray looked heavy, filled with copper pots and bowls. They were steaming and aromatic, making me also want to tear into the bread with my teeth bared. I was suddenly aware of how hungry I was.

As she began placing the copper pots on the table, describing each dish, James turned his animal desires to her, the bread ragged and forgotten on his plate. The way he stared at her breasts as she leaned over looked like something you'd see in a movie, not the behavior of even the most lascivious modern male. At least not in the world where I lived. There were surely men like him all over the planet, but you didn't often see them sober at lunchtime in New York restaurants. How on earth had Diana decided this guy was a good fit for our group? He was a creep in every way.

"You have strong arms," he said.

Ignoring him, the server placed the jasmine rice at the center of the table.

"Do you work out?"

"Are there any questions about the food?" she asked.

James laughed. "Are you ignoring me? It's very cute but not the best approach, considering you're working for tips."

I felt as if he'd punched me in the stomach. My previous thoughts of him seemed excessively fair in the face of this. I admired her for not reacting to him.

"That tray is a lot of weight for a little thing like you."

The server gestured to the pork vindaloo I'd ordered and warned us it was extra hot.

"Like you?" James asked.

"Please stop." Her voice had a tremor, but he didn't seem to notice.

"I'm just being friendly. Right, Alexandra?"

"No. You're being rude and inappropriate."

He glared at me. "Lighten up. Is that the world we live in now? A guy can't even flirt with a gorgeous woman who's placing enticing, flavorful food in front of him?"

"I'm not interested," the server said. "Are there any more questions? Do you need anything else? More naan?"

"For someone who comes from a culture with hot food, you're an icy gal."

She glared at him. "Fuck off." She turned and walked away.

I scooped rice onto my plate, eager to get some food into me before he made a scene, and I'd end up walking back to my office with a snarling, empty stomach. After filling my plate with Aloo Gobi, Bhuna Paneer, rice, and a small scoop of the pork, I looked up. James' face was not the red of a wounded ego turning to rage that I'd expected. Instead, all the color was gone. Even his lips were white. His pupils were tiny dots despite the dim lighting.

"She's not getting away with this," he said.

"Calm down."

"That's not how you treat customers."

"You were being a creep. Just enjoy the food. Let's talk about Pauline."

"Who the hell is Pauline?"

"Our client."

"Who does that girl think she is? No one uses that kind of language and attitude with a customer. She's the most unprofessional waitress I've encountered in my life."

I took a bite of Aloo Gobi. "It's delicious. The best I've ever had. You made a good choice."

He gave me a vicious look. His plate remained empty.

I picked up the serving spoon and placed some rice on his plate. I arranged the pork vindaloo next to it.

"Don't serve me like I'm a child."

"You're acting like a child. A bully first, and now a toddler throwing a tantrum. This is supposed to be a business lunch."

That seemed to re-orient him. He must have realized I could tattle to Diana as easily as he could. He seemed to compose himself. He finished filling his plate and began eating. He didn't speak or look at me but steadily shoveled food into his mouth. He chewed and shoveled in more before finishing the previous bite.

When he filled his mouth with pork vindaloo, I saw the reaction in his watering eyes and quivering lips before he said a word. "What the ..." He let the food fall out of his mouth onto the plate. "What the hell is ..." He grabbed his water glass and took several gulps. "That's like eating burning coal."

"Don't exaggerate."

"Are you trying ..." He drank more water, then shoveled rice into his mouth. He ate more naan, chewing furiously.

"Where did you grow up?" I asked.

He swallowed thickly. "We covered that in my interview."

"We talked about your education. Not your childhood."

"You're going to analyze me now?"

"Just curious. Making conversation, not trying to uncover land mines."

"What land mines?"

I laughed. "It was a simple question. I'll start. I grew up in Oregon."

"Spokane."

I wondered if Spokane was a backward-leaning place or if it was specific to his family. Definitely the latter. All distortions are specific to the family. I should know.

"Why does that matter?"

"As I said, curiosity. What was your family like?"

"I have no idea what that question means." It was clear he was still angry, and since he couldn't pick a fight with our server, I was the next best thing.

Then, a new server came to our table. He asked if we wanted more naan or tea.

"You're not our waitress," James said.

"Her shift ended."

James let out a single burst of laughter. "I bet it did. Maybe she was fired. She should be."

"Can I bring you anything else?" the server asked.

"Nope. I've had more than enough." He shoved his plate forward, crashing it against the copper pots.

"Should I wrap these up for you?"

James shook his head. He grabbed his water glass and drank the rest of the contents.

"I'll take them," I said.

"How frugal of you," James said as the server collected a few of the containers and turned to leave.

"I love leftovers."

"Whatever."

"So you didn't tell me what your family was like," I said.

"Almost done?" He stared at my plate.

"I don't like to rush."

"We need to get back."

"Not right this minute." I took a large forkful of pork vindaloo. "I thought we were here to get to know each other."

"Only on your terms, right?"

"Not necessarily," I said.

"I'm the oldest of four kids—three boys and a girl. My dad was MIA, and my mom was a music teacher. Satisfied?"

"Do you play any instruments?"

He sighed. "I'm ready to head out. We'll have to try this again, another time when we're both in better moods."

My mood was fine, but I didn't argue. I finished the food on my plate, waited for the replacement server to put the leftovers in cardboard boxes, and then allowed James to pay. I thanked him, but he was rather ungracious about it.

CHAPTER 13

*J*ames and I walked back to our building without speaking more than was required for navigating the crowds on the sidewalks and the streets we had to cross. I carried a brown paper bag with straw handles, heavy with all the food we hadn't eaten. At the entrance to our building, James paused, then took a few steps away from the door. "You go on up. I have something to take care of."

I shrugged and went inside, rode the elevator up, and stored my haul from lunch in the fridge. When I lived alone, I would have looked forward to diving into it while enjoying a martini and a TV show or an entertaining channel on YouTube or just letting my mind wander, focusing on the flavors wrapping themselves around my tongue and weaving their way down my throat.

Now, I wondered how I would navigate my desire for leftovers with Eileen's likely dinner plans that would include food she'd already purchased and was well on her way to preparing. Maybe I was looking at lunch behind my desk the next few days. Unless I could persuade Eileen to put her meal plans on ice.

I grabbed a bottle of sparkling water, went into my office, and pulled up the executive summaries for several new clients. I sipped water and read the information, eager to get busy with a steady stream of photo sessions. I hadn't realized how much the never-ending fighting with Stephanie had distracted me from what I liked doing—getting people to relax while my camera lenses stared them down. A surge of fresh energy rushed through my body, and I lost myself studying our clients.

At three o'clock, I went into the break room for a cup of coffee. James was there, making a fresh pot. As I entered the room, I could feel his mood had done a one-eighty from his leering, racist, combative behavior over lunch. "Thanks for making coffee," I said.

"I have a servant's heart." He gave me a beatific smile.

"That's good to know."

"It should be obvious."

"I'd love a cup of coffee."

"Absolutely." He took a clean mug off the shelf and filled it with steaming liquid. He held it out to me.

Our eyes met. I considered commenting on his changed demeanor. He looked almost triumphant. In fact, it looked as if he wanted me to ask why he was in such a good mood. He gripped the handle of the mug, unwilling to yield it to me as if he wanted to keep me standing in front of him. "Thanks."

"Sorry lunch went a bit off the rails." He relinquished the mug. "Raincheck?"

"Sure."

"You don't sound enthusiastic. But you didn't the first time, either." He laughed sharply.

"I don't normally socialize a lot with co-workers."

"Don't like mixing business with pleasure?"

I left my face neutral and let the innuendo dissolve in the air around us. "Something like that." I took a sip of coffee.

"I handled it badly," he said.

"You did."

"But not as badly as she did."

I said nothing.

"I went back to the restaurant and took care of it."

"That's good."

He gave me a leering, eager smile.

"I need to get back to it," I said.

"Me too."

I took another sip of coffee."Thanks for this." I walked slowly out of the room and across the hall. At my doorway, I turned and glanced back. He was facing the window above the small table in the alcove beside the sink. Something wasn't right, but I couldn't figure out what it was. I didn't think he'd done what he should have, which was offer an enormous tip along with an apology when he'd returned to the restaurant.

At five-thirty, I took my bag of leftovers. Instead of heading toward the subway, I walked the six blocks to where we'd eaten lunch. The door swung open easily, and I went inside. The man who had finished serving our lunch stood at the hostess stand in the foyer.

"May I help you?" He glanced at the bag I was carrying. "I hope there's nothing wrong with the food."

"Not at all. The food is amazing. Some of the best I've ever had."

He grinned as if he'd prepared it himself. "I was here for lunch today with a—"

"I remember you," he said.

"I wanted to talk to our server," I said. "The one whose shift ended before we were finished."

"Rada."

"Do you know how I can get in touch with her? Or can I leave a note?"

"What's this about?"

"I'm just … I wanted to make sure she was okay. To apologize for what happened. The guy I was with—"

"You don't need to apologize at all. We let her go." He raised his hands, responding to the horrified look on my face. "Not me. Those decisions aren't mine to make. But your lunch date was—"

"It wasn't a date. Co-worker."

His brow wrinkled in a way that if I hadn't been staring directly at the spot that houses the supposed third eye, I wouldn't have noticed. He spoke smoothly, without emotion. "He was very upset."

"He was hitting on your employee and making racist comments. Isn't that something you want to prevent?"

"This is Manhattan, we expect certain people to—"

"I know where we're located," I said. "But he had no right to treat her like that."

"We expect our staff to roll with it." Hearing him speak these words in his precise, articulate accent took my attention off the conversation. At the same time, I couldn't get my head around their policy that expected women, or any server, to put up with harassment.

"Racism?"

"Well, it …" He glanced over his shoulder as if he hoped to be rescued.

"He was disgusting."

He shrugged. "The customer is always right. I mean, not the racist comments, obviously, but we're supposed to … she didn't mention … we're still supposed to treat them with respect. So I guess they are always right. No matter what."

"That's not true."

"If you want to stay in business, there are many hard truths."

His firm belief in this caused a thought to flash through my mind, whispering that perhaps you could never remain true to yourself and be employed by another person. The only answer was total control over your financial stability and your destiny. Hadn't I already learned that lesson when I studied our clients, searching for common elements that resulted in their phenomenal success? I pushed the thought aside for future consideration. "Do you know how I can get in touch with her?"

He narrowed his eyes, his gaze probing mine, trying to figure out why I cared so much. "That's not appropriate."

"Why not?"

"Because her contact information was given to us in circumstances of trust. It's part of her employment record which we're required to keep private."

"My co-worker paid the bill, and he didn't tip her. I'd like to make up for that."

"That's a very generous gesture and very unnecessary."

The door opened, and a group of three women and two men entered the foyer. The man I was talking to—Khalil, according to his name tag—stepped from behind the podium and greeted them. "Do you have a reservation?"

"No." The woman with short dark hair laughed as if not having a reservation was the funniest thing she'd heard all week. "But we're easy. You can stick us right by the kitchen doors or the bathrooms. Wherever. Ian said your food is the best Indian in New York, so we had to come. We're only together for one night. Please." She gave him a gooey, almost seductive smile.

It gave me pause. Sex has a way of seeping unexpectedly, sometimes unnoticed, into many human interactions. I was an expert in that, probably more than most. I used it often enough because it worked. It's as close to a guarantee as you can get. And it worked in this case. Khalil swept them into one of the side rooms, telling them they absolutely had to try the pork vindaloo, and the man, whom I assumed was Ian, loudly agreed.

I waited, hoping Khalil wasn't going to find other tasks and send someone else to man the entryway, leaving me to start all over again, trying to elicit information that no employer would release to a casual inquirer. After three or for minutes, he returned. He didn't seem surprised to see that I was still there, which made me feel like I'd won a small victory. Very small.

"So, can I get her contact info?"

75

"I told you I can't do that. But if you'd like to leave a gratuity, I'll see that it's included in her final check."

I pulled out my wallet and removed two fifties. I held out the bills, but he didn't take them. "That's too much. It's inappropriate."

"For a man who knows everything that's appropriate and not, you sure seem okay with a customer sexually harassing one of your employees. He put an immediate end to her income, not to mention damaging her chances of finding another position."

"We don't pass on the reason for her leaving, so she'll have no problem with that."

I stared at him, not sure either of us believed that, but not wanting to get off onto something that had nothing to do with what I wanted in that moment.

I moved the fifties closer to his hand. "Please take these."

"It's too much."

"Hasn't anyone ever left your servers excessive tips after they had a memorable, delightful experience? Sometimes the dollars don't equate to the service, but to the experience."

He rolled his eyes.

"She earned it," I said.

He took the bills, pinching them from my fingers and letting them dangle from his own as if they were toxic.

"I won't tell anyone you gave me her contact information," I said.

"That's not the point."

I smiled. I widened my eyes. It wasn't as effective as usual because I was hyper-conscious of the woman who had given him an inviting smile moments earlier to assist her in getting a table without a reservation.

"You can leave your card," Khalil said. "If she's interested in talking to you, she's free to get in touch."

"Perfect." I looked directly into his eyes, giving him the warmest, most grateful smile I could manufacture.

Without seeming to respond to my charming smile, he folded the bills. He held out his hand, waiting for a card.

I didn't have any. I dug around in my bag until I found the tag I'd cut off a top I'd bought on the way to a club the weekend before. I took the pen off the stand in front of me and wrote my name and phone number. I added my work email address. It was more information than I liked to pass around, but this was important. And she was a stranger. So was Khalil. Sometimes, often, strangers are safer than people I know.

CHAPTER 14

I'd accurately foreseen the future in which I didn't get to enjoy my leftovers. The apartment smelled like garlic when I stepped inside. I went into the kitchen, where Eileen had bowls and utensils scattered across the counter, two steaming pots and a frying pan on the stovetop.

"I'm making garlic chicken and pasta. And a fruit salad. There's Chardonnay in the fridge if you want a glass." She glanced at the large bag I was holding. "What's that?"

"Leftovers from lunch. I thought—"

She laughed. "They'll have to wait. Ned's coming over. I hope that's okay."

It didn't matter to me one way or the other if Ned was coming over. It did matter that my delicious lunch was once again shoved to the side because someone else had an agenda that sucked me into its vortex. I opened the refrigerator and began unloading containers from my bag onto the top shelf.

"That's a lot of food," Eileen said.

"I went out with James. Our lunch ended suddenly."

"Why?"

I realized this was exactly the kind of thing I did not want to be passing along to a roommate. I had no idea what would come of the situation with James. It wasn't as if I was planning to get rid of him and already covering my tracks, but I'd be lying if I said there wasn't a soft, distant whisper in the back of my brain that it might come to that. "We had to get back to the office."

She laughed. "You ordered all that food, and then there was a sudden emergency in someone's career advancement?"

I shrugged. "Do you want a top-off to your wine?"

"Sure."

I added a splash to her wineglass and poured a small amount for myself. I folded up the bag and shoved it into the recycling, chattering about how nice the weather was, how it would be great to eat outside sometime soon, anything that came into my head that might fill the room with words, forcing all thoughts of my aborted lunch out of her head.

"What can I help you with?" I took a sip of wine.

"Nothing. Go relax."

I took my glass into the living room, turned the chair slightly to face the window, and settled down to enjoy the divine taste. It was so delicious there was a risk of drinking it too fast. I held the glass up to the light and admired the silky golden yellow. I swirled it around. I put my nose over the rim and inhaled. I allowed myself a very tiny sip.

Right then, I wanted a cigarette. I'd found myself wanting them less and less, which was good. It had become easier and easier to run longer distances. But when I had something to drink, I sometimes craved that hit of nicotine, that burn of smoke in my lungs, and the satisfying exhalation of a graceful stream of smoke. And if for no other reason than because, without a cigarette between my fingers, I tended to keep sipping. There were no distractions.

Of course, this apartment didn't have an easily accessible roof garden, so it wasn't as if I could indulge that desire even if I wanted to cave to my weakness.

In the kitchen, Eileen was talking to herself, discussing the steps of her recipe, humming a little, then telling herself what ingredient she needed next in a singing voice. It was a little creepy because she sounded like she was slightly insane, talking and singing, banging pans and utensils, and chopping as if she were stabbing the cutting board.

I took another sip of wine, then heard the front door open. So ... Ned had a key to our apartment. I hadn't been aware, and I felt a prick of annoyance that Eileen hadn't thought she should mention this to me.

"Hey! Good to see you, Alex." Ned came into the living room, waved as if he were calling to me from across the street, then turned toward the kitchen. This was followed by several long moments of silence, which I assumed was filled with kissing, the singing and humming sealed off for now.

I took another sip of wine.

A few minutes later, Ned returned to the living room and sat on the couch, placing his wineglass on the coffee table. He took off his shoes and shoved them under the table. "Hope you don't mind. I hate wearing shoes indoors."

I smiled and said nothing. He seemed to feel quite at home. It made me wonder why Eileen had agreed to share an apartment with me. He must have suggested she move in with him, but for whatever reason, she'd said no. Our lease was for a year, so she must have been quite confident that she would be staying put for that time. But then, she'd handed him a key.

"How was your day?" Ned asked.

"Good."

"Are the new employees acclimating? Any interesting clients you can tell me about?"

"Everything's good." I picked up my glass for another sip and saw it was empty.

"Let me refill that." He jumped up, grabbed the glass out of my hand, and whisked it away to the kitchen.

When he returned, he seemed to hold onto the glass a moment

longer than necessary, giving me repulsive memories of James. There was a subtle struggle before he released it into my hand. He gave me a smile that I couldn't interpret, but it made me wonder if the two of them cut from the same cloth.

During dinner, he and Eileen talked non-stop, the flow of words unbroken as if their speech cadence and even their thoughts were so aligned their minds had become a single flow of consciousness. I listened. They didn't seem to notice I wasn't stepping into that flow, which was fine with me. It was the first time I'd eaten a meal with the two of them, so I preferred being an observer. Especially after that thing with the wineglass.

What I observed was that they interacted like a couple who had been married for a decade. I wondered if that was because Ned was so much older, and the force of his twenty extra years pulled her closer to the middle years of her life. He seemed very devoted to her. At the same time, he was so overly certain in his beliefs about the world and what he wanted in life that he didn't seem inclined toward compromise. Not that I'm a marriage expert or even a relationship expert. I'm certainly not the poster child for compromise in a relationship. I'm the furthest distance possible from that. I do sometimes wonder whether I might eventually find a man who I'd like to be around for an extended period of time, but the compromise thing could be a problem. This pushes me to observe closely, trying to figure out how things work. What I have observed is quite a lot of compromise.

I wondered why Eileen was drawn to a man so much older. It was hard to imagine they shared similar tastes in music and other kinds of entertainment, but maybe I was making ageist assumptions about Ned.

As the evening progressed, I realized that Ned was spending the night. Finally, he stood and swallowed the last of his wine. He poured his remaining Scrabble tiles from the game we'd been playing back into the box and said, "I hope we don't need to lock our bedroom door, Alexandra."

"Ned." Eileen laughed and looked anxious at the same time.

He gave her a sharp look. "You know I like to be straightforward."

She said nothing.

It was a strange way to phrase it. Wouldn't the natural statement be—*I am straightforward*? That's the straightforward way of expressing it. Did he realize he was suggesting that he had to work at being straightforward, and therefore, it was put on?

He looked at me, meeting my gaze with a slight smirk that I'm absolutely sure Eileen did not notice. "I think Alex has a stealthy quality. She's like a cat that suddenly shows up when you had no idea she was in the vicinity. A stealthy person might consider peeking in on us while we're in bed."

I laughed.

"Ned!" Eileen's face was flushed and blotchy.

"It's my impression, that's all. I don't think I'm offending her, am I, Alex?" He gave me a wicked smile.

If it were anyone but me, they would be offended. But he was right. "You didn't offend me," I said. "Maybe you gave me an idea."

Ned moved his head slightly, agreeing with himself, gratified he'd spoken the truth and elicited more.

Eileen stared at me. She looked horrified, and I'm sure it was at what I'd said more than the words that tumbled out of her fiancé's mouth. "You … you're giving me a hard time, right?"

"It was his idea," I said.

He put his hand on my head as if I were a child. "There's a lot going on in that little head, and I think the pieces that make it out into the world are infinitesimal. And you always get what you want because you've planned it all ahead of time."

"Have I?"

"I don't like this conversation," Eileen said.

Ned kept his hand on my head. There was nothing sexual about it, and I don't think Eileen perceived it that way either, but she looked more upset than I'd ever seen her, maybe even including the moment when she'd learned her mother was dead.

"Always plotting, getting your way, and making sure people fulfill their usefulness to you," he said.

"You're making her sound awful," Eileen said. "She's one of the kindest and most interesting people I know."

"Interesting, yes," he said. "Kind?" He let the word hang there.

I couldn't figure out what I'd said or done to get him talking like this. How had he figured out that much about me in the few brief times we'd spoken to each other? It made me wonder if I was outmatched. It didn't hurt my feelings as Eileen feared, but it made me think more deeply about all the things I'd given up for a larger, nicer apartment.

If Ned thought I was using people or whatever it was he meant to suggest, did that mean he'd been observing me without my being aware? Was he going to note every time I wasn't home or went out late at night, disbelieving whatever story I told?

He took his hand off my head. Eileen kissed my cheek and gave me a hug, something she'd never done before. I froze slightly, but she didn't seem to notice. If she did, she didn't give it away. They went into her bedroom and closed the door. I heard the lock turn. I was absolutely sure it was flicked quickly to be certain the sound was loud enough for me to hear if I was still standing closer to the bedroom door than I should have been.

I went into my room and closed the door.

I would have to be very careful around Ned. I didn't like knowing that. For several long minutes, I wondered if I'd made a terrible mistake in deciding to share an apartment with Eileen before learning more about her fiancé.

CHAPTER 15

 ortland, Oregon

* * *

My given name is Laura Alexandra Mallory. But once, there was another Alexandra Mallory.

The situation with our names is difficult to explain because it suggests there was something seriously broken in my parents' minds.

But after everything that happened, I cherish the name Alexandra because it keeps me tied to her. Forever.

Even on our gravestones, she and I will be connected. She's the only person on this planet I wanted to be tied to, and she's the one person I was denied.

I was given the name Laura Alexandra on the day I was born. The only thing I can figure out, based on what happened after, was that by the age of one when my sister came into the world, my parents already wanted a do-over. I can't imagine what they saw in me that caused this. They already had three boys, so they must have been familiar with the differing behaviors among children with

84

their unique personalities and desires. You would think they might write off some of it—whatever *it* was—to their first experience with a female child, but they didn't.

They must have believed I was trouble before I spoke my first word. Before I could drink milk from a cup. They thought I was trouble within a month of my victorious effort of pushing myself to my feet and toddling across the living room to steal a token from my brothers' board game.

When their second girl was born, a precious gift from god, another flower for my father to protect and nurture in his hothouse, they realized how much they loved the name Alexandra.

In one of the strangest parenting choices I've ever encountered, they named my sister Alexandra Laura.

As the family legend goes, my brothers had already taken to calling me Alex. It's possible they couldn't figure out how to relate to me unless I had a male nickname. I really don't know, and the *why* of the story was lost to time if it ever existed.

My parents gave both my names to my sister, placing their favorite one in front, in a clear message to me. Obviously, I wasn't aware of this at the age of twelve months and three days, but they weren't shy about re-telling pieces of this story on a regular basis. They told it on her birthday and mine. They told it when missionaries from overseas stayed with us and asked about our family. And they told it each time someone new came into our home.

It didn't matter much to me, but trying to explain it to others painted an image that was a freak show of twisted thinking. On their part, not mine.

From the moment I first spoke her name, I called my sister Lexy. Another family story, lost by the time I turned six years old, was that I articulated this nickname perfectly the very first time. Lexy was the name my brothers quickly adopted, but my parents refused.

When she began talking, Lexy called me Alex. Another family story was that I refused to respond to any name but Alex. My parents punished me by making me sit in my room alone. They deprived me of desserts and playing outside. I didn't give in. They were not going to take my name away from me, and I didn't care how bored I got. I wasn't giving in.

My parents complained about this often. They wanted their girls to be called Laura and Alexandra, not these ridiculous nicknames, these too-short words that featured the x-sound. But eventually, they were forced to yield because I simply refused to respond.

My father worshiped that little girl. He took her out of my mother's arms so he could be the one to carry her into church every Sunday. He marched down the center aisle, holding her near his shoulders so everyone could see her face as if carrying her to the altar for sacrifice. He held her on his lap through the entire church service. Her high chair was beside his seat at the dinner table, and he was the one to come into our room and shush her at night when she cried.

But he hated the name Lexy and always called her Alexandra.

So we began to grow up—Lexy and Alex—two girls with slightly confused identities, but clinging with iron grips to the identity each knew. We refused to give up that inner strength and confidence that all children are born with, and many yield too easily.

This strength and confidence were things that my parents often wailed about, snapping at each other about our stubborn resistance to their world where children obeyed their parents without question. They were terrified that Lexy would follow in my cloven footsteps.

Behind their closed bedroom door at night, when they thought I was asleep, not crouched just outside it, they worried themselves sick. They prayed loudly and fervently that evil forces would remove their talons from our shoulders. Before their prayers started, they talked about their worry. After their prayers, they picked up the same conversation, clearly not confident their prayers would be answered, that not even a single request had been noted.

Because of all this worry, both discussed and explained in their prayers, which were simply more eloquent worries, I was surprised they allowed my sister and me to share a bedroom. I suppose practicality won out. Maybe they figured they could keep a closer watch if we were always together.

It's also possible they didn't think separating us would accomplish anything. Separation might create a forbidden fruit situation. This was warfare in the realm of the supernatural. This was not something that could be fixed by human effort. The evil strain that had taken root in me from birth, and was slowly worming its way into my sister, was for god and the angels to take care of. God would make it right. They would follow his directives, wait for his guidance, and trust that our hearts would be purified.

Lexy's heart was utterly pure. But they couldn't see that. My parents lived in terror of the eternal fires of hell. Terror can drive people to do terrible things. I suppose it's self-preservation.

CHAPTER 16

 ew York

* * *

Two days after James harassed and bullied our server out of her job,
I still had not heard from Khalil regarding whether he'd given my
contact information to her. I was pretty sure he thought I'd
forgotten all about her.

I told my colleagues I was taking a late lunch. A few minutes
before three, when the restaurant was less likely to be scrambling to
hustle diners in and out, I walked to the restaurant. Inside, the host
station was unoccupied. I leaned on the front edge of the stand and
peered into the various rooms of the restaurant, all of which were
visible from that spot. There were three or four occupied tables in
each room, servers moving at a casual pace without feeling pressure
to accelerate the transaction of eating lunch.

Finally, an older man appeared in the lobby. "Table for one?"

"I'm looking for Khalil."

"Who should I tell him is asking?"

"Alex."

He waited for me to give him the rest of my name, a pleasant expression on his face.

"He won't recognize my name."

He waited another half-second before conceding. "I'll check."

After ten minutes, I began to wonder if he'd described me to Khalil and learned I was trying to interfere in their employment policies. Then, Khalil appeared. "I remember you." He didn't look thrilled.

"Did you give my contact information to Rada?" I asked.

"I did."

"I assumed you would let me know what she said."

He stared at me with a tiny smile at the corner of his lips as if to say he owed me nothing.

"What did she say?" I asked.

"We didn't discuss you."

"Did she say she'd call or text me?"

"That's none of my business. I passed on your message and your gratuity."

"Did she say it was okay for me to call *her*?"

"You're very persistent."

"What happened to her isn't right. I want to fix it."

"Do you think you can fix things in the world that have nothing to do with you?"

He seemed to realize this might have more to do with me than the server. Any woman who's treated unfairly *is* me. Or a potential form of me. I know I shouldn't think in those terms, but it's wired into my brain for some reason I can't explain. I don't know if it's about my sister, something unique to my psyche, or something else entirely. I try not to analyze it more than necessary. Some things simply are. "You never know," I said.

"Who gave you that right?"

Who *gave* it to me? It was such a strange question, I almost couldn't process what he was asking. He seemed to think my desire was a directive from a higher being. It wasn't like that at all. It was a sense that when everyone does their part to gently shift the world in one direction or another, society and the human race evolve. Of course, it's often evolving in circles, but eventually, those circles expand.

"I think she'll want to know that I'm making up for the way he stiffed her. I really don't see why I can't get her phone number. It's not like I'm asking for her address because I'm going to her apartment to stab her to death."

He looked horrified. I probably shouldn't have said that last part, but there it was.

"You don't know this woman. You can't assume your help is welcome."

Why on earth would it not be welcomed? She'd lost her job. This guy's attitude seemed to explain why she'd been fired. They truly did live to serve customers. And only customers. Still, I would have thought that if you were concerned that much about one group of people, you would also have concern for the people who took care of that first group. Food wouldn't be delivered without servers, dishes would be left uncleared without kitchen staff, not to mention the preparation of the delicious food itself.

"I really can't help you any further," he said. "If you'd like a late lunch, I can seat you."

I shook my head. I went to the door and pushed it open, blinking my way into too-bright sunlight after the dim, atmospheric interior. I stood there for five minutes, letting the timer on my phone count down the seconds.

Then, I returned to the restaurant. I found the host stand deserted again, as I'd expected at this time of day. I slipped quickly into the first dining room to my left. Like the others, the room was lavishly decorated—fabrics woven with gold threads draped across the ceiling, large brass pots standing in alcoves in the wall and on pedestals, some filled with wild grasses. There were eight tables of varying sizes. Only two were occupied. I lingered near a pedestal with a brass pot that towered over me.

After less than two minutes of hovering, a server approached the two-top table closest to where I stood. In another stroke of luck, the server was female. As she spoke to the men seated there, I edged my way toward her, keeping out of her line of sight. When she turned away from the table, I followed her quickly. "Excuse me."

She turned, smiling. It was shocking. Most people don't do that. The natural instinct is to turn with wariness.

"How can I help you?" She glanced around the room as if there must be a table with new customers she hadn't noticed.

"I'm trying to get in touch with Rada."

She frowned.

"I had lunch here a few days ago. The man I was with created the situation that got her fired."

She gave me a stern look. "What do you want?"

"I want to give her the tip he cheated her out of."

"She needs a lot more than a tip. She has to find a new position, and now she has a large black mark on her job history."

"I know. It's disgusting. She was professional all the way." I gave her a sympathetic smile. "But she still deserves the tip, even if it's not all that helpful for what she's facing."

She nodded. "Why didn't you say something at the time?"

"I did. I tried to get my colleague to stop being a jerk, but …" I gave her a knowing look. "I tried talking to the manager."

She sighed as if, despite her suggestion, she'd known I couldn't have expected anything but a concrete wall.

"They won't give me her number," I said. "Khalil said he passed my contact information to her, but if it wasn't explained clearly, she might be worried about what I want. She might think I'm coming after her because of how awful my colleague was."

"That would be my reaction."

"Do you mind giving her number to me?"

She studied my face. "What did you say your name was?"

"Alexandra Mallory." The words sounded strange in my ears, two words I'd spoken ten thousand times, but in that moment, I felt like I was exposing more of myself than I ever had.

"Okay. Let me get my phone." She went through the double doors leading to the inner workings of the restaurant. She returned a moment later and asked for my number. Maybe this was the reason for the strange feeling of exposure that had come over me a moment earlier. I went out of my way to avoid giving out my number, even though it technically belonged to Fly Higher because that's where the bill was sent. She would likely delete it the moment I left, but I couldn't know that. People sometimes hoard what comes into their phones, clinging to data and photos and calendar appointments until the end of time. Or what seems like the end of time, as images and words from our lives drift into the cloud and remain there until someone wants to take the time to remove them. And since those pieces of us aren't taking up space that gets in our way, they fall into an out-of-sight-out-of-mind void.

I thanked her for the number, assured her I wouldn't tell anyone she'd given it to me, and left.

Back in my office, I closed the door and opened the text window. I tapped out a message to Rada, telling her who I was and that I wanted to make things right with her tip, even though that one right thing wasn't going to fix her problem.

There was no response. I tried to get busy with work, studying the profiles of new clients and making notes about what I might focus on in their photography sessions. I had a meeting with Diana about the next round of clients ready for their photographs. I dodged James in the break room, twice. I chatted with Fallon and surfed the web for restaurant reviews. I texted Eileen and asked if she wanted to meet for dinner. She had plans to spend the evening and stay over at Ned's. I put down my phone, pleased by the thought of an evening alone.

At ten minutes to six, a message appeared from Rada.

You are so, so sweet. I could kiss you. But Khalil already gave me your too-generous tip.

I texted back — *What my colleague did was inexcusable. You deserve more.*

Rada: *I can't accept it.*

Alex: *Please. I want to. And I had a little windfall, so I want to share.*

Rada: *I'm soooo grateful for your kindness. I would love to meet. Does tomorrow work?*

For the second time in three days, someone was calling me kind. I stared at the words, impressed by my skill in human interaction. I sent her the name of a wine bar and told her I could give her what she was owed and say goodbye, or we could have a glass of wine and talk. My treat.

She replied with—*See you there.*

I assumed she felt awkward or apprehensive and wanted to see me again before deciding. Or maybe she was always vague.

CHAPTER 17

*T*ess and I hadn't had a video chat in months. I was glad Eileen would be out that evening, leaving me free to say whatever I wanted without her curiosity perched on my shoulder like a bird of prey.

Tess had arranged this call with more planning than usual, suggesting we mix martinis to sip while we talked, even though it would be noon the following day in Australia to my seven o'clock in the evening. I followed her directive and mixed my drink. I carried it to the living room and propped my tablet on the coffee table. I sat on the floor where the tablet could capture my face, and I was hands-free to sip my luscious drink.

I made a premature toast to myself and took a tiny sip.

When Tess's face appeared on the screen, I felt like I was spinning backward in time. Looking at her sharp, interested smile and commanding eyes, none of the events since I'd last seen her seemed real—the people I'd killed, the guys I'd had sex with, the games I'd played, the photographs I'd taken. We raised our glasses and took simultaneous sips.

"I have news." Tess placed her glass somewhere out of range of the camera and leaned forward slightly, filling the frame with her dark hair and eyes. Since leaving the corporate world to run her own business as a marketing consultant, she hadn't toned down the heavy eye makeup she wore. Now, she worked from home a lot of the time, taking casual meetings in cafés and sometimes in pubs. I supposed she still favored the dramatic appearance for her frequent video calls, maybe now more than ever.

In the background, I heard Damien echo her words in his raucous voice—*I have news!*

I smiled and took a sip of my drink. I missed that bird.

"You'll probably think I've lost it," she said.

"I doubt it." I plucked an olive off the stir stick and ate it.

"I'm getting married."

I was surprised and, at the same time, not at all surprised. I raised my glass to the screen. "Congratulations!"

She grinned. "Thanks."

"I don't think getting married is losing it unless you met him two days ago."

"Nothing like that. He was a client. We've known each other for more than a year."

"Then what's the losing it part?"

"He's American."

"So?"

"He's not an American living in Australia. He lives north of San Francisco. He's the co-founder of a cyber security company. I've been working a lot with him as a consultant, and I'll be joining as Chief Marketing Officer. Not that it's such a big deal since the company has forty-three employees."

"You're moving back to California?"

"Yes. We're getting married in Napa Valley. Probably early spring next year."

"All of that sounds rational." For someone who thought well of marriage, who loved to market technology, her plans made perfect sense.

"You don't think it's funny that I moved to Australia, and instead of meeting an Australian, I might as well have stayed home?"

I laughed. "Well, you didn't move there just to meet a guy."

"True." She looked slightly perplexed as if she was seriously questioning her judgment. She always had second and third-guessed all her choices. For someone oozing confidence and who had always held powerful roles, she did a lot of self-examination, often without reaching a solid conclusion. "Who understands the ways our lives unfold? Right?"

"You sound mellow. For you."

"I'm the same as always. I don't think of any of my choices as mistakes."

I wasn't sure Tess was being truthful with herself. She wouldn't debate her choices and constantly reconsider them if she wasn't so concerned about mistakes. The only mistakes I worried about were ones that could get me incarcerated. Mistakes that couldn't be fixed. Making one choice or another never looked like a mistake to me. Just a choice. I could make a different one the next time.

"Well, thanks for being excited for me."

"Not everyone is?"

She shrugged. She took a sip of her drink and stared into the glass, avoiding eye contact with me for a moment.

"But you're happy?"

She looked up, smiling. "Absolutely."

"Then I'm thrilled for you. What's his name?"

"Marcus."

"Tess and Marcus. It has a nice ring."

She smirked. "Why do people say that?"

"Because our instincts override our brains. Sounds and patterns are more compelling than what people are saying. Our subconscious minds pick up on it."

"Is this valid psychology you learned from Trystan, or is it something you made up two seconds ago?"

I laughed. I had no idea why I'd used that cliché about it having a nice ring. I suppose I wanted to assure her I was accepting her relationship at face value. I hadn't heard this theory about gut instinct around things like name combinations expressed exactly as I'd just said it, but it made sense. I certainly knew from my work that people operate on a lot of beliefs and habits that they don't even realize they have.

"When are you moving back?" I asked.

"We haven't set a definite timeline. Probably this summer. It depends on the date of the wedding. You'll be a bridal attendant, of course."

I laughed.

"Why are you laughing?"

"I'm not sure I'm bridal attendant—"

"You have to. You're one of my closest friends. I'd feel half-dressed without you standing beside me."

"If you say so." If I was one of her closest friends, I wondered about the others. She knew almost nothing about me, although I suppose she thought she knew quite a lot. And that was true of everyone in my life, for obvious reasons. I couldn't see myself in a popsicle-colored dress matching other women, smiling and holding flowers, tossing birdseed, and hosting showers and bachelorette parties. I sighed. Maybe it would all be a west coast thing, and I could fly in at the eleventh hour. It was almost a year away. I didn't need to give it another moment's thought, for now.

"So ... what's new with you?" Tess asked.

"Getting adjusted to having Diana in charge. We're hiring new people."

"Is there a guy in your life?"

"There is no guy." I took a sip of my drink and ate the second olive. I would need to correct that soon, but for the time being, I was absorbed with too many other small matters that had the potential to mushroom—James, Ned, Eileen, Rada. Clearly, Rada didn't need to be my issue. I'd invited *her* into *my* life, but it was necessary.

"It's always good to have time to clear your head between relationships," Tess said.

"Yes."

"How are the new hires?"

"One is a problem. I didn't want to hire him. He's a misogynist who thinks he's evolved."

"That's the worst."

"I had lunch with him the other day, and he hit on our server. She blew him off, and he threw a fit to the restaurant management. She was fired."

"There must have been something else. No one gets fired anymore for standing up to harassment."

"I think you're wrong."

She sighed. "You're probably right. In large companies with solid HR departments, maybe. I suppose in a restaurant that's not a national chain ..."

I nodded. "I tracked her down, and I'm going to give her an inflated tip. He left her nothing."

"Don't get sucked in."

I laughed. "I don't get sucked into anything."

"Sometimes, you do. By your own self, not that anyone can twist your arm. Ever."

"Anyway, I told Diana right away he wasn't a good fit. I told her I had concerns. He called me sassy." I made a repulsed face. "She didn't care. She says she wants the absolute best person, regardless of what they're like or how they fit in with the others on our team. Supposedly he's it—the best."

"Isn't that why she has you?"

"Okay, sure."

"That's admirable, really."

"To a point. He gives me the creeps. I hope he gets bored and leaves."

"I thought the best part about your job is most of your time is spent out with clients. How often do you need to talk to him?"

"We go over the photographs together, and he gives me micro-expression insight. So it's pretty regular, even if it's not all the time."

"Just try to be professional. Be cool, be polite, say as little as necessary. Be efficient."

"All good advice. But it's difficult to be polite when someone can't keep his mouth shut and feels the need to explain women to themselves."

"Just don't kill him."

I laughed. She laughed with me. We sipped our drinks. There was a tiny little whisper in the depths of my brain, wondering if she knew more about me than I'd realized.

CHAPTER 18

Rada was standing outside the wine bar. She wore jeans and flip-flops and a tight black top that showed a line of skin between the hem and her belt. Her face was entirely free of makeup, and she was stunning without it. I imagined James hadn't been the first person to treat her like he deserved to have her. I wondered if he was the first who had cost her a job.

She gave me a tentative smile. "This is a little embarrassing. I feel like I'm taking a handout, but I really can't say no to extra cash right now. And Khalil gave me the cash you—"

"Do you want to have a glass of wine? My treat."

"You already—"

"Don't worry about it. I want a glass of wine and I want company." I gave her a smile that I hoped looked a tiny bit lonely.

It succeeded, or else she was just waiting for encouragement because she grabbed the door handle and pulled it open. "That would be great. Thanks a bunch."

We were seated at a booth for two with partial walls that made it feel quite private. A thin silver light hung over the table, offering a glow that was bright enough to see the menu but didn't glare in our eyes or make our faces look harsh and unwelcoming. The aroma of garlic filled the room, that enticing scent that makes you hungry for a lavish meal even if you just ate two hours earlier.

We ordered two glasses of Pinot Noir and a bowl of assorted olives as well as button mushrooms sautéed in herbs and garlic. When I ordered the olives, she claimed to adore them, which made me think even more highly of her.

I'd put the cash that went far beyond the tip James had stiffed her out of into an envelope. I placed it on the table between us.

She took it more quickly than I'd expected, given her earlier suggestion of shame. She looked inside. "Oh, this is too much. Way too much." She started to pull out a bill.

I pushed her hand away from me. "Keep it. Consider it hazard pay."

She laughed. "Why are you doing this?" She narrowed her eyes and placed the envelope on the table in the exact center. "What do you want?"

"I'm doing it because the man I was with was utterly disgusting. And it's outrageous that you lost your job because of him. The restaurant should have had your back."

"They never take the servers' side. We're part of the decoration. Don't you know that? We're like the food—there to be consumed."

I laughed. "It's not funny, but it is."

"I know."

This girl was fun. I felt like her big sister. It was a strange sensation, and I wasn't sure what to do with it. I didn't need to take responsibility for another human being. That was the last thing I wanted in my life. When I wanted to have an impact on a woman's life, I preferred to slip quietly in the back door, do my thing, and leave. But she made me laugh. And that's not a quality you find as much as you'd like. I certainly hadn't found it in my co-workers, or my neighbors, for a long time.

"It's not like he's the first man to make rude comments. I hear it every day."

"I keep thinking society is changing … that the mix is shifting. That men are getting it."

"Not for servers. Not for people who don't have money. And power. Like I said—"

"You're there to be consumed." I finished the sentence for her.

"But he's the first one to go out of his way to cause trouble for me. Usually, they don't tip, and that's the end of it. Sometimes they walk out and don't pay the bill. A few times, that got taken out of my check because the guy said I'd treated him and his friends so badly, which wasn't true. But no one has ever done something like this. I don't know what he said to them. He probably threatened to destroy their reputation somehow."

I sipped my wine. I ate a Greek olive and then a Spanish olive. I stabbed the tiny fork into a mushroom and ate that when I'd swallowed the olives.

"Where do you work?" Rada asked.

"A place called Fly Higher. We coach women who are at the top of their careers but are stagnating or want to achieve more."

"I could use some of that."

I didn't want to tell her it was far more expensive than a year's worth of tips. Besides, she didn't have the kind of career we were set up for. "Are you going to find another server job or try to get into something else?"

She shrugged. She ate five mushrooms and stared at a spot to the left of my head, avoiding my gaze.

"I hope they won't give you a bad reference."

"I'm not sure. I might leave it off my resume. I've only been there nine months, so I could make it look like I took some time off. I haven't figured it out yet." She took a sip of wine.

"Do you like being a server?"

Again, she shrugged.

"Are you in school or anything?"

She gave me a hard stare. "See, everyone asks that."

"What?"

"You don't think it's a very good job. You assume it's only something I would do for a while, on my way to something better, something important."

"Maybe. It's hard work."

"It can be really great pay. If you're at the right place. If you have regular customers who get to know you."

"Do you like it?"

She laughed. "I hate it. Actually, I was going to school, but … life." She shrugged and ate a few mushrooms.

I thought she might start crying. I really hoped she would not. I liked her witty, sarcastic tone. I didn't want to have to make her feel better. I wasn't good at that at all. "What do you want to do?"

"I need money, so what I want to do isn't the main thing."

"Yeah."

"I'm interested in science. I was studying biology, but I wasn't sure what kind of career I could have with that." She shrugged. "I don't know. Anyway, my parents always said, *you have to get good grades. Study hard. School is important.* But they never told me why, and they never talked about what my options were or asked what I wanted to be. Now I realize they assumed I'd get married, and they just didn't want me to be ignorant."

We sipped our wine for a while, not talking. I wondered if Tess had been right. I was getting sucked in. And yet I didn't want Rada to be left hanging. Nothing that happened to her had anything to do with me, except maybe not fighting hard enough with Diana, making her see that James was not going to do anything to make our company shine. I wasn't sure why I'd caved to her desire to be so accepting and inclusive. It wasn't like me. I would never have given in before, even if she chastised me for not getting along, even if she acted so in-charge and certain that she was right that I had to stop picking fights. Usually, that kind of thing makes me fight harder.

Besides, I don't actually pick fights. All I do is stand my ground, and other people fight back.

I wanted to keep my job. I couldn't imagine something more interesting than taking photographs, at least not right now. Eventually, I might get bored. Eventually, I probably *would* get bored, but I wasn't yet. I liked the variety of people and that there were so many of them. Everything about taking photographs of hungry, ambitious clients kept me from getting bored, which is the thing I hate most. I wanted to work with Diana. I wanted to see the company succeed. I wanted more potential for increasing my income, which was in my contract. Each time Fly Higher reached specific financial targets, I would get a nice bonus.

And I'm lazy. I didn't want to move out of New York yet and I didn't want to look for another job. I didn't even want to figure out what that other job might be.

And, I was aware that things with Stephanie had gotten out of hand. For all those reasons, I'd caved to her decision to hire James.

I didn't blame myself for this girl's job loss. But I did think I was in a position to fix it, and for that reason, I couldn't let it go. There was a tiny part of me that thought she would do really well with Fly Higher consulting, but I knew Diana would laugh that off the minute I said the word *server*.

"It's really nice of you to take such an interest in me," she said.

"No worries."

"Most people are so busy with their own problems they hardly have time to even smile at another person, much less try to fix something that isn't even their fault. Or to just listen."

"I'm not really as nice as you think I am."

She laughed. "Of course you are."

It wasn't something to argue about. "I wish I knew someone who owned a restaurant and could offer you an interview. Maybe, someone who was so impressed with your experience, they didn't care about the details on your resumé."

"It's fine. It's nice that you listened to me. It's nice that you're trying to think of ideas. It's really nice that you bought me this." She took a few sips of wine. "I haven't had a glass of wine in forever. Too poor for that." She laughed. She picked up the envelope of cash and shoved it into her purse. "And thanks for this. It helps." She drank the rest of her wine.

"Good."

"Honest—thanks so much." She stood and slung her purse over her shoulder.

"If I come up with any options, I'll text you."

She smiled. I could see in her eyes that she thought I was just being ridiculous now. She was trying hard not to laugh, or cry. In her mind, there were no ideas. She had to figure out a way to explain the time she'd worked at her recent job as time off work and find a new serving job at a restaurant that would accept her explanation. She would continue working as a server and meet more men who would treat her like she owed them more than a few drinks and a plate of food. Before she knew it, she would meet a guy and have a kid, or three, and be too old to even remember that she'd ever thought about options.

CHAPTER 19

I went for a five-mile run through Central Park on Sunday. Although I listened to a pop music playlist the whole time, I hardly noticed the words that were supposed to keep me from thinking too much. Instead, I thought non-stop about Rada.

By the end of my run, I did have an option for her. I marveled over how right Tess had been—I was the one sucking my very own self into Rada's life. But I couldn't stop. Maybe it's because I'm so easily bored that I get sucked into situations where I shouldn't. Maybe it's my unrelenting curiosity—wanting to know other people's business ... things I shouldn't.

But I did have an idea. It was a simple idea, with the potential to get me into more trouble with Diana than fighting with her about what James might have done. I'd caved on one thing, and now I was poised to do something far worse than argue and challenge her authority. And I couldn't stop myself.

As planned, I showed up late Monday morning at the Angel Orensanz Foundation for an exclusive fashion show featuring models from Pauline's agency. It was a luncheon for publicists, bloggers, and fashion influencers. The food promised to be amazing and would be served with high-end champagne, not the stuff that's splashed into orange juice.

I was there to photograph Pauline interacting in her element. The goal was to catch her absorbed in her work, unselfconscious and unaware. I hoped that I wouldn't be so busy focusing my camera on her face and her body language that I wouldn't have time to look at some of the trendy clothes her models would be parading down the runway. The heat in Manhattan had been unrelenting and oppressively damp. I was in the mood for a few new outfits that were light and whimsical, that would make me feel fresh even when I was sweating. Of course, high-fashion clothes rarely do that. They're mesmerizing on someone trained to show off interesting angles and sweeps of fabric but aren't necessarily comfortable. Still, they might inspire me.

I settled myself at the corner of the horseshoe table arrangement. It framed the runway coming out from a stage draped with black velvet curtains and lit with gold lights. I placed my camera on my lap and picked up the glass of champagne that had been served the moment I pulled out the chair. I took a sip and reminded myself I was there to work.

Pauline was talking to several women who were seated, sampling appetizers arranged on long narrow plates at the center of the table. She was laughing, then lifting her head to sweep her hair off her face. I stood and took several photographs, moving away from the table, so the servers didn't have to zigzag around me.

As I continued taking pictures of her, I watched her move alongside the tables, talking to each person as if they were her best friend. I wondered if I was mistaken in assuming I would get a few minutes alone with her. So far, she hadn't seemed to notice I was there, which was a good thing for what I was supposed to be doing but not good for my plan to talk to her about Rada's career.

The fashion show began, and I ate my lunch, letting the camera rest because Pauline was now seated in the darkened room, and there was no way to get any photographs without disrupting the event. I gave myself over to the loud thumping music, letting it pulse in my ears and vibrate through my bones as I watched the rhythm of the models strutting down the runway. They behaved as if they were completely unaware they were inches away from a precipice where they could fall five feet onto a table filled with expertly sharpened knives, as well as glassware that would rip their flesh as it shattered beneath them.

I sipped champagne, making sure I paced myself to keep to my promised two glasses.

After an hour, during which I saw five skirts, two pairs of pants, a dress, and several shirts that I wanted to own but couldn't begin to afford in my current situation, the lights came up, and the music was softened to a level that allowed people to resume talking.

I slugged down the last of my champagne and popped a slice of melon wrapped in tissue paper-thin prosciutto into my mouth. When a man appeared with a champagne bottle, poised to refill my glass, I smiled and shook my head.

He looked hugely disappointed.

I made my way toward where Pauline was talking to one of the models, positioning myself so I could photograph Pauline from the side, capturing only the corners of her lips and eyes, her gestures and the tightness of her jaw, cutting the model out of the image. From the corner of my eye, I saw the model glance at me every few seconds. It was a shock to her system, having the camera avoiding her when she was used to it following every breath she took.

Finally, the model took a step closer to me, turning so that I couldn't avoid capturing her. "What are you trying to do?" she asked.

I lowered the camera. Pauline looked at me, confused and slightly self-conscious.

Pauline had been explicit she wanted our work to be private. I should have been prepared for questions, but I hadn't thought about the mindset of a model. In her world, this was completely upside down. "Just taking some publicity shots," I said.

Pauline smiled, her face relaxing. "Thank you."

"Do you work for HMA? I've never seen you before," the model said.

"Nope. Sorry to be in the way." I took a few steps back and turned to look directly at Pauline. "When you have a minute, can I get some time with you, Pauline?"

She gave me a single nod. I retreated quickly, feeling darts from the model's eyes in my back, knowing she didn't fully believe my story, knowing she was upset that she hadn't been the one who attracted my attention. Why would PR shots involve her boss and not one of the focal points of the show? Why would I want to take photographs of a middle-aged woman instead of a woman who was paid to look beautiful, who lived to present a perfect face and body to the world? She was absolutely stunning, but she was clearly worried that it wasn't quite enough, anxious she was already losing her edge.

It was a horrible way to make a living. I wondered what Eileen really thought about her career and what she planned to do with the rest of her life. Not that I was a poster child for planning a career path. But I had time, she was close to the end of the runway.

I returned to the chair where I'd been sitting, put my camera in my bag, and picked up the glass that still stood beside my plate. Miraculously, the same waiter appeared. He filled my glass eagerly, and I took a sip before I slung the bag over my shoulder and went to wait for Pauline to make time for me.

After about thirty minutes and another inadvisable glass and a half of champagne, the crowd began to thin. The champagne, of course, loosened my tongue, which was good for Rada but might not be so good for my position with Diana, if this ever got back to her, but I charged ahead. I maneuvered Pauline away from the tables and the runway, away from the beautiful women who towered above me, and the bold and talkative women and men who were TikToking and Instagramming about the show. "I'll get right to the point since I know you're busy."

"I'm finished now. Did you get the shots you needed?"

"Yes. This is a personal favor."

She raised her eyebrows and waited.

Pauline was also taller than me. I wore three-inch heels, but so did she. I had to look up slightly. "I won't go into the details unless you want me to, but I met a woman who's a server. A customer was harassing her, and when she didn't stroke his ego, he went to her supervisor and got her fired."

She narrowed her eyes but said nothing.

"Until now, most of my professional contacts have been men, so that's why I thought of you right away, even though I hardly know you. I was wondering if you have any friends in the restaurant business who might be willing to give her a chance. Knowing she will have a rough spot in her work history."

"I don't know … I …" She turned her head, looking across the room.

I couldn't tell if she was plotting her escape, annoyed that I'd put her in an uncomfortable position, angry that I was trying to take advantage of her when I hardly knew her, or mentally sorting through her connections. I could have easily placed a bet on any of those.

Wanting to help Rada was turning into a need that was eating at me. I wanted it almost as badly as I wanted to be the only photographer at Fly Higher. Maybe I saw a sliver of myself in Rada. Like me, she was simply trying to do her job. She hadn't done anything wrong, and all of a sudden, she'd been attacked by someone riddled with insecurities that spilled out onto other people. Not that I saw myself as a victim. But I did see that I was being treated as the one at fault when I'd simply tried to uphold a standard for the job I was passionate about. When Stephanie decided she wanted something she couldn't have, she attacked me for being better than her, for having what she wanted and couldn't get.

Pauline turned her attention back to me, putting a stop to my intricate self-analysis.

"I could ask around. But I…"

"I know I'm putting you on the spot. I wasn't expecting an answer right this minute. With your attention on all of this." I waved my hand around. "And a thousand other things." The mild flattery seemed to be working. Pauline looked mildly sympathetic. I cranked it up a notch. "She's sharing an apartment, but she's living paycheck to paycheck … I don't mean to burden you with her problems. I just want to help. It was so creepy what this guy did to her. All because his tiny little ego was wounded when she wouldn't flirt with him."

"I don't need her whole life story."

"No. Anyway…" I moved away from her. "I know I'm crossing a line here, but you know how it is to start out working for other people and fight your way up. She's really smart. Funny."

She smiled. "She hasn't been able to find anything?"

"This just happened. I'm trying to get things moving fast for her."

"She's a friend?"

"Yes."

"I'll let you know if I think of anything."

There wasn't much to hang onto there, but she hadn't said no. "Thank you so much." I thought that most women might have lunged in to give her a hug, but I didn't, and I imagined she appreciated me not being that type. If she even thought about it. I left slightly dissatisfied. I wasn't confident she was convinced.

CHAPTER 20

*a*t four that afternoon, Diana, James, and I met to review the micro-expression analysis process Diana wanted to implement. Four o'clock is not the best time for a meeting under any circumstances. On a pristine summer afternoon, following a delectable lunch and a few glasses of champagne, it was a miserable time for a meeting. Add James into the mix, and I knew I would be challenged beyond anything I faced on a long run or lifting heavy metal plates at the gym. I decided the best course of action was to say as little as possible to avoid my tongue running ahead of my brain.

I settled into my chair, my laptop open in front of me on the table, to make it look as if I were deeply engaged with the sections of our internal repository that Diana wanted to review. I had a large latte that I'd gone out for right before the meeting started. The latte was a mistake because it immediately introduced a problem.

"I made a pot of coffee," James said. "Why did you go out for coffee?"

"I wanted a latte."

He nodded but looked annoyed that I needed something so fancy.

Diana settled herself at the head of the table. She went through her plans, outlined on the slides displayed on the screen in front of us. James talked more than she did, interrupting her every other sentence, but she seemed to love it. After ten or fifteen minutes, she looked directly at me. "Don't you have any thoughts, Alex?"

"It all sounds good to me."

She gave me a curious look, waiting for me to say more.

I took a sip of my drink.

"Nothing at all?"

"Nope."

"That's unusual."

"I like that you're making the process more structured."

Her smile grew tighter. She didn't believe me.

James had the same disbelieving look on his smug face. "You always have opinions."

"Not always."

"Every time I've spoken to you."

"Not this time."

"Is something bothering you?" he asked.

"No." I took a sip of my drink.

It was not fun sitting in a room with two people who literally made careers out of studying facial twitches and slight shifts in eyelids and lips. They were reading things even if I wasn't communicating them. Even when my face was a blank screen, they were certain they saw something they didn't like. I took another sip of my drink, although I knew that, too, was probably being interpreted as suggesting I had something on my mind that I was withholding from them.

Diana moved to her next topic while James stared at me, his gaze growing more intense and challenging by the minute. He wasn't going to let me relax into the numb state of a weary brain, exhausted by champagne and a desire to escape as soon as I possibly could.

Every time Diana paused, she looked at me, expecting a reaction.

Each time I refused to give one, they both grew increasingly agitated, as if my non-response meant that I was deliberately sabotaging the meeting.

For the most part, the things she was saying were common sense. There truly was nothing to say. I had no opinions.

Trystan had run our organization primarily by intuition. Diana wanted structure and process, and while I agreed that was a good thing to a point, I could feel it weighing us down. As each process took its place, the solidness of it caused us to sink imperceptibly. Eventually, we might never rise to the surface again. So much for flying higher.

"How are things going with Pauline?" she asked.

"Good."

"What does that mean?" James asked.

"It means they're going well." I could feel the heat increasing in the room, could see his breathing growing shallow, his pulse quickening, and I could feel Diana's frustration. "The photography session in her office went smoothly. She took a while to forget the camera, but once she did, I got an excellent variety. Have you had time to look at them?"

"Remember," James said, "The new process requires us to wait until everything's loaded onto the site before we review anything. So we don't form advance judgments that color our view of future images."

"Well, that process is just being implemented now, and you've already looked at some. We'll have to start that with future clients." I sipped my latte. "The fashion show today was a great opportunity. A unique environment. And there will be one more session where she's scheduled to deliver an inspirational talk to her models."

James grinned, one degree shy of a leer. "I'd like to sit in on that."

"No," I said.

Diana shook her head, agreeing with me, but didn't speak. He didn't seem to notice her head moving.

"A room full of models? Come on. Have a heart."

"I don't have a heart," I said.

His leer sank into his face.

"It will distract her. The point is for me to become invisible so she forgets I'm there."

"I know what the point is," he said, "And I can do a pretty good job of becoming invisible."

"No," Diana said. "That's not how we do it."

He pouted, but he stopped arguing.

They talked around and past me for another fifteen minutes. Finally, Diana ended the slide show and closed her laptop. I pushed my chair away from the table and stood. James stayed rooted to his spot.

"I'd like a minute with you, Alex," Diana said.

"Uh oh. Someone's in trouble," James said.

Diana glared at him.

"Anything else?" he asked.

She shook her head. He got up and left, moving as slowly as he could as if he hoped she would start our private conversation while he was still able to pick up a few juicy morsels.

"What happened at the fashion show?" Diana asked the moment the door was closed.

"It was impossible to take any photos during the show itself. It was too dark, and getting close to her would have been disruptive."

"But you got what you needed?"

"I think so."

"What else?"

"That's it."

"What did you talk to her about?"

"Nothing important."

"She tried to call your cell phone after you left, but you didn't pick up."

I held her gaze. I'd thought that telling Pauline I was asking a personal favor, and my subtle comment acknowledging that I was crossing a line had let her know I preferred she not mention my request to Diana. I wasn't sure if she'd missed my subtlety, didn't care, or was deliberately trying to get me in trouble. She didn't seem like the malicious type, but what did I know? She was a stranger. I thought I'd read her well. Maybe I hadn't.

"Why are you asking personal favors of our clients?"

"I don't think it's a big deal. She doesn't have to—"

"It's a big deal."

"Why?"

She leaned her forearms on the table, and once again, I found myself missing the jangle of the bracelets she used to wear. All the fun had gone out of her. "We're here to serve our clients."

"But I usually connect with them, and when I do, we end up talking about other things. It's natural."

"Only to elicit facets of their lives that will help us coach them."

"So we're manipulating them?"

"Not at all. We're *coaching* them. They're paying us for a service. You aren't BFFs."

"I didn't say I'm BFFs with her. I thought she might know someone who could—"

"Find a job for a waitress? What's wrong with you?"

The look of disdain on her face was almost embarrassing. I didn't like that she acted as if a waitress didn't deserve my time or wasn't worthy of Pauline's consideration. I got it that it wasn't professional, that I shouldn't have done it, but it was the fault of the man she hired who had acted like a sleaze. The problem was, I couldn't tell her that. It wouldn't go well. No matter how all of this turned out, it wouldn't go well for me. It was better to let her be angry at me now and then move on.

"You need boundaries."

"Maybe."

"Not maybe. I need you to apologize to her."

"Fine."

"With sincerity. And I emailed you a podcast about professionalism."

"Are you serious?"

"Yes. And do not ask her for help finding a job for this waitress. If she brings it up, tell her you are deeply sorry for imposing on her, and you won't discuss it any further."

I stared at her.

"Are we clear?"

I continued staring.

She raised her eyebrows. "Now you seem to have some thoughts. Would you like to share them? I don't want things simmering. I want everything out in the open. I want clear communication among everyone on the team."

"You're doing all the talking. And you're telling me what to do. I don't see a lot of room for other opinions."

"I want to know what you're thinking."

"Why do I need to say it? You already know what I think. I thought it was okay to ask if she knew anyone in the restaurant business. I thought she and I had a connection. We'd talked about other personal things, and I didn't think it was a big deal. She was free to say no."

"She was not."

"She owns one of New York's top modeling agencies. I think she knows how to turn down a request for a favor."

She glared at me.

"Now you know what I think," I said.

"Do you *want* to work together?"

"That's a big leap."

"You seem to have this need to argue about everything. And you think you can do whatever you want and argue your way out of it. I'm not Trystan. I have a different vision. I thought I'd made that clear."

"I get it."

She pushed her laptop away from her.

I took a sip of my latte. It was now lukewarm. I wanted to leave, but she seemed to want to argue far more than I did. It didn't seem like a good idea to point that out.

"You manipulated Trystan."

I laughed. "Probably."

"It's not funny."

I smiled. It was funny, and her distress was also a little funny. I wasn't sure why she was so upset with me. Maybe she wasn't sure what she was doing and felt she needed to control everything. Maybe James was putting worms in her ear, and she wanted to put me in my place to be sure there were no more employee turf wars. I'd thought she and I got along. And maybe that was the problem. Maybe she wanted to sabotage our relationship because she thought it would interfere with being in charge.

Whatever it was, I needed to figure out how to manipulate her more effectively. I had no doubt I could find a way.

CHAPTER 21

 ortland, Oregon

* * *

Every year, our church spent months planning a huge mid-summer camping trip. People donated equipment to make sure those who couldn't afford it were able to join. An entire room at the church was dedicated to organizing the dinners, stocking it with bulk food and cooking supplies. Dinners on our camping trip were cooked by teams of women so that we all ate together. Daytime activities were organized, and evening campfires included mini-sermons, songs, Bible readings, and stories for the kids, all chosen ahead of time to fit the theme.

Each family loaded tents and food, and sleeping bags into their minivans and cars, no RVs allowed, and we drove in a caravan to the Rogue River in southern Oregon.

There were over a hundred people every year. We reserved an entire campground exclusively for our group. The minister—Pastor Joshua—liked it that way. There would be no ungodly influences on the teenagers—no loud music, no weed-smoking, or booze-drinking sinners to contend with. No foul language, no wild *antics*, no nothing.

At the age of five, I didn't know most of this, but I picked up on the idea that *bad stuff* wasn't allowed. The children just weren't informed about what this *bad stuff* consisted of. It gave me the idea that everyone in our group was good and the people who would normally be camping were bad. Like the characters in the church-authorized children's movies we were allowed to watch. Good. Evil. Nuance never factored in.

Our family tent was large. But even with its zippered windows and door, including screens, it was crowded inside that canvas cave with two adults, three good-sized boys, and two little girls. My sister and I slept near the back with our mother beside us. My father was close to the door, so he could protect us from wild animals and other unnamed threats. The boys lined the sides. There was space in the middle where all our duffel bags were piled. Clothing constantly spilled out of the bags no matter how often our parents told us to put everything away and close them up so bugs wouldn't creep inside.

I liked camping. I liked the tent. I liked my warm, snug sleeping bag. I liked burrowing inside with a small flashlight and pointing my finger through a learn-to-read book, figuring out how to seal the edges of my bag so no light leaked out, giving away that I wasn't asleep. I liked waking in the middle of the night and whispering to Lexy, nudging her into consciousness and inviting her into my bag, where we whispered softly. The snores of the others told us they were in another world, deep inside their heads, where they couldn't hear us.

I liked listening to the crickets outside our tent, and I liked hearing the raccoons and other nighttime creatures scurrying through the forest. The screeches of the raccoons sounded like the demons our church loved to discuss. Their cries made it sound as if those sly, furry bandits had risen out of the depths of the earth and were coming for all of us in the dead of night. No one ever mentioned this during the day, but I wondered if they trembled in their tents, nothing between those wicked claws and razor teeth but a sheet of canvas.

The days were filled with a mixture of Bible stuff and outdoor fun. When we were younger, the Bible stuff wasn't so bad. There were gripping, violent, back-stabbing stories of sin and victory. And crafts. Even on a camping trip, we did crafts. The kids sat at a cluster of picnic tables grouped by age. This meant Lexy and I were not at the same table, which I didn't like.

The theme of the trip, when I was five years old and Lexy was four, was obedience. The craft on the first day involved painting macaroni shells and gluing them onto small cardboard boxes. These boxes would be used to hold scraps of paper on which we wrote the things our parents expected us to do. Since our parents were the stand-ins for god, we were to treat every word out of their mouths and every request they made as a command directly from the lips of god. Disobeying god not only broke his heart, it made him so angry that if you did it enough, or did something awful enough, he tortured you with fire until the end of time, which was basically forever. As I got older, my mother tried to explain to me that I wasn't understanding the finer points, but I was pretty sure I understood it exactly right.

Painting each macaroni shell was fun. It took a long time, which was probably the point. The only problem was that powdery yellow pollen drifted out of the surrounding trees and stuck in the paint. Still, since the macaroni had its own fine powder, the results were already slightly gritty.

After this, we went for a hike, then ate a picnic lunch of peanut butter sandwiches and apples. We had quiet time in our tents, then we got to wade in the river. Lexy collected pebbles and stuffed them in her pockets until she looked like she might fall over from the weight. When she was full up on stones, she started picking up bird feathers, insisting I use my pockets to help her carry them back to our tent.

The grownups had their own Bible studies along with hiking and volleyball, frisbee, and softball games. I wondered if the grownups who supervised the kids wished they were with the other group or if they preferred it that way because we were more fun and they liked the stories more than the Bible lectures and long prayer sessions. I couldn't imagine prayer outdoors was any more fun than the hours of praying that went on indoors. Besides, in the forest beside a languidly flowing river, you had to deal with mosquitoes. With your eyes closed, the preacher droning like a mosquito himself, they were sitting like trays of Swedish meatballs on an open buffet.

Everywhere we went, I kept my eye on Lexy. This wasn't only because my parents told me to, which they had. And, of course, I'd printed this demand on a piece of paper and put it in my obedience box. It was one thing I didn't have to be told to be obedient about. I would have done it anyway. My little sister was the most interesting person in the world, and I never wanted to stop listening to her talk or watching what she did.

I didn't like it when they put me at a picnic table with my back toward the table where Lexy was sitting. There was another table between us, so even when I turned, I had to lean to the side to see her. And, of course, when I leaned, the grown-up at our table barked at me to be careful because I was going to knock over the cups of paint. They also didn't like that I kept turning around because it disrupted the others at my table.

When I explained that I had to keep an eye on my sister, they said they were keeping an eye on her just fine.

"My parents told me to," I said. "I'm being obedient."

"Don't give me any sass," the grown-up said.

I stared at her. She stabbed her finger into my shoulder. "Come on now. Get back to work." When she was called away to help a girl who had gotten paint in her hair, I turned again to check on Lexy. She wasn't there.

I jumped up from the table, and as the grown-up had predicted, I knocked over a cup of paint.

"Sit down! You need to clean that up."

"I can't see my sister."

"That's not your responsibility. Someone is watching over her."

"Who?"

"Sit down."

"I can't find her." I walked toward the table where she'd been seated. She definitely wasn't there. I asked the grown-up overseeing that table what happened to her.

"Mr. Caruthers needed her help with something."

"What?"

"It's not your problem. Go back and finish working on your box."

"My parents told me to keep an eye on her."

She smiled. "She's helping him get something that rolled under the seat of his car." She patted my head. I ducked from under her hand. "He needed someone with a little arm and a little hand to fit under there." She laughed. "She's being a good helper."

"Where did she *go*?"

She waved her hand in the air. "To wherever his car is. Go back to your table."

I stood my ground. She glared at me, no longer charmed by my obedience to my parents' command, but she didn't seem to want to go so far as to shout at me or drag me back to my seat. "I'm asking you to do what I said."

"I'm supposed to obey my parents."

"You need to watch your tone."

"We're supposed to be obedient. It's like doing what god says."

"I can see you've been a good listener, sweetie. But now you need to be obedient to me." Her voice was cheerful and so shrill I thought of the witch pretending to be a kindly old woman in Hansel and Gretel.

"What if god tells me to do one thing, and my mom tells me a different thing, and my dad says do something else, and you say—"

"That's enough." Her sugary smile dissolved. "Go back to your table. I'll let you know when your sister is finished. Mr. Caruthers is an elder, and we need to do what the elders ask. You should know that. She's already serving god at such a young age. Isn't that beautiful? She has a willing, obedient spirit. You should learn from her." She beamed at me as if my sister had transformed into an angel with a shimmering halo.

I started walking toward the parking area. I hadn't taken more than five steps before I felt the shadow of the grown-up fall over me. Her hand locked around my upper arm, squeezing so tightly I thought she might twist it right off my body. "You need to listen, young lady." She yanked me back toward my table.

I stomped my foot, sending up a cloud of powdery dust.

"Don't stomp your foot at me. It looks like you haven't learned anything at all about obedience."

"I'm *supposed* to keep an eye on my sister."

"There are plenty of people to do that. I think you misunderstood your parents' meaning."

"I didn't misunderstand."

She dragged me back to the table, my feet making scuff marks in the loose dirt, creating more clouds of dust. She picked me up and tried to force me onto the picnic table bench, but I kept my knees locked. I think at that point, she realized she was in danger of causing a huge mess—all the cups of paint tipping over, colors running onto the other children, irritated parents who had packed a limited supply of spare clothing, a loss of control that was infinitely more entertaining than painting macaroni. She pulled me off the bench and tugged me away from the other kids, dragging me until we were behind one of the cinder block buildings that housed toilets and showers.

We glared at each other for several minutes. "Are you ready to return to the group and do what you're told?"

I softened my voice, making it sound wet with tears. "I want my sister."

She must have realized she wasn't going to win and that, in the end, I wasn't her problem. "If you don't cooperate, I'm going to tell your father. Is that what you want?"

I stared at her.

We stood there for quite a long time, staring, both of us waiting for the other to back down. I began to realize she was stalling. I knew this because I'd been accused of stalling quite a lot. She wanted to keep me away from the other kids where my bad attitude might infect them. She was probably praying with all her heart that my sister would return from her stupid chore of crawling around in some guy's car.

After she got tired of staring, she looked at her watch. "Why don't we see if we can find your sister?"

She took my hand. I let her, squeezing as tightly as I could. I heard a tiny sound of pain come out of her, but she didn't try to pry my fingers loose. We walked in a circle around the picnic tables. If she hoped the other kids had forgotten about us, she was disappointed. The other children held their paintbrushes in the air like tiny colored lights as they watched us walk by. We wound through a group of trees toward the parking area.

Before we reached the cars, I saw Mr. Caruthers and my sister. She was walking beside him, a look on her face that I imagined looked exactly like my own face.

Later, while we ate our sandwiches, Lexy whispered to me in a voice I couldn't hear. I leaned closer, and she said, "Mr. Cruthers car is sticky."

I whispered back. "What?"

Another girl sitting beside us demanded to know why we were whispering.

"We're sisters," I said, we have secrets.

"Secrets are bad," she said.

I took a bite of my sandwich and chewed with my mouth open, letting her see gooey, saliva-filled peanut butter and bloody-looking jam. Lexy laughed and copied me.

The girl stuck her finger in her mouth, pretending she was gagging herself. "You're disgusting." She turned away.

Lexy and I giggled. We each took a bite of apple to get rid of the stickiness from too much peanut butter.

"Why was his car sticky?" I asked.

"Not sticky. *Icky*," she hissed.

"Why?" I licked peanut butter off the corner of my lip.

"I had to look for this." She dug in her pocket and pulled out a plastic cap with something sticking out of it that was like wood, but softer, like the inside of a tree after it falls down and is starting to come apart. Too smart for her age, she held it close to my knee so no one else could see it. She wrinkled her nose. "It smells icky." Keeping it cupped inside her fingers, even smaller than mine, she held it to my nose.

The smell wasn't awful. It was a little bit like something my mother used to clean with, but not really. Sweeter. She shoved it back into her pocket.

"You took it?"

She scowled. "He's mean."

Both of us thought a lot of the grown-ups at our church were mean. Our brothers thought the same thing. Some of the church people seemed more like the bad people in the Bible stories than the good ones. "He poked my butt. He said hurry. Hurry. *Hurry*. In a mean voice. And he said, don't tell anyone. If you tell anyone, you're in big trouble. God will know if you break your promise."

"He poked your butt?"

She stabbed her index finger into the fleshy part of my hip. "He smelled icky too. Like that thing I looked for. I said I couldn't find it. He was mad. But then he acted like he was nice and held my hand. It was wet." She made a face and took a large bite of her sandwich.

She chewed for a long time because of all the peanut butter. I wondered if she was going to get in trouble. I wasn't sure how, but if grown-ups wanted children to find something and they didn't find it, they got mad. They would say it was right in front of your eyes. If she got in trouble, I might get in trouble. Whenever Lexy did something wrong, my parents figured it was my fault. They were probably right.

CHAPTER 22

*N*ew York

* * *

The woman taking photographs of Hunter Pierce's boss had been in his thoughts since the moment he first saw her. Supposedly, her magical photographs were intended to reveal some secret sauce holding Pauline back in her career. As if she'd been held back.

It was humor worthy of a meme. In his mind, the whole thing was a bit of a con. But more power to them. Pauline Herrera had nothing holding her back. She was at the top of the food chain. She owned one of the most elite modeling agencies in New York City. She was still gorgeous at forty-five, and she had more money than she could possibly spend in her lifetime. But she needed photographs to reveal hidden flaws, along with hours of counseling and role-playing and all kinds of bullshit to try to *fly higher*.

He wasn't sure the photographer bought into it. There was something cynical about the way she smiled, but her boss was deeply, maniacally serious about the entire business.

When he arrived at the office, the photographer was standing outside his building. It was six-fifteen in the fucking morning. A time when he could count on having the entire space to himself. When he could drink his coffee hot, without interruptions for questions that could be answered if the person asking paused to think for two minutes. A time when he could sort out his agenda for the day without a non-stop gush of conversation flooding his head.

He did not expect to see someone stalking him. And showing up at that hour of the morning, outside his office building, was surely taking a step over the line into stalking territory. Was it still stalking if you were thrilled to see the stalker? He wasn't sure.

He shouldn't have been surprised. That photographer had stared him down like she wanted to climb onto his lap right there in the conference room. It wouldn't have bothered him, in a different setting, obviously. She was hot, and she looked like the kind of girl who would be up for anything without making a lot of demands. She looked fun. She looked interesting. And there was something about her eyes, like she could read his mind. Obviously, she couldn't, but he couldn't shake the feeling that she could if she wanted to.

He wasn't sure if it was because she stared at him almost without blinking or if there was something clicking between them. He didn't believe in those sorts of things—love at first sight, soul mates, or instant connections. He wasn't sure he believed in love at all. He believed in having a good time and good sex and not getting tangled up in a relationship that turned into a fucking horror show, which too many seemed to.

Some were violent, dramatic, bloody horror shows. Others were the silent, creepy, bone-chilling kind where you never knew when they might turn dangerous. The kind that killed you slowly, where you might not even know you were dying until your throat was slit and there was more blood outside your body than inside.

Why the hell was she waiting outside his building? At sunrise?

She didn't try to pretend it was a coincidence either. She walked right up to him and blocked his way as he approached the doors. "Hi. Remember me?"

He gave her a single nod. "Pauline won't be in until about eight, eight-thirty."

"I'm here to see you."

"Why?"

She shrugged and smiled. She had blonde hair that was dyed. Not cheap dye, it was the high-end salon kind. Most people would think it was natural, but you don't work with models all day for years and not learn to recognize what's real and what's not. The rest of Alexandra was definitely real. She had on a silky white top and a black suit jacket and short pleated skirt and black, very high heels. It was a lot more eye-catching than what she'd worn to the photography meet-and-greet. So, she was there to catch his eye.

She still hadn't answered him. He pulled open the door and stepped inside. She followed him into the building.

"Do you want to get breakfast?" she asked.

"I already ate."

"I'm starving."

He took a sip of his coffee as he started across the lobby. Was she trying to find out more about Pauline behind her back? Hitting on him? He couldn't get a read on what she was after, and it seemed as if she was planning to follow him to the elevators and up to the floor occupied by the Herrera Modeling Agency. "Do you have a question or something?"

"I already asked it. About breakfast."

He pressed the call button. It seemed as if she wanted to flirt, but it was such a strange time and situation for flirting, he was completely off balance and wasn't sure how to get back on. It was an unfamiliar feeling. He wasn't in the mood for flirting, and didn't like it that she seemed to be in control of whatever was going on between them. "Do you need more background on the agency? Do you have some questions about Pauline? Is there a problem?"

"No." She smiled and stepped into the elevator with him. She pressed the button to close the doors.

"If you're planning to wait for Pauline in our lobby, you can't. You need to wait for—"

"I told you, I'm here to see you."

"I came in early to get work done."

"Do you want to go out sometime?"

"You had to ride up in the elevator to ask me that?"

She laughed. "You weren't being very forthcoming."

"You were vague. You asked me to breakfast."

"I thought you would take it from there."

"It wasn't clear if you're here for business or something else."

"Something else." She had a large leather bag over her shoulder. It was kind of scruffy and didn't go with her slick, expensive-looking outfit. She pushed it to the side as if she wanted to get it out of the way.

"You should have been more specific," he said.

"I guess so. But I don't mind riding in the elevator with you." She gave another one of her charming but slightly disturbing smiles. Once again, suggesting she had figured out what he was thinking. "You have very interesting eyes."

"Thank you," he said. "So do you."

"Do you like Indian food?" she asked.

"Love it."

Her hand slithered into her bag as the doors opened. He stepped out into the HMA lobby, and she followed. She pulled her phone out of her bag. "What's your number? I'll text you the details for the restaurant."

He gave her his number, once again feeling like she was way ahead of him, unsure whether or not he liked that. It was different, that was for sure. He continued to feel off-balance, and it was both uncomfortable and slightly exciting at the same time.

"Are you finished photographing Pauline?" He shoved his phone back into his pocket.

"No. There's one more event where I'll capture her in action."

"This seems like a conflict of interest."

"Are you worried she'll fire you?"

"No. But maybe you should be worried about your job. She wanted to keep this private," he said.

"I'm not telling anyone. Having dinner with you doesn't mean anything."

"Just checking. In case you like your job."

She laughed. "I'm not going to talk about her over dinner. I'm sure you won't either."

"She doesn't know that. Your boss doesn't know that. I'm fine with it, but I thought your team was all about confidentiality. I had the impression she gave you a lot of personal information."

She dragged her finger across her lips as if zipping them closed.

He shrugged. "If you say so."

"See you tonight. At seven?"

"Sounds good."

She twirled around, her skirt flaring out, and walked to the elevator. She pressed the button and waited. He stood watching her. The entire time, she never checked to see if he was still there, to see if he was watching. When the elevator arrived and she stepped inside, she turned slowly and looked directly at him, giving him a final smile. He knew she'd known he would still be standing there, and it made him feel as if she'd won another point of some kind.

Dinner would be interesting.

He walked down the hall toward his office, sipping his coffee. She was strange and aggressive, and so hot. There was something almost frightening about her. There was definitely a conflict of interest in the two of them going out to dinner, or anywhere else, but he had no plans to tell anyone about it. He was in the habit of keeping his private life to himself. And he wasn't worried about her. That was her own risk. Hers seemed far greater than his.

Seated at his desk, looking out over Manhattan, still methodically sipping his coffee, he found all his thoughts for the day had turned to sludge. He could only stare at the time on his phone and calculate the hours until seven that evening.

CHAPTER 23

*C*hoosing the Indian restaurant that had fired Rada for my dinner date with Hunter was a spur-of-the-moment decision. With all the spectacular restaurants in New York City, I'm not sure why I chose that one. It was delicious, of course, but there were plenty of others. I suppose Rada was still occupying a large part of my mind, for one thing. Or maybe I wanted to keep my eye on them. The restaurant management was to blame for her job loss almost as much as James. Some might argue they were entirely to blame.

Even though she'd told Diana what I'd done, I hoped Pauline would come through for Rada. Ratting me out didn't mean she wouldn't try to help. I was almost certain she hadn't done it to get me in trouble. She'd done it because she seemed to be oblivious to the repercussions, unlike Hunter. Maybe she had only a superficial impression of Diana and didn't recognize how finicky she was about *professionalism*. Or how she defined it. Maybe it was defined differently in the modeling business.

Since Diana was already irritated with me, I figured going after Hunter wouldn't matter. She couldn't be any more upset for crossing yet another line. Unless she could be. But it was worth the risk. Besides, I couldn't picture him giving a call to Diana. In what context would that even happen? Talking to him confirmed my instinct on that point. He wasn't the kind of guy that let information flow out of his lips without restraint. Like Ned, for example. Or James.

I like guys who keep their thoughts to themselves. They're more challenging. And less tedious. It's almost like a game, trying to find out what they're thinking, trying to determine whether they're telling the truth.

When I walked up to the restaurant, Hunter was approaching from the opposite direction. Both of us right on time. I wondered if he'd thought about dinner all day as I had. It was impossible to know. I liked to think he had.

He was carrying the same tablet bag he had that morning, and wearing the same clothes—dark brown brogues, faded jeans that rode loosely around his hips, a dark green T-shirt, and a midnight blue jacket. His hair was kind of messy so I guessed he'd walked there, but there wasn't a single drop of sweat visible on his skin, even though it was still in the mid-seventies and muggy as always in summer.

"Hey." He pulled open the large door with brass facing, and I stepped inside.

We said nothing else until we were seated at the table I'd reserved. It was a private booth with carved oak walls. The menus lay open in front of us.

"This isn't how I expected my day to end when I got up this morning," he said.

"I did."

He laughed but didn't meet my gaze, keeping his attention on the menu. "Do you want a drink?"

"Sure."

When the server returned, I ordered a vodka martini with three olives.

"I'll have the same," Hunter said.

"Extra olives, sir?"

"Absolutely."

A chill ran down my spine. Was he trying to charm me, or did he like martinis as much as I did, relishing the vodka-soaked olives with equal glee? I studied his expression, trying to figure out if he was mimicking me, too lazy to think about what kind of drink he was in the mood for, or just being polite. He smiled without revealing the answer to any of those questions and returned his attention to the menu.

We ordered enough food to feed us for the next three nights. The server pointed out that we might have quite a lot to take home.

"We don't want to leave hungry," Hunter said. "That's an unforgivable sin."

I laughed. "Is it?"

"The food won't go to waste," he said.

We sipped our way through two martinis and tasted our way through every spice imaginable. It was the most erotic dinner I'd ever experienced. Each time Hunter tried a new dish, he held out his fork to me and offered a bite. He waited for me so we could chew together. He insisted we describe the flavors we noticed and rate the heat of the spices on a scale of one to five. The erotic part was the way he put the fork in my mouth, pulling it out slowly. He looked into my eyes as the flavors burst across my tongue, holding my gaze for several seconds longer, waiting for me to start chewing, and continuing to gaze into my eyes after that.

"Do you always eat dinner this way?" I asked.

"What way?"

I drank some water before taking a sip of my martini, a very small one, since the second drink was almost gone. I ate the last olive, which was not a good place to be in, but I could no longer resist the need for it. With all that stalling, he was still looking at me, waiting for me to clarify exactly what intrigued me about the way we'd consumed our meal. "Feeding your date."

"Am I making you feel like a pet?"

I laughed. "It hadn't crossed my mind."

"Does it bother you?"

"I like it."

"I thought you would."

He withheld his feelings about it, leaving me to guess.

"I've rated restaurants, but never each dish," I said.

"Comparisons are good. And it's all subjective, so it means nothing. You might rate the Bhuna Paneer a five, and I might rate it a three, and it will still tell us nothing about how the other experiences it."

I desperately wanted another martini. I wanted it like I hadn't wanted something in a very long time. It meant breaking my rules, but isn't that how the cliché goes? His glass was also empty. My stomach wasn't completely full, although our pace of eating had definitely slowed.

"Still hungry?" he asked.

"A little."

"And what are our plans after dinner?"

"Don't we have more immediate decisions to make first?" I asked.

He tipped his head a fraction of an inch to the side.

"Like whether we want another drink."

"Is that a decision that needs to be discussed?" He signaled the waiter and ordered two more martinis. At that moment, I knew how the rest of the evening would go. His smile told me he knew the same. But both of us had known that hours ago. Maybe days ago.

When we stood to leave, I felt the alcohol flood my body. I picked up my water glass and took several long swallows before turning away from the table. With the cool water coursing through me, I was able to walk easily toward the entrance, although I had that hyper-awareness that comes from too much alcohol. I felt the pressure of the floor beneath my heels and the movement of my hips and the cool air on my skin as we approached the lobby. I felt my hair swaying across my shoulders, and most of all, I felt Hunter behind me, his eyes on my body, and in my imagination, his own hyper-awareness.

He had already ordered an Uber through the app. A champagne-colored Lexus sedan was waiting for us when we stepped out into the still, muggy evening air. He asked where I lived. I smiled and said, aren't we going to your place? He gave the driver an address on Third Avenue, and the car eased away from the curb, pushing me gently toward him, but I resisted falling all the way against him despite the vodka pumping through my blood vessels.

Even though the warmth and solid presence of him, the sound of his breath, and the words he spoke consumed me, we rode the entire distance without a single kiss. This had the effect of making every inch of my body ache for him. I'd never met anyone like him, and I knew he was pulling me into something that was completely unfamiliar. I sensed I was losing control.

I'd been the one to approach him, to demand he take me out, but I'd done it out of some strange compulsion. I had to know him. I had to talk to him. I had to sit across from him and look into the bottomless pit of those eyes and try to pry inside that brain, locked tight beneath that beautiful wavy blonde hair.

In his apartment, I wanted to notice his furniture, study the layout, figure out who he was and what he was about from the things he surrounded himself with, but I couldn't be bothered. He had a single light on in the living room, and when he began kissing me, I closed my eyes to blot that out.

Once we moved to the bedroom, all I noticed was an unframed acrylic painting of something tropical, a window open to the night air, tiny model cars lined up on the sill below, and a nightstand with a lamp that was nothing but a post, the top half glowing like a magic wand.

And then we were in bed, and all I saw was his face and his body. I was in way over my head. So deep I was drowning, but I liked it.

CHAPTER 24

*T*he new furniture for our apartment was being delivered on Saturday morning. The temperature was already in the mid-seventies at eight-thirty in the morning. The delivery guys, although one was a female, had to lug it out of the truck in hot, humid air, so I imagined they were grateful for our icy cold lobby and elevator.

There was a lot of stuff to transport up to our apartment. We were getting an incredibly smart TV, a couch, two armchairs, a few living room tables, track lighting that would be installed for us, and a dining table with eight chairs. I'd also purchased a larger ash dresser for my bedroom. The lighting and TV actually came from different stores, but we'd been lucky enough to arrange for everything to arrive on a single day. It was a miracle of timing on the scale of the parting of the red sea.

It took them nearly four hours to unload, relocate to our floor, arrange things in their places, and unwrap the protective foam and straps and enough plastic to smother quite a few people.

When Eileen and I were finally settled on our beautiful new couch, scenes of Roman ruins sliding across the TV screen to a playlist Eileen had chosen, we settled back with iced lattes and smiled at each other.

"I've waited all day," she said. "Now you have to tell me about your secret date."

"Why do you think it's a secret?"

"Because I didn't know it was happening."

"That doesn't make it a secret."

"I didn't even know there was a guy. You haven't said a word."

I sipped my chilled coffee and leaned my head back on the couch. It was the kind of couch that would be difficult to leave. I liked the luxury of comfortable furniture, but I could see how it could take over your life and end up being your enemy if it was too lush. Gradually, without your noticing, even things that were fun might become battles—whether to go out dancing or watch a movie, when you knew that in the end, dancing would definitely be more exciting. But the welcoming form of that couch held your body in such a wonderful state of bliss that your bones and muscles and slug brain wanted nothing but to remain there indefinitely.

"Start talking," Eileen said.

"I met him at the first client meeting for Pauline Herrera. He's cute and seemed interesting, so I asked him out to dinner."

"He must have been absolutely fascinating since you didn't get home until almost two-thirty."

"Are you keeping track of my schedule?" I shivered as more cold coffee ran down my throat.

She laughed. "We're roommates."

"What does that mean?"

She frowned. "Is there a reason you don't want to tell me about this guy?"

"What do you mean, *we're roommates*? I asked if you were keeping track of me, and you said, *we're roommates*. So, what does that mean? Do you think roommates have a right to know each other's every move?"

"God, Alex. Why are you so wound up? Roommates usually

know when the other is coming or going. They know each other's schedules. That doesn't mean I'm spying on you or whatever it is you think I'm doing. I heard you come in. Just like I hear when you're in the shower. It doesn't mean anything." She laughed, then stopped suddenly. "You're kind of giving me the creeps. What are you so worried about?"

"I'm not worried. I didn't understand what you meant."

She stood and picked up her latte. "If you don't want to talk about your date, just say so. I'm going to have a glass of wine." She went into the kitchen. I heard her take a bottle of wine out of the fridge. I wasn't sure I was ready for a glass of wine this early in the afternoon. Not when my body was still recovering from three martinis.

I shouldn't have worried. She returned with a single glass of Chardonnay and didn't offer me one. She picked up the remote and clicked the TV to the menu screen. She began scrolling through the latest offerings.

"Don't sulk," I said.

"I'm not."

"You are. And now you're lying about it."

She laughed, but there was a bitter edge to it.

"You didn't offer me a glass of wine."

"Do you want a glass of wine?" Her voice was deliberately robotic.

I sighed. I stood and went into the kitchen. I didn't need a glass of wine, but I figured I needed to be social. We were supposed to be celebrating the thousands of dollars she'd spent furnishing our apartment. I didn't want to piss her off. I liked living there. And I liked her. I just didn't like being watched or crowded.

I returned with a very large glass containing a very small amount of wine.

I clicked my glass against hers. "His name is Hunter." I settled beside her on the couch.

141

We faced each other, and each of us took a conciliatory sip of wine.

"I don't know why he grabbed my attention. He's not shockingly good-looking, but he's cute in a unique way. Kind of skinny, but tall, which is nice. His hair is longish, but not really styled. He's quiet. Funny. He seems smart."

"What does he do?"

"He's the head of PR."

She nodded.

"We had a really good Indian dinner. Drank too much." I laughed.

"And you had sex on the first date?"

"Why not?"

"You've done that before?"

"Yes."

"That's …"

I sipped my wine, waiting for her to finish her thought.

"I'm not judging you. It seems … I guess it doesn't matter. If you like the guy and you hit it off. Maybe it's game-playing to wait. But how do you know if you like him that fast?"

"I always know. And sometimes, it's not about that. Sometimes, it's just sex."

"Oh."

She stared at me without actually making eye contact. I wondered what was circling inside her brain. Was it the stories her mother had told her about how women should behave according to the rules of god? Or was it something else entirely? For all I knew, she was jealous and wished for the same freedom herself.

"Did he call or text today?" she asked.

"No."

"How annoying."

"It's fine."

"Do you think it will go anywhere?"

I shrugged.

She uncrossed her legs and drained her wineglass. I held out my empty glass to her. She got up silently and went to the kitchen. When she returned, she had the wineglasses on a tray with a small bowl of potato chips that she placed on the coffee table. I ate two chips and took another sip of wine, wishing I had a glass of water instead.

"Do you want it to go anywhere?" she asked.

I shrugged again. "I'm more into him than any guy in a while."

She smiled. "I'm sure he'll call."

"If he doesn't, I'll call him."

"You don't worry much about following the rules, do you."

"Didn't you already know that about me?"

She smiled. "Yes, but it still surprises me, every time."

What I didn't tell her, and probably never would, was that I was more into him than any guy *ever*. I couldn't stop thinking about him. I wanted to know everything about him. More unsettling, I found myself with a strange impulse to tell him all about me and my life. Not everything, obviously. But more than I should. This was a very dangerous situation I was in. I had to make sure to squash that impulse. I'd never experienced it before, and I liked the thrill but wondered how I was going to make it work. I put down my wine-glass. "I should go for a run."

"Now? It's …" She picked up her phone. "It's eighty-seven degrees out there. And you just had a glass of wine."

"An easy run."

"I don't think that's a good idea. You could make yourself sick."

"It will clear my head."

"It's too hot."

I stood. "The gym, then. I'm going to lift weights. I need to do something."

"You didn't finish your wine."

"You can have it."

"What's wrong? Did I say something to upset you?"

"Not at all. I was up late, and I drank more than usual. My muscles are twitchy. I need some exercise."

"Ned and I are going out to dinner. I hate leaving you alone, waiting for him to call."

I laughed. "I'm fine. I'm not waiting for anything. I'll go lift some weights, do yoga, and eat some of my leftover Indian. We split the leftovers, and even my share is a bucket-load. I'll have a feast."

"I'll put your wine in the fridge."

"If you want to." I went to my room and stripped off my shorts and T-shirt. I put on spandex everything with a sleeveless workout shirt on top.

When I returned to the living room, it was empty. Eileen had apparently retreated to her bedroom, so I left without saying good-bye. I sent her a text message as I left our building, telling her to have a great dinner with Ned. I jogged to the gym, keeping one hundred percent of my attention on dodging pedestrians.

CHAPTER 25

*W*hen I returned from the gym, it was six-forty-five. I'd found some inner reserve that allowed me to do three complete circuits. Despite alcohol still oozing through my muscles from the night before, despite the damp heat my skin had absorbed as I jogged on pavement, dodging sweating bodies that were disinclined to move out of my way, my body had been alive with a desire to work itself hard.

I'd thought the heat would bring a crowd into the air-conditioned building on a Saturday afternoon, but that wasn't the case. Maybe the heat had filled everyone with lethargy instead. Even better than the energy firing through me, I had the free weights almost entirely to myself. It felt divine to push my muscles to the extreme, perspiration oiling my skin, resting after each set, closing my eyes, and easing into the thump of the music coming from speakers in the ceiling.

At home, the moment the apartment door swung wide before I glimpsed the interior, I felt the presence of someone inside. Eileen should have been long gone. I was ready to take an indulgent shower, put on a summer dress, and relish my feast of leftovers.

"You're still here," I said.

She was seated on the couch, her face a hard knot of anxiety. Her purse was on the floor, her phone on the coffee table. She gave a single nod.

"Ned's running late?"

She shrugged. She looked like she was putting forth a monumental effort not to cry.

I took off my shoes and started toward my bedroom.

"What are you doing?" she asked in a quiet, meek voice.

I turned back. "Taking a shower."

She nodded.

"Have fun, if you're not here when I get out."

"I think I will be," she said.

"Did something happen?"

"I don't know." Her voice was a whisper.

"Is he okay?"

"I don't know." Her voice was softer still.

I returned to the living room. "What's going on?"

She shook her head. "He was supposed to be here at six. I haven't heard from him and he's not answering my messages. My call went right to voicemail."

"It's not even seven."

"He's never late."

"Everyone's late once in a while."

"Not him."

"Are you worried something happened? Are you worried he—"

She gave a hard laugh. "I don't think he had a heart attack or a stroke if that's what you're imagining. He's not that old."

"Lots of guys that aren't that old have heart attacks."

"He was different yesterday. I think he's—"

"He's not the kind of person to ghost you. He would tell you. You know that. He says what he thinks. Come on. Why are you being like this?"

"We had a fight."

"All couples have fights."

"This was weird."

"Okay. Some fights can be weird. Maybe all of them are."

"Weird as in creepy."

"Oh."

"It was about you."

My stomach rumbled, and I thought about my Indian food. I thought about the half-full bottle of chilled Chardonnay, which I was definitely ready for now. I thought about my sweaty skin and that I really wanted to be clean and wearing something different. I edged toward the short hallway leading to my room.

"Because you said that about peeking in at us when we were having sex."

"I was kidding."

"He thought you were serious."

"I was kidding."

"Anyway. He said I should watch my back with you."

"Maybe you should."

"Alex! Why would you say that?" Tears filled her eyes. "I don't understand why you said that. Or the other thing."

"It's good advice, don't you think?"

"No. I don't treat my friends like I expect them to stab me in the back. I trust people until they prove they don't deserve my trust."

"You can trust people and watch your back at the same time."

"No, you can't. But I don't feel like arguing about this. I'm too upset." She grabbed her phone and tapped the screen. "I don't know why he's not answering me!" Her voice was a genuine wail.

I didn't know what to say. I really wanted my shower. I couldn't imagine Ned dumping her in this way, and I thought she was over-reacting when it had just now been an hour. It could be anything. Maybe he was stuck in traffic with a dead phone or on a subway without a signal. It could be ten different legitimate reasons, and I didn't think I needed to list them all for her. She was acting like a heartbroken twelve-year-old. "Have a glass of wine. The minute you pour it, he'll probably show up. Isn't that how things usually work?" I started toward my bedroom.

"Why are you so unsympathetic? I feel like you don't even care!"

"Because there are a lot of good reasons he might be late. You're overreacting."

"I'm not. He *never* does this."

"I really think you should have a glass of wine and calm down. Did he break up with you after your fight?"

She shook her head.

"Did he say he would see you today?"

She nodded.

"Have you heard from him since the fight?"

She looked confused. "I … yes."

"Then not hearing from him has a reasonable explanation." I went into the kitchen and splashed a bit of wine into a glass. I returned and handed the glass to her. "Chill. Have a fabulous dinner, and I'll see you whenever. I need a shower right now. Say *hi* to Ned." I left without looking back, and I ignored the tiny whimpering sounds that came from her.

The silence of Eileen's desperation that filled the apartment as I stripped off my clothes seemed to seep under my bedroom door and slither its way into my space, snaking up the bathroom walls. I felt like Eileen's gaze was boring through the ceiling, staring down at me as I turned on the water, adjusted the temperature, and stepped into the shower. I lathered my skin and closed my eyes. Hot water ran over my shoulders and steam filled my lungs, but I still sensed her in the other room wanting something from me. I sensed her anxiety like another presence. I wasn't sure how I was going to enjoy my feast if she was still there when I got out.

If he hadn't shown up by the time I was clean and dressed, tears would be running down her cheeks.

Sure enough, when I opened my bedroom door, the tiny whimpers she'd been emitting earlier had grown louder. I heard the click of the wine glass on the coffee table.

In the living room, I found her bent over, hugging her knees, her hair covering the sides of her face. What had happened to her? Since she'd gotten out of her toxic relationship with the guy I'd eliminated, who then surprised her with his repentance from the grave by making her a moderately wealthy woman, I'd thought she'd slowly transformed back into a strong, confident human being. She was in control of her career. She'd stopped starving herself to fit a certain standard and was still doing well. She seemed happy with Ned.

Now, one delayed text message, and she was dissolving into a morass of spoiled fruit.

Ned wasn't that spectacular. He was slightly, or quite a lot, full of himself. And he was a little old for her. There's no explaining who people fall in love with or hook up with. For some people, twenty or thirty years might be nothing, but with these two, something was slightly off. He didn't seem worth all of this. But, I knew absolutely nothing about love and rejection and relationship landmines and broken hearts. All I knew was that it was better to keep my opinion of Ned to myself. For now.

I picked up her glass off the table. I went to the kitchen. It was seven-twenty. I put a bottle of Chardonnay in the freezer and then decided maybe Eileen wasn't overreacting. Unless the subway had broken down entirely, leaving him in a cell tower dead zone, Ned couldn't have been without a signal all that time. Maybe she had some gut instinct telling her something that was causing her to know it was more than a small hiccup in their relationship. Offering a listening ear wasn't an impossible task for me. And it would be good to have a little more information about their fight. I was curious simply because I was curious, but I also wanted to know what Ned was thinking about me. If their relationship wasn't over, I needed to watch my own back.

I took the wine bottle out of the freezer, put it into the fridge, and got busy mixing two martinis. In a lavish display of indulgence, I garnished both of our drinks with four large olives. I put potato chips in a bowl and some jalapeño dip in a smaller bowl. I turned my attention away from the containers of Indian food. It could wait, and there was plenty for Eileen to enjoy with me.

With our glasses and chips on the table, I sat beside Eileen, who was still holding onto her knees for dear life. I put my hand on her back, an unnatural gesture for me, but it seemed like something most women would do in a situation like this. She sat up immediately, so I guessed she was aware of how strange it was for me to behave like most women.

"Let's have a drink," I said.

"I shouldn't. It's too much…we'll have wine with dinner and—"

"Maybe he's not coming."

She stared at me. Instead of bursting into tears as I'd expected, her eyes were cold. "Why would you say that?"

"Isn't that what you think?"

"I don't know. I thought you said there were a million reasonable explanations."

"I said ten."

She didn't laugh or even offer a tiny smile.

I picked up one of the martinis and handed it to her. She sipped it eagerly. I tasted my own drink. "If he's broken your date, it doesn't mean things are over. You had a fight. He needs space. It can be worked out. Couples fight."

She ate three of the olives, one after the other, hardly finishing the one she was chewing before popping another into her mouth. I watched in shocked fascination. At the same time, I wondered why I was always compelled to pace the consumption of the olives in my martinis. It wasn't as if more weren't readily available. Still. I left mine untouched and took another sip of my drink, enjoying the warmth of the alcohol in my bloodstream, the chill of the drink in my throat. "I'm not offended that he told you to watch your back with me."

"You're my friend. And I live with you!" Her voice rose close to the point of hysteria. "I don't want to feel I have to be afraid of someone I've trusted with a key to my home, who sleeps twenty feet away from me. Who potentially has access to my credit cards and knows everything about me."

"Everything?"

"It's a terrible way to live. He acted as if I should be concerned that you might hurt me."

"Why does he think that?"

"I don't even know! That's what we were fighting about. He can't tell me. He said it's just a feeling, that you seem cold. I'm sorry." Her eyes filled with tears. "I shouldn't be telling you this. I don't want to hurt your feelings. I don't want you to think badly of him. And he already thinks badly of you. What a mess. I hate it!" She took a long swallow of her drink.

"Why does he think I'm cold?" I gave her a smile that I was trusting to fill my eyes with warmth.

Her face wrinkled like a crumpled tissue and, for a moment, looked as if it were about to dissolve completely. "He said it's just a feeling. That was part of what the fight was about. How can you say something so awful about a person and then have nothing to back it up except a feeling?!" She ate her last olive.

It sounded as if Ned had good instincts, that's how he could say it was just a feeling. I could also see that she was so caught up in the unfairness of his assessment of me that she couldn't stop herself from spitting out more words. I urged her forward. "There must be something I said, or did, that caused him to think that. Was there something else, besides the joke about watching you have sex?"

"He said it wasn't that. It didn't surprise him at all when you said that. He thinks you're always watching him."

"I wonder why he thinks that?"

"Are you?"

"I'm not exactly sure what he means by *always*." I laughed. "I'm not stalking him."

She didn't smile. "Did you do something to make him angry?"

"How on earth would I know that? And if I did, that's not my problem, it's his."

"It depends on what you did."

"Really? Is that what you think? If a person gets angry, it might be the other person's fault?"

She dragged a potato chip through the dip, took a tiny bite, then checked her phone for messages. "I guess he's not coming. And he's not even going to tell me he's sorry, or explain why. Or, he's dead." She started sobbing, and I wasn't sure whether it was over the thought of him being dead, or the withholding of an explanation.

It was possible he could be dead. I wouldn't say that to her because she would cry even more, and then I would have to reassure her that he probably wasn't. But it was strange that he hadn't let her know he was canceling. He was not a guy who kept his thoughts to himself, as he'd proven quite a few times. If he didn't want to have dinner for any reason, he would have had no problem telling her to make other plans.

CHAPTER 26

*A*fter a seemingly endless night of Eileen's tears, as well as two martinis, wine, and all of the food I'd brought home from my dinner with Hunter, I wasn't sure how I was going to survive the rest of the weekend with her. When we went to bed at one-fifteen Sunday morning, she still hadn't heard from Ned.

I was rescued at nine-thirty-four, just as my brain was starting to flicker with consciousness, by the vibrating of my phone. I thought it might be a text from Hunter. Feeling for a brief moment as if I had turned into Eileen, I *wanted* it to be a text from Hunter. I rolled onto my side, took my phone off the nightstand, and looked at the screen.

Rada: *Want to meet for a cup of coffee? My treat because my kind-hearted roommate hooked me up with a mini loan.*

She added a winking face beside a face with a green tongue sticking out featuring a dollar sign.

I texted back, *sure.* I threw off the blankets. I couldn't wait to escape my spacious, nicely-decorated, previously tranquil apartment. I'd never felt this claustrophobic in my former too-hot or too-cold and occasionally-startled-by-a-large-roach-staring-me-down apartment as I had the night before.

The weather was promising the mid-eighties, so I put on a white skirt, a dark brown top with lots of crisscrossing straps across the back to let in the barest whisper of a breeze, and dark brown gladiator sandals. I would probably regret them once the temperature started to climb and wish I'd worn flip-flops, but they looked cool with my white skirt, so I would just have to remember the last glance in the full-length mirror when I felt sweat pooling under all those leather straps.

I grabbed my water bottle, filled it, and left the apartment like I was escaping a one-night stand before someone tangled me in his web. I texted Eileen from the elevator while the doors were open, ensuring I still had a good connection. *Heading out for a brunch date. With a female! See you later. Try to distract yourself.*

I doubted her inevitable hangover would allow her to distract herself with anything but the TV. Based on her mood the night before, I doubted she even wanted to put forth the effort to distract herself. She was determined to think her way toward imagining every single thought that might possibly be circling inside Ned's brain, putting them in order so she could analyze each one and then carry on an equally imaginary conversation with him.

Thinking about it gave me a headache. I took a long swallow of water and walked quickly toward the subway.

When she and I were seated at a table, Rada got right to the point. "Did you think of any ideas for how I'm going to find an amazing new job?"

"I did." I took a sip from my water bottle. "I spoke to a woman who knows thousands of people. Literally."

Her eyes widened.

"She's going to check with a few people."

"What does that mean?"

"We'll have to wait and see."

"Are you sure your friend will come through for you?"

I took a sip of my coffee and a bite of the blueberry scone she'd also treated me to. "She's not a friend. She's—"

"Then what's her reason for helping me, if she's not a friend? What if she changes her mind?"

"She's the type of person who wants to see other women succeed because she's climbed so high in her own career." I wasn't sure Pauline was this type of person at all, but it was possible. Anything was possible. Maybe that was why she was bored with her upward climb.

Rada blew on her coffee drink which was even more ineffective than blowing on hot beverages is under normal circumstances because hers was topped with a thick layer of whipped cream. As she recognized this, she stuck out her tongue and lapped at the cream. "You got my hopes up. It doesn't sound like a sure thing."

"I said I would try. You shouldn't put all your hope in someone you don't know." It sounded harsh, but I didn't like that she immediately turned my offer into an obligation.

"You were the one who chased me down."

"Yes, but you need to be more cynical. I said I'd *try*."

"Trust me, I'm cynical. But you said you'd have *options*. Not just one person who *might* help because she has a thousand friends. I'm officially out of savings. I'm scared." Her eyes filled with tears. She lapped at the cream some more. It was so thick, she hardly seemed to be getting any, but she kept lapping as if it comforted her.

"Don't panic. It's never helpful."

"Maybe you could set up a meeting with us. If she met me, she might be more motivated. Right now, I'm nothing to her."

This was true, but she was misunderstanding if she thought Pauline would consider meeting her. Although the moment I had that thought, I supposed I shouldn't assume so. Maybe Rada was right. Maybe seeing her and hearing first-hand how she'd been treated, and seeing her funny, intelligent side, would motivate Pauline. Maybe seeing Rada's face and realizing the flesh and blood outrage of what James had done just because, apparently, he could, would fill her with the same need to change the situation as it had me.

155

"Is that a yes?"

"Is what a yes?"

"You didn't answer. That means you're thinking about it."

"I am, but apparently, I already got your hopes up about options. It sounds like everything I say I might try to do gets your hopes up, so it's not a good idea to say I'll arrange a meeting when I have no idea whether she'll agree." I took a large bite of my scone.

"Does that mean you will?"

"I'm not going to say."

"You kind of just did."

"No, I didn't."

She smiled as if she'd won. "Did you tell your co-worker I was fired?"

"No."

"Why not?"

"It's a waste of energy."

"He's actually the one who owes me. Not some other random woman."

"Yes, but Pauline might be able to help you find a job. James won't do anything except double down on saying he did nothing wrong. So you would have to sue him. Chances are, that would go nowhere or cost a fortune. If you can even find an attorney who—"

"Maybe I should."

I shrugged. "You could try."

"You wouldn't bother, though. If it were you."

"I'd figure out how to get myself to a place where a man can't have that kind of power over me ever again." I wondered if I'd truly done that in my own life. Just because I worked for a woman didn't mean I was immune to that kind of stuff. And women can do worse, given the right situation, when they're the ones with the power.

We talked about other things. I half-listened while thoughts about James bubbled below the surface. No matter how much my mind circled the question, I could not understand why Diana had hired him. Sometimes, being good at what you do isn't enough.

Surely there were others who were equally qualified. Absolutely, there had to be others who had his skills. She hadn't tried hard enough. She'd taken the easy path. She'd interviewed people she'd already known. A closed circle. There might be ten or twenty people, maybe more, who had equivalent expertise in micro expressions for all she knew. Maybe hundreds. I got it that she was in a hurry to get momentum with our rebirth. I got it that she wanted to focus on new clients, not on hiring staff, but we could have done alright for a few weeks, even a few months.

Now, we were stuck with this creep who had the ability to destroy everything she was trying to build. It was as if she were constructing a beautiful steel tower, and as fast as she raised the beams and glass into the clear blue sky, he was down below ground, cutting away the foundation.

She wanted to focus on female clients, but she had hired a man who saw women as adorable wind-up toys, décor to embellish his world. He was not going to get away with what he did to Rada. Fly Higher owed Rada for bringing him into her vicinity. In my view, that justified one of our clients helping her find a fabulous new job.

Most people would consider it intrusive to text a client on a Sunday morning, but I figured Pauline would have more mental space to give some thought to a desperate woman than she would during the week. If she was outraged that I'd invaded her weekend, I hoped I could spark further outrage in her by revealing the gruesome details of what James had done. Surely she'd experienced predatory men in her long career. Especially in her modeling days. It was a given.

After Rada and I said goodbye, I took myself to a bookstore. I bought a book about career planning that I planned to give Rada, then walked to Central Park. I sat on a bench in the shade, watching joggers and families with strollers, and people with every breed of dog known to the planet. I sent a text to Pauline.

I bet you stepped over a few lines to get where you are, so I'm stepping over the line again for Rada—the unfairly unemployed server I told you about. Any chance you have an hour to meet for a glass of wine to talk about what she needs?

She answered immediately, and I knew that her complaint to Diana had been taken as something threatening to our reputation when it was nothing like that. An hour later, Pauline and I were sitting across from each other. On the table between us was a piece of slate with three minuscule selections of cheese, six grapes, four pecans, and three slices of flatbread.

"You seem very driven to fix your friend's employment issues. Has she been applying for new positions?"

"Yes, but I was hoping to get her something where there might be upside opportunities. And make it happen faster. She's really smart."

"What do you mean by upside?" She took a sip of wine and ate a grape. She looked at the cheese with an expression that suggested it was a cancerous growth on the piece of slate.

"Maybe a position in a kitchen where she might start learning how to cook."

"To what end? Becoming a chef in a high-end restaurant, if that's what you're thinking, requires training. An apprenticeship. And education is not inexpensive. It sounds like your friend needs a monthly paycheck as soon as possible. It might not be the right time for her to be pursuing her career aspirations at the same time."

"She does need an income. But what happened was so unjust, it would be nice to see her come out better than she was."

"You're somewhat of a control freak, do you know that?"

I smiled and swiped off half the offering of blue cheese, smeared it on a cracker, and ate it. Pauline looked at me with a mixture of disgust and unfettered jealousy. I suppose years of modeling engrain not eating so deeply into a woman that she spends the rest of her life viewing food as an enemy to be wrestled into submission at every meal. "Do you want to meet her?"

"That would be awkward."

"It might be less awkward if you get to know her. You'll realize how much she has to offer."

"You're quite confident in asking me for favors."

"Isn't that what women do? Support each other in their careers?"

She took a sip of wine. I waited for her to respond, but she said nothing.

I took the extended silence as an open door and told her what James had done. As I talked, her neutral expression shifted until she looked slightly angry.

"I understand why you're so engaged." She took a sip of wine and settled back in her chair, glancing at the piece of slate and the remaining food. She took a grape and ate it. "Have you spoken to Diana?"

"It's a difficult situation. Please don't mention this to her."

She looked at me over the rim of her glass. She swirled the wine around, letting it dance up the sides of the glass. "I'm happy to help, but I'm not going to be her mentor or whatever you have in mind. I can't be finding opportunities for a girl I've never met simply because some guy was a creep. I hate saying this, but there are a hundred thousand women in New York City telling that story."

"Would you like to meet her?"

"Alexandra, if you haven't noticed, I run a large, successful modeling agency. I have a lot of responsibility to the women whose careers I represent. I don't have time to take on more. I do know two people who own restaurants and one who's an investor in a whiskey bar. I'll check to see if either of them needs a server, but that's all I can do."

"That would be great." I pulled out my credit card and slipped it into the holder that had been placed beside me only a moment earlier. I noticed Pauline notice the gesture. I also noticed she didn't make the slightest move toward her purse. I hadn't expected her to, but it made me smile inside that I'd called it right.

CHAPTER 27

*P*ortland, Oregon

* * *

Lexy slept with that stinky whiskey cork under her pillow. Of course, I didn't know at the time that it belonged to a whiskey bottle. Alcohol was forbidden in our church, so I'd never even smelled it because my parents never had any. I didn't encounter whiskey fancy enough to have a cork until I was out of college and slithering my way from job to job, looking for the perfect place to hide my avocation.

In the morning, after she swiped it, my little sister tucked the cork with its plastic head into her jacket pocket. She carried it around all day, moving it from her jacket pocket to the pocket in her shorts when it got hot.

She treated it the same way she treated the tiny plastic animals from our toy farm. She loved talking to those animals, and each week she favored a different one with her undivided attention, carrying it in her pocket and talking to it throughout the day, setting it by her plate at meals, pretending it was enjoying the foods she didn't like but was made to eat.

"Here little sheep, you like *green* beans. Eat a *green* bean, little sheep. Be a good sheep and try the *green* bean." It was funny listening to her because she put the emphasis on *green*, making the word sound unique and slightly ominous as if the bean were somehow mysterious and possibly dangerous because it was green.

Now, she talked to the cork, although she had a unique instinct for a four-year-old that told her to keep the cork in her pocket instead of placing it beside her milk cup. She whispered into her lap, telling it not to be scared in the darkness of her pocket. She promised to get a snack for it later.

The weather changed that day. I remember it clearly. I remember a lot of things from that trip much too clearly.

The adults supervising our crafts were flustered and short-tempered. Although they'd complained repeatedly about the heat during the previous three days, worrying about the effects of sitting in the sun, now they complained that it was impossible to work on our new project with a dry, warm wind whipping across the picnic tables. It blew pine needles and finely powdered dirt into the modeling clay we were shaping into crosses and crowns of thorns.

When the pine needles embedded themselves in one smooth crown, the girl with stylishly short hair seated to my right said the pine needles made better thorns than those we were shaping out of modeling clay. The woman supervising our table told her to copy the design sitting on a cardboard box at the center of our table. That was what our crowns were to look like.

Then, the girl asked why we were making crowns with thorns when Easter had been months ago.

I looked at her, amazed by her question and surprised that she was asking a question not meant to be asked. We were often reminded that god wanted children to listen and learn. That was our job. It was how we were supposed to serve god. The teacher smiled with infinite patience and explained that we should always be aware of the pain that our savior suffered. Every day was good

Friday, she said. In every moment of our lives, we should be thinking about how we might endure suffering on his behalf and how we might show humble gratitude for his suffering.

We returned to rolling tiny thorns from dark brown modeling clay. We stuck the awkward thorns to our crowns, where half of them immediately toppled over and rolled down the side onto the table, picking up pieces of grit.

My crown and cross were finished, and I was watching the girl next to me stick pine needles into her cross when I was suddenly aware of a shadow over the table. I turned and saw Mr. Caruthers behind me. He was standing between my table and Lexy's, which was now closer after the previous upset. He had his hand on Lexy's head. "You need to come with me."

I started to climb down from the picnic bench.

"Not you," he said.

"I'm supposed to—"

"I heard that song and dance already. Your sister is perfectly safe with me. There's nothing to worry about. Your parents want you to watch her when there aren't adults from Pure Truth around. You completely misunderstood them. Now sit down." He grabbed me under my arm and lifted my shoulder as if to help me back onto the bench.

I yanked myself away from him. "My mother said I should."

"No back talk. Or I'll tell your father you have a smart mouth that needs dealing with."

The girl with the pine needle-infested cross held it up. One of the adults swooped in and began plucking pine needles out of the clay. Mr. Caruthers walked away, gripping my sister's wrist. I guessed that she had refused to let him take her hand.

I'd barely had time to show my cross and crown to the teacher for approval before my sister returned. She climbed onto the bench beside me.

"What did he want?" I asked.

"He said not to talk about it."

"Why?"

"Because gops is a sin. Girls do it too much."

"Gops?"

"GOPS!"

"What are gops?" I asked.

"You're saying it wrong. Goppiss."

"Gossip?"

She nodded.

"No one will know if you tell me."

She grabbed a piece of my clay, rolled it, circled it into a lumpy crown, and stuck a thorn as fat as her thumb into it. The project was too difficult for a child her age. That was easy for me to see even as a five-year-old. I knew what my abilities were compared to my sister's. I knew how her coloring had improved since the beginning of summer. I remembered how she couldn't cut a straight line with scissors, and then, suddenly, she could. But her hands were still not able to roll tiny bits of clay into slender thorns and make them stick to a coil. I suppose they wanted to keep our hands occupied all morning. But instead, half the children were frustrated and no longer paying attention to their crowns. They were rolling the clay into balls and throwing them at each other or playing games with the gathering piles of pine needles.

Later, while we ate our lunch, I told Lexy she needed to tell me what Mr. Caruthers said. "We always tell our secrets to each other. Remember?"

She nodded. "I forget what a secret is."

"When you only tell one person."

She nodded.

"What did he want?"

"He wanted to know where the thing was that I found. Miss Dinky Dinko."

"What?"

She pointed to the lump in her shorts, barely visible at the edge of her top. "That's what I named her. Miss Dinky Dinko. He said he knows she was in his car, and he wants her back, and he knows I took her."

"What did you say?"

"I said I don't know. But he was mad."

"Why didn't you tell him?"

"I like talking to her. She eats food I don't like." She pouted. "He's mean. He said I'm a bad girl for lying."

"What did you lie about?"

"Not finding Miss Dinky Dinko. He said I must've found her 'cuz it was there and I took it and lied and I'm a bad girl. He said give it back. He said bad things happen to bad girls."

"What bad things?"

"He just said bad things. Maybe hell."

"That's after you die."

"Bad girls that lie get stoned."

"What?"

"God says to throw rocks at bad girls 'til they're died."

"No."

"That's what he said."

I put my hand on her head. It was hot and full of life. "Those are stories. The bible is really old. So don't be scared he'll do that."

"I'm not." She put her hand in her pocket, and I saw the outline of her knuckles through the fabric as she fiddled with her new toy. I wondered why Mr. Caruthers was so worried about it. I wondered what he was going to do if Lexy didn't admit she had it and give it back. I wondered how long it would be until my parents found out.

CHAPTER 28

ew York

* * *

I didn't expect to hear from Pauline with job offers for Rada right away on Monday, but of course, I'd hoped to. I didn't realize I had this hope until I found myself checking my phone every thirty minutes, followed by an increasing impatience that her name hadn't appeared in email, text, or voicemail.

My impatience grew. I started to wonder if she didn't want to help. It seemed selfish. It was such a small request. Pauline did know thousands of people, and I was sure that there must be dozens, or more, who owed her favors.

When James appeared in my doorway, looking smug before he even opened his mouth, I did not keep my cool.

He leaned against the doorframe and hooked his thumb through his belt loop like he thought he was a cowboy in a 1950s film. I half expected him to pull a pistol out of a leather holster and twirl it around his finger.

"How's it going, Miz Alexandra?"

"Fine."

"You've been keeping to yourself."

"I've been busy."

"Busy doing nothing?"

"Busy working. Do you want something?"

"I want to catch up. You've been chilly since our lunch date. Brr." He shuddered and laughed.

I gave him a smile without showing my teeth and turned my attention back to my computer screen.

He walked into my office, adjusted the chair facing my desk, and sat down.

"I'm working."

"I doubt you have a deadline, since I don't have any immediate deadlines, and your work lands on my desk when you're finished with it."

"I like to stay on top of things. I set my own deadlines," I said.

"Diana wants team players. We need a re-do on our lunch so we can get better acquainted and smooth any ruffled feathers."

"We're acquainted just fine."

"We didn't even finish our lunch, thanks to ..." He rolled his eyes and laughed. "But I took care of it. You shouldn't have to deal with that when you're out having a nice meal with your colleague. I'm sorry you were treated to such rudeness."

I pushed my chair away from my desk. "The only rudeness was on your side."

He laughed.

"Your little fit got her fired."

"Really?" He looked satisfied. "I didn't think they'd go that far. Interesting."

Maybe waiting on Pauline wasn't the way to go. Rada was right. James was the one who had torn her life apart, he should fix it. And he should face the consequences from Diana. What if he went around the city treating people like that, and they found out he worked for Fly Higher? I gave him a tight smile and raised my voice to a level I knew would carry through my open door. Since Diana left hers open much of the time, there was a good chance she would hear me. "You harassed her. She was totally professional, and you treated her like a piece of meat."

"I was being friendly. It's too bad a guy can't be friendly to a girl anymore."

"You were not being friendly, you were creepy. And now she's out of work."

"That's not my fault. It was her supervisor's call."

"Because you complained."

"He didn't have to fire her."

I wasn't aware of any movement in the hallway. I wished I'd waited. Now I sounded like I was play-acting. I stood and moved toward the doorway.

"Where are you going?" he asked.

"I want a cup of coffee."

"You forgot your mug." He grabbed it before I could and held it out to me. I took it from him, and as I did, he turned his hand slightly and brushed his fingers against mine. I wanted to smash the mug across the top of his head.

"I like it when you get feisty."

I stepped into the hallway and glanced toward Diana's office. She was seated at her desk. She was looking directly at me, and it was clear she'd heard us. Why wasn't she getting involved? Was she planning to wait until we were shouting at each other? I didn't understand her. I didn't understand why she seemed to have changed so dramatically since she'd taken over the company. She was micromanaging some aspects and completely ignoring an issue that had the potential to destroy us.

I went into the break room, and a moment later, I felt James standing behind me as I poured coffee into my mug. "You should go back and tell them you made a mistake."

He laughed. "I'm not doing that."

"She lost her job because of you."

"That is not true."

"It is. Don't you care about that?"

He cocked his head to the side and studied my face. "From what I've observed, nothing about you has suggested you care a wit about anything. So why now? Why this girl? Just to mess with my head? Trying to make me look bad to the boss-lady?" He cackled.

"I'm asking if you care about someone losing her job. If nothing else, I'm wondering if you're concerned whether it reflects badly on Fly Higher."

"How would it do that? We don't provide consultation services to waitresses."

"Maybe we should."

"They can't afford us."

"Maybe we should model ourselves after attorneys and offer pro bono services."

He laughed. "You're funny when you're pissed off."

"So you don't feel any responsibility for her job loss?"

"Why do you keep blaming me? It's highly unlikely I'm the only person who complained. I expect what happened is that she had a long string of unhappy customers, and I was the final straw. No one loses their job over one customer complaint."

"You don't know that. And it was unjustified. She did nothing wrong."

"She's paid to keep customers happy and add to the ambiance of the dining experience."

"She's paid to take customers' orders and serve their food."

"Well, we have a difference of opinion on that."

I glanced to my left and saw Diana in the doorway. She had a neutral expression on her face. James didn't follow my gaze, and I wondered if he'd known she was there for several minutes, as if he had a sixth sense, always aware of her proximity.

Why did Diana think so much of this guy? It was baffling.

"What's going on?" Diana asked.

"A friendly disagreement," James said.

She smiled. "Anything I might be interested in?"

"James hit on our server at lunch the other day, and she gave him a verbal smackdown. He complained, and she was fired."

Diana's expression didn't change, at least not that I noticed. Maybe James picked up on a few nuances. But no matter what her microexpressions might be saying, it was clear she wasn't concerned about the situation. This guy could act like the biggest creeper in New York City, and she was going to tolerate it. Because he was that good? Or was there some other connection between them she hadn't told me about?

I stared at her, suddenly seeing her in a different light. I turned my attention back to James. All of his obnoxious behavior flashed through my mind under a much different filter.

"That's too bad," Diana said.

"That she was fired?" I asked.

"Yes. What's the disagreement?"

"He treated her like a piece of meat. He should tell them he over-reacted, that she was very professional, and ask them to rehire her."

Diana raised her eyebrows slightly. "I'm sure she's used to overly friendly male customers. And I'm sure it wasn't as bad as you're making it out to be."

"He—"

She held up her hand. "We all know you can be dramatic."

Her comment was unfair, but I wasn't going to nurture her opinion by objecting. "You aren't concerned it could reflect badly on Fly Higher?"

"Is that what the argument is about?"

"*Friendly disagreement*," James said.

Diana laughed. "Right."

"You're okay with your employees behaving like misogynistic thugs? When our mission is to build *women's* careers?"

"She's a sassy one, isn't she?" James asked no one, clearly directing the question to himself, then smiling at his observation. He seemed perfectly content without any reaction from Diana.

Right then, I made my final decision that I was going to rid the world of him. Permanently. I also was aware it would be even riskier than I'd realized, because I was almost certain he and Diana had a connection that I didn't understand.

"Women need to be tough and self-reliant. We can't expect the world to adapt to our sensitivities," Diana said.

"Indeed," James said.

"Don't worry about Fly Higher," Diana said. "We want a reputation as a group that helps women grow stronger, that helps them get to the top with hard work and grit, not by getting favors and exceptions. Women shouldn't be looking for environments that shape themselves to fit their needs, however they define those needs. When you're at the top, then you get to create the environment that pleases you. Until then, you play by the rules, and you win, fair and square.

I could get on board with that. I would play by my rules, and I would beat James. Fair and square.

CHAPTER 29

The following day Diana and I met with Pauline to review her photographs. I told Diana I had a dental appointment and I would meet her at Pauline's agency. I arrived half an hour early, certain I could figure out a way to run into Hunter, but the receptionist had a different idea.

She informed me that our appointment was at four p.m. and until the clock struck four, I was not allowed to leave the lobby area. I was there to meet Pauline in her office, and it was not okay to wander around any of the three floors occupied by the Herrera Agency. When I asked if that meant I wasn't allowed to use the restroom, she gave me a spiteful look and asked if I needed to use it. I said I might, and she offered to call an escort for me.

For twenty-six minutes, until Diana walked through the doors, I did nothing but stare at the live tree in the opposite corner and think about how I might successfully lure James to his death.

When Diana interrupted my thoughts, there was a brief moment when I forgot who we were there to meet. She sat beside me, checked her text messages and email, and flicked through the transcripts of her voicemail. While still looking at her phone, she spoke in a low voice, reminding me that she would do the talking and I wasn't to comment on any of the photos unless she asked me a direct question.

"If Pauline asks you a question, defer to me. Is that clear?"

"Yes."

How could it not be clear? It was a basic statement without any confusing details. We'd done it already with four other clients. She was in charge. I did hope I would remember that fact.

We were escorted to Pauline's office. I hooked up the laptop and displayed the images to the monitor on the wall facing Pauline's conference table. We moved the chairs so we were clustered on one side of the round table and began looking through the images. Diana described to Pauline what James had seen in her facial expressions. It was somewhat remarkable, and I wondered how much of it was accurate and how much was his fancy.

According to him, Pauline was mourning her lost youth. Her eyes were sad, and the grief was evident in the set of her mouth. She was feeling stagnant in her ownership of the agency because she missed modeling. She knew she could never go back, but that desire to go back was preventing her from moving forward.

Every fiber of my being was yearning to ask Diana how much of that analysis came from James and what aspects of it had come from her. I was willing to admit, to believe that he'd seen some form of grief in her expression. I was not willing to admit he had the insight to recognize that her desire to go back was preventing her from moving forward. It seemed almost beautiful in its simplicity and its completeness. I refused to believe he had the ability to think of something that poetic. But I couldn't ask. Not then, or ever.

The line between James and I had been drawn, and if I was going to be rid of him, I needed to quickly change Diana's perception of my relationship to him. Any more attacks or criticism would have to be swallowed live, left to thrash around in my belly like so many squirming eels.

Pauline stared at Diana as if she'd seen a vision. She glanced at the photographs. She searched the images of her face, looking for secrets that she hadn't been able to ferret out herself, wondering at the magic, maybe. Or maybe she thought it meant nothing. It was hard to say because she hadn't spoken a word, and her current expression hadn't changed at all.

"Interesting," she said, after a very long pause that had worked its way up to the edge of awkward.

Diana pushed her chair away from the table. "I'll get us some coffees from your café while you look at the final selection. Our microexpression expert has labeled the most telling photographs. He's noted some of the shots from the fashion show where your body language suggested an attitude of defeat. That's another area we need to dig into." She walked toward the door. "I'll be back in about ten minutes."

I was used to this maneuver also. It was Diana's way of letting clients think through the comments on their own without her telling them how to interpret the results any further, letting them absorb the insights. I was there to keep them from getting diverted to email or phone calls, but under strict instructions not to talk.

However, I had another plan.

The moment the door closed, I leaned my elbows on the table. "That's a lot to work with—defeat and a desire to go back in time. I imagine it's a little shocking, and overwhelming."

She nodded, then slowly looked in my direction. Her eyes were glassy, and I was startled to realize she might be ready to cry.

This was good. She would be eager for a distraction. I doubted she wanted to cry and leave her beautifully designed face smeared with makeup. I doubted she wanted to cry in front of me at all. I spoke quickly. "Have you made any progress in finding something interesting for Rada?"

She recoiled visibly as if I were a viper, striking at her throat.

"That's … inappropriate. This is a meeting to focus on my future success. I don't think Diana would appreciate you—"

"I know. And I know you won't tell her. I thought you'd like to have a chance to take a deep breath. She hit you with a lot, and you need time to process everything."

She laughed sharply. "You did get that right."

"I know I shouldn't be doing this, but I just thought you were eager to help, remembering how it was when you were young. When men could harass you, and you had absolutely no power."

"I get that, but you're pressuring me, and I don't like it."

"She has zero income."

"People need to save their money. Manhattan is an expensive place to live."

"I'm sure she knows that."

"It's not going to happen any faster because you keep pushing me. I said I would help, and I will, but asking me repeatedly is irritating. It's making me wonder why you're so eager. Your need to help this girl is almost painful."

"I thought it was an easy request for you, so I've gotten impatient. That's all."

She nodded. "I think there's more to it, but okay." She glanced at the screen. "I need to look at these photos."

"But you'll put her next on your to-do list?"

She turned her chair toward me, her eyes hard, the shimmer of tears completely evaporated. "Why are you *so* concerned about this? You'd think this woman was your sister or your closest friend. You're almost acting like you need to atone for some sin of your own."

"Nothing like that at all."

"Are you sure?"

"Absolutely."

"Then why are you so intense about it? Why are you risking your own job over this? And you are risking it, are you aware of that?"

I was pretty sure I wasn't risking that much. Getting smacked down hard by Diana, sure. Getting put on probation, maybe. Being forced into more time with James—that thought sickened me and was also probably true. She might even cut my pay, but I didn't think Diana would fire me over this.

"So why the intensity?" she asked.

As if I could hear her high heels clicking in the hallway, even though no sound came through the thick office door, I sensed that Diana would be finished ordering coffee drinks and would be opening that door any moment. I needed the conversation to end. I needed Pauline to at least glance through the photographs. It had been a mistake to pull her away from them so completely after all.

"A man should not be able to walk into a restaurant, make rude comments to a woman about her body, expect her to get all excited about it, and then get her fired when she doesn't respond," I said.

"Men can mostly do as they please. Especially men with money ... white men with money. Surely you know that."

I could feel Diana getting closer. "You'll let me know? Tomorrow? Thursday?"

She snorted softly. "Don't give me a deadline. I'll do what I can, but people are busy." She turned her attention to the photographs and James' comments on the screen, studying them as if they were the dead sea scrolls.

The door opened, and Diana stepped inside carrying a small tray with three lattes in pale green ceramic mugs. I went to the door and took the tray from her. She thanked me and seated herself at the table.

I placed the drinks on the table. I sat down. I studied my fingernails, admiring the dark purple color. I wondered why I was so determined to do everything I could to be sure Rada got another job. A good job. Maybe I could feel James breathing down my neck, threatening my own job, eventually.

CHAPTER 30

*A*fter I left Pauline's offices, I took a cab home. It was too hot to walk to the subway, and I felt like splurging, and I wanted to go for a run. That line of thinking was not at all contradictory. Running in the heat when I was wearing light nylon shorts and a sports bra and my hair was swept off my neck in a ponytail, and the sweat was telling me my muscles were working while music was pounding into my brain was a lot different from walking in high heels, wearing a skirt and blouse, carrying a jacket and a bag with a laptop, my hair bunched up with a clip, but still clinging to my face and neck. Not to mention crushing against people going up and down the stairs to and from the subway.

Eileen wasn't home, which I appreciated.

I stripped off my clothes and dropped them on the floor, changed into running clothes and shoes, and left, still shoving my phone into the strap that hooked to my arm as I locked the front door. I walked quickly to Central Park, did some warm-up stretches, and started an easy jog. The air was cooling very slightly, and I was glad I'd stuck with my decision.

Halfway into mile two, I felt someone running near my left side, about two feet behind but keeping perfect pace with me.

They were close enough that I kept seeing a blur of arms and glimpsing their head and torso. It was annoying, the way they were matching my pace exactly, but keeping out of my full range of sight. I had the urge to swat them away, as if a big, blood-fattened mosquito were buzzing in my ear. Instead, I forced myself into a burst of speed. The mosquito copied me exactly.

Without warning, I stopped. The bottoms of my shoes skidded on the pavement, and the mosquito kept running. When she realized I was gone, then stopped and turned, I saw it was Rada. She walked back to where I was standing. She was breathing hard. "Hi." She grinned.

"Hi."

"Why did you stop like that? You scared me."

"You were running too close to me."

"Oh. I thought it would be fun to go running together."

"By suddenly appearing beside me?"

She smiled. "Oops."

"How did you know I was here?"

"I saw you go out."

"What do you mean?"

"I saw you go out of your apartment building."

I stared at her. I wasn't sure what to think. Was she socially awkward and simply eager to be friends, or was there something about her that should concern me? How had she figured out where I lived? I wanted to know, but I didn't want her to know I was concerned. "I don't recall giving you my address."

"I followed you from work."

She looked slightly guilty, which was a good sign, I suppose.

"I probably should have told you," she said. "I guess it looks a little creepy."

"Yes." I tried to remember if I'd mentioned the name of my company. If I hadn't, maybe James had. That didn't seem quite as intrusive, so maybe this was almost harmless. But she'd followed me home? That was weird. Far from normal. And when had this happened? "I wasn't at my office this afternoon."

"I followed you last week. I know it's really weird. I'm sorry. I should have said *hi* and been a normal person. Losing my job has ..." She laughed softly. "Sorry. Still friends?"

I glanced at my wrist. My fitness tracker was nagging at me for standing still for too long.

"I'm interrupting your workout," she said.

"You can explain while we run." I didn't want her running with me. I didn't want anyone running with me, ever. But I needed to know what was going through her mind, and I didn't want to give up my run, so there weren't a lot of options.

"That would be awesome." She began jogging in place in a way that made it look almost as if she was jumping with excitement.

"Not on a regular basis. Just today."

"Absolutely."

I grimaced.

We started a slow jog. "I know what I did was a little creepy. Not working, sitting in my apartment all the time, has messed with my head, I think. I wanted to see where you worked, and I saw you leave, and I just got a little obsessed with curiosity and decided to follow you. I'm sorry."

In a way, she sounded like me. Curiosity getting the upper hand, taking control of her sanity. I'd experienced that often enough. Maybe I shouldn't think anything of it. But I still didn't like her knowing where I lived. It made me feel trapped. And I already felt more trapped than I wanted with a roommate and her overly curious boyfriend getting familiar with my habits. How was I going to keep doing what I did when I had all these people circling the edges of my life? It made me think I was being watched on all sides, and I might never have the same anonymity again.

"You live in a nice building."

"Thanks."

"And you're a photographer?"

"Yes."

"I guess that pays pretty well."

I was not going to tell her I had a roommate. I was not giving her more information about my life. She was fun to be with and interesting to talk to, but her deepening interest was still concerning.

"You probably think I'm stalking you. Or that I want you to give me a job."

I had not thought that at all. About the job. Now I really wondered what she was after. Had I made a critical mistake in trying to help her? I could set her free from James, that should have been enough. It wasn't my place to become a job placement service for everyone who was harassed out of their job and had to fight against an unexplained termination to find something new. Maybe Pauline had insight into me that I was blind to—why *was* I so invested in trying to find a job for a total stranger? I couldn't answer that question.

It had become an obsession. But now I felt like I'd stepped into something that had the potential for spiraling far out of my control. I'd been whirling around in the sky, like a small child clutching the tail of a kite, whipped this way and that, without any way of getting my feet firmly back on the ground.

Rada knew where I lived.

She didn't have my apartment number, but how hard would it be to get that? A hot, twenty-something woman like Rada could easily talk our doorman into giving her all kinds of details about the residents of our building. I shivered as an image of myself stepping out of my apartment door to see her standing across the hallway flashed through my mind. I imagined coming home in the darkest hours of the night, fresh from killing James or someone else, and finding her waiting for me.

I let out a small gasp.

"Are you okay? Do you need to rest?" she asked.

"I'm fine. If you don't mind, I'd rather not talk anymore so I can push myself harder."

"Absolutely. I should do that too."

We ran for another mile and a half, and she kept pace with me the entire time. She didn't try to break her vow of not talking, and she didn't seem to get tired. When we'd circled back to the West 59th Street entrance to the park, I told her I needed to head home.

"I thought we could grab some dinner," she said.

"Can you afford to eat out anymore?"

She looked utterly ashamed, and I knew she'd not only thought we'd grab dinner, she'd thought I would fill her hungry belly again. Risking my reputation with Diana by pressuring Pauline was already going above and beyond.

"Have you had any interviews?" I asked.

She shook her head. "I thought you—"

"I am, but you should still be looking also."

She nodded. "I will."

"You will, or you have been?"

"A little. I just thought … you sounded so …" She looked like she might cry.

"I'm working on it, but you need to look. Don't depend on me. Okay? I'll give you a call next week." I said goodbye, turned, and began jogging toward my apartment, almost breaking into a run once again.

All the way home, I thought about her standing outside my office building, outside my apartment. I wondered how long she'd stood there, trying to figure out which windows belonged to me. I wondered what she wanted, I wondered if she thought we were on the cusp of a friendship. I also thought about how funny and clever she'd been when we first met. The downhill slide in her stability was sharp. Was it only the lack of work, the worry about money, or was there more?

The only thing that kept my thoughts from brooding over Rada for another hour was a buzz from my phone that made me stop before I entered the elevator. A message from Hunter. And it had been worth the wait.

Best date ever. Lather. Rinse. Repeat?

I sent back the bar of soap emoji.

Then I stepped into the elevator and rode to my floor, thinking about Hunter and not caring if Rada wanted to set up a tent across the street and aim binoculars at my window for the rest of the summer. Eventually, she'd get bored and go away. My life really was not that interesting to the casual observer.

CHAPTER 31

*W*ithout a job, Rada did clearly have too much time on her hands because the following evening, when I left work, she was standing just outside the doors of our office building. I wasn't sure if she'd planned to follow me again or she wanted to talk, but it no longer mattered because whatever she'd come for, had turned into a street drama.

She was crying so ferociously, her whole body shook. People were steering a wide path around her, crushing against each other in their effort to give her plenty of space. A few had even stepped into the gutter, risking confrontations with traffic. They stared at her in fascinated horror, then looked away, eager to keep some distance before they were sucked into whatever was happening.

James stood facing her, talking a mile a minute. Whatever he was saying only made it worse because she continued sobbing like a heartbroken child, emitting small, periodic shrieks of despair.

My first thought was to turn and run as fast as I could toward the subway entrance.

My second was to kill James in broad daylight.

The one I acted on, my third thought, was the impulse that almost always caused me problems. I indulged my curiosity. I needed to know what James had said to cause such extreme emotion. Until that moment, aside from her stalking, she'd seemed like a fairly calm, centered person. I also needed to know why a steady flow of words continued to gush out of his mouth. I couldn't imagine what he had to say to her.

I approached them, keeping myself out of his line of sight until I was in a position where Rada could see me. But she was so deep in her misery, her eyes so flooded with tears, she didn't notice me. I stood there, willing her to look up, willing her to catch her breath and focus.

When she didn't, I took another step forward.

From the corner of his eye, James saw me. "The cavalry has arrived." His voice sounded like that of a man bellowing to passersby at a county fair.

Rada looked at me. "Hi." She gulped and gasped for air. "I wasn't stalking you." She gasped again. "I promise."

James laughed, although I had no idea what he thought was so funny about that, unless he'd known she was outside the building on other occasions.

"What's going on?" I asked.

"I wanted to talk to him. I thought he could speak to my supervisor and tell him he made a mistake. I thought now that a little time had passed, he could apologize and say that I didn't do anything wrong. Maybe they'll hire me back. It's impossible to find a job. The first place I applied wanted references, obviously. When I didn't put my most recent position, they said there are a hundred applicants, and they don't need to bother with someone who's trying to hide something."

"She should have thought of that before treating her customers like they have an infectious disease."

"I didn't do that. I was trying to be polite. But you—"

"You can't dress like you do and not expect men to notice, so cut the BS," James said.

I took hold of Rada's upper arm. "Let's go get a cup of coffee."

"But I didn't dress in … I was wearing regular clothes. Nothing—"

"That tiny little skirt?" James laughed. "Leaning over the table so I could see your tits. You wanted me to look, and then when I did and was nice enough to compliment you … well … you whip out the foulest word in the English language."

"I—"

"Let's go," I said. "This isn't going to turn out well."

"I need a job!" she wailed. "Please. I'm literally begging you. If you just tell them you made a mistake. What's the big deal?"

James laughed again, more sharply this time. "I didn't make a mistake. You get up every day and paint your face with pouty little lips and make your hair all silky soft. You put on that short skirt and low-cut top, and I'm supposed to pretend I don't notice. If you don't want me and every other normal guy to look, why are you doing all that? You want us to look, and then we get punished for doing exactly what you want. Usually, it's the men who lose their jobs."

"You can't … I have to look good for my job."

"Stop talking to him," I said. "Let's go." I tugged her arm, but she stayed rooted to the pavement as if she truly believed he was her lifeline and that there was some way of convincing him to help her. The more she talked, the more he rooted himself to his own spot.

"Are you her benefactor now, Alexandra?"

"Just a friend," I said.

"You should watch who you choose to become friends with."

"My personal life is my business."

"I can't get a job because of what you did," Rada said. "I don't understand why you're doing this to me."

"Because you were a little bitch when I was trying to be nice, and you're proving it again right now."

I squeezed her arm so tightly she yelped. "Let go. You're hurting me."

"Because you're not listening. He's not going to talk to your supervisor. Let's go get something to eat, and you can calm down."

184

"How can I calm down? I don't have a job! My rent is due in five days, and I have less than six hundred dollars. I—"

"What did I tell you?" James asked. "Someone working for tips should be much more focused on making their customers happy."

"Please stop talking," I said. "I'll handle this."

James snorted softly. "Do you have a hero complex or something? I didn't know you were so altruistic, Alexandra."

I began dragging Rada away from him. Her flip-flop slid off her foot, and she stumbled toward me, leaving her shiny pink shoe sitting on the ground. A woman walking past immediately stepped on it. The woman kicked it to the side, shot me an irritated look, then kept going.

"Cinderella lost her slipper," James said.

I let go of Rada's arm and ran back. I picked up her flip-flop, returned to where she was standing, balancing her bare foot on top of the other, and handed it to her. She slipped it on, and we started walking. I half expected James to follow us, but I resisted the urge to turn and check on his whereabouts. When we reached the Chinese restaurant that served the best Beef Chow Fun in midtown, I didn't see him anywhere in the area.

We went inside and were lucky enough to get the last booth. I ordered two martinis without asking what she wanted. She didn't object when she heard me place the order. When our drinks arrived, I didn't offer a toast. I took a sip and opened the menu.

"Thank you," she said.

"No worries."

Her face was still red from the inflated crying. She took a sip of her drink. "This is good."

"Vodka martinis are better than gin."

"I've never tried one before."

"Enjoy."

"I don't understand why he's doing this to me." She took another sip of her drink.

"You punctured his ego. And it's very large and very weak."

"Nothing like this has ever happened to me before."

"That's a good thing, isn't it?"

"Yes, obviously. But now … I'm living in a bad dream. A nightmare. I had a good job. I made great tips, awesome tips, sometimes. And I … I don't know what to do. I thought he would apologize. I thought he'd be over it by now. I don't get why he's so upset."

I took a long, steady swallow of my icy drink. The alcohol ran through my head and scrubbed away the memory of James' self-important voice. It dissolved his entitled attitude and helped me see the situation more clearly. I wondered if it would do the same for Rada. "What did he say that made you so hysterical?"

"How can he be allowed to work in a job counseling people about their careers? He's a monster," she said.

"Yes."

"I didn't think men like that worked in professional jobs."

"They do."

"He treated me like I'm practically a …" She took another sip of her drink. She pulled out the stir stick and ate one of the olives. "I'm starving."

"The food will be here in a few minutes."

She ate another olive.

"What did he say?" I asked.

"A bunch of stuff. Does it matter? I just want him to tell my supervisor he made a mistake. I just want my job back."

"I'm working on getting something else for you."

"It's taking too long. My rent—"

"I heard about your rent. Hopefully soon."

"I appreciate you looking out for me. I really do, but I can't wait. And you don't owe me anything. But he does. I realized I keep leaning on you, but he's the one—"

"I know."

"It seems like he wants to destroy me. I don't *get* it."

"Why were you crying?"

"He said I shouldn't be a bitch to customers. That it's my job to make them feel good. Stuff like that. He acts like I owe him something. I've had lots of men flirt with me and hit on me. I've had men grab me, ask me out, say rude things. But no one has ever told my boss to fire me."

"Were there other complaints, and this was the final one?"

"No. I guess I shouldn't have told him to fuck off. But I've said that a few times before. Other guys get it and leave me alone. No one ever told my supervisor."

Our food was delivered, five or six plates of steaming noodles and rice, chicken, beef, and shrimp. The server hadn't even settled the last dish on the table before Rada was spooning fried rice onto her plate. I scooped a serving of chicken salad onto mine. Once we'd both taken the edge off our hunger and satisfied our thirst with ice water, she leaned back and put her hands over her face. A moment later, her shoulders were shaking as she started silently crying again.

"What, exactly, did he say?"

She was quiet for a few seconds. She sighed and slowly lowered her hands to her lap. "He said girls wear makeup and high heels and short skirts and tight jeans because they're selling themselves to the highest bidder. Anyone who doesn't understand that is too stupid to live." Tears ran down her face. "I really don't think that's what I do, but now I'm not sure." She pushed her plate away from her and drank the rest of her martini.

She didn't say much after that.

I didn't push her to talk. Instead, I returned to the question I'd failed to answer when I was sitting in Pauline's lobby—How could I successfully lure James to his death? And the key word was not lure, as it usually was. The key word was *successfully.*

CHAPTER 32

*P*ortland, Oregon

* * *

Every night of the church camping trip, there was a big campfire that lasted for almost two hours. It took place in a large circle surrounded by rocks to make sure no one got too close. Spread out beyond the ring of rocks were more rings formed by logs sliced in half with stubby legs to create benches.

The campfire was the best part of the day. The flames from the fire were taller than most of the grownups, forcing everyone to look up to see the tips of them reaching up into the sky. I also liked the campfire because it was at night. I liked staring into the sky and seeing so many stars. It felt like there might be a million tiny little eyes looking down at us.

A few people played guitars, and we sang songs. The minister told stories, and we sang more songs. The stories were interesting for kids because the campfire was supposed to be enjoyed by the whole family before we all went off to our tents and crawled into our sleeping bags.

The same day that Mr. Caruthers told Lexy she was a bad girl, and that bad girls had stones thrown at them, he came walking up to my father as soon as Pastor Joshua said *amen*. The flames were still leaping with loud cracking and popping noises. The faces of everyone sitting in the first row of log benches glowed orange.

"Brother Mallory." Mr. Caruthers slapped my father's back. "You're raising the two most obedient little girls in the entire congregation."

"Glad to hear it," my father said.

Mr. Caruthers put his hand on my shoulder. I tried to wriggle away from him, but he squeezed tight, talking loudly. He put his other hand on Lexy's shoulder. "This big sister looks after the little one like she's the good shepherd Himself."

"Is that right?" My father gave him a bright smile.

"I have a small treat for your girls. I think obedience should be rewarded, not just by the parents, but by the church body. Do you agree?"

"Of course," my father said.

"I'll just whisk them away for a few minutes and bring them back to your tent, if that's alright with you."

"What kind of treat?" my mother asked.

"I can't say, sweetheart. That would spoil the surprise." Mr. Caruthers laughed so loudly I felt the growl of his laugh coming through the bones in his fingers, right into my body. It was not a good feeling. I wanted him to take his hand off me. I wanted my father to tell him to take his hand off me and his other hand off Lexy. I wanted my mother to tell him treats weren't allowed before bed. I wanted god, if he existed, to make Mr. Caruthers go away, to fall into the river and get washed out to sea.

But god didn't hear me. I'd already started to suspect he didn't listen quite as hard as all the people at church said he did.

"Let's go, girls." Mr. Caruthers began walking.

"I don't want a treat," Lexy said.

My father laughed. "Since when?"

"We had cookies after dinner. We don't need more treats," I said.

"Who are these strange girls? What have you done with my children?" My father was laughing as loudly as Mr. Caruthers now, and I wasn't sure which one of them I hated more.

Soon, we were walking away from those enticing flames into the thick, silent darkness of ancient trees. We walked for a long time. Lexy and I took turns asking where we were going and announcing boldly that we didn't want a treat.

Mr. Caruthers didn't say a word.

It was so dark I could hardly see the shapes of the tree trunks as we wove through them. The stars had all disappeared now that the thickness of the branches overhead blocked them. It felt like the trees had all grown into each other, forming an enormous tent that covered everything. I wanted that man to tell us where we were going, but he refused to speak. We were wearing jackets, but the cold air on my face and hands made me shiver even when I tried not to.

"I'm scared," Lexy's voice trembled. "It's too dark."

"Stop whining," Mr. Caruthers said.

Lexy whimpered slightly, then stopped.

I felt his body move suddenly as he yanked her arm. "I said stop it. You girls are little liars, but I'm going to get the truth out of you."

"You said we get a treat," Lexy said.

He laughed. "I can lie as well as you. And you won't be telling your parents. I'm in charge here. Your father respects the authority given to the church elders, and he's not going to believe you. So shut up and walk faster. It's up to you how long this takes."

As he dragged us along, I thought about kicking him, but I knew he would just hold on tighter. I wasn't sure what he was going to do, but I was very sure he was right that my father was not going to believe anything bad we said about Mr. Caruthers. I wasn't as sure about my mother. It was hard to know with her. She usually believed the things we told her, but she thought it was her job to do what my father said. Later, she would hug us and kiss us and tell us that god was looking out for us. Everyone had a job, and god had given fathers the job of making sure children grew up the way god wanted them to.

When we were so far away from everyone else that we couldn't hear any human sounds, or see any bobbing flashlights from people walking back to their tents, Mr. Caruthers stopped.

"I'm going to stay calm because we don't need a lot of ruckus here. Sit down."

"Where?" I asked.

"On the ground."

"It's cold. There are bugs," I said.

"Sit."

We sat. I took Lexy's hand.

"You found something in my car, missy. I need you to give it to me. No more games."

"I didn't," Lexy said.

Part of me thought I should make her give it to him. I knew my sister was stubborn. More stubborn than me probably, although I don't think anyone but me knew that. They always called me the stubborn one. Maybe because I was loud about it. Most of the time, Lexy smiled more and seemed more agreeable. She just did what she wanted. I thought she was going to get in a lot of trouble from him if she kept refusing to give back the thing he wanted. But I sure wasn't going to tell him she had it. I wasn't sure if she'd fallen in love with the little thing now that she'd given it a name, or if she was just so angry at him she was never going to give him the satisfaction of getting what he wanted.

Still, I couldn't understand why she was scared enough to cry, but not scared enough to do what he wanted. I leaned close to her and put my mouth against her ear and whispered. "Are you okay?"

"Stop whispering!"

She squeezed my hand.

"Where is it?" Mr. Caruthers shouted, breaking his own rule about creating a ruckus.

Suddenly, Lexy let go of my hand. She pushed herself to her feet. "I want my mommy. I have to go potty."

All the fire went out of him as if someone had poured huge buckets of water on the campfire, and nothing remained but wet ash. He sighed, then made a hissing sound. "If you're lying, something very, *very* bad is going to happen to you."

"Stones?" she asked.

I shivered. I wished she would stop saying that. It wasn't real.

"Get up!" he said.

I stood.

Again, he took one of our arms in each of his hands. We walked, too fast, back the way we'd come.

"Where's our treat?" Lexy asked when we were almost to our tent.

"Your treat is that you didn't get a spanking," he said.

"Mommy will ask what our treat was."

"You're a good little liar," he said. "You'll think of something to say." He let go of us and disappeared into the night. We walked the rest of the way to our tent alone. Neither one of our parents asked where Mr. Caruthers had gone, and my mother didn't ask about our treats.

CHAPTER 33

*N*ew York

* * *

The mysteries that live within the relationship between any couple are inscrutable. I knew that as a child, observing my parents, and I've seen it in every couple that has crossed my path. And, I have no doubt that the relationships I've had with men create questions in the minds of those who know me.

So I shouldn't have been surprised when I came home from work to find Ned sitting on our couch with a glass of Chardonnay in his hand, a smug look on his face, and his stocking feet on the coffee table.

Eileen hadn't said a word about them patching the cracks in their relationship. With all her crying and her certainty that he was either dead or had dumped her, I was genuinely shocked she hadn't mentioned that things were so lovely between them that she was cooking him dinner; and he was settled into our cushions as if he were the man of the house. He seemed more certain of his position

CATHRYN GRANT

than ever. In fact, it felt as if I'd walked into a home where I was the guest.

"Hello, Alex," he said. "How was your day?"

Those words ran like cold water down my spine. I made an instant decision that I should conjure up plans to eat dinner somewhere else. "Good. Just came home for a quick change before I head out for dinner."

Eileen walked into the living room. "You can't go out." She pouted. "I made tacos. I bought extra everything for you. I bought your favorite Chardonnay."

She hadn't mentioned Ned was coming to dinner. She hadn't mentioned that all was forgiven with Ned, and he was cozy in our apartment whenever he felt like it. I wondered what else she hadn't mentioned.

"Did we make plans to eat dinner together?" I asked.

"Yes."

"Don't be rude." Ned stood and walked toward Eileen. He kissed the top of her head, then downed the rest of his wine. "Didn't your mother teach you it's rude to change your plans because you like the second offer better than your previous commitment?"

"I'm meeting someone for—"

"You promised," Eileen said.

"I know I did not promise because I don't make promises."

"That's not surprising," Ned said.

"I made this especially for you."

I looked at the two of them. Maybe I'd acted too quickly with my fake dinner plans. It was probably better to stay and find out what had changed so dramatically at some mysterious point during the past five days. Keep your enemies closer and all that ...

I went into my bedroom and changed into jeans and a comfortable shirt. I left my feet bare and brushed my hair into a messy bun. I washed my face and put lotion on my hands and forearms. I laid on my bed, crossing my ankles and closing my eyes. After a few deep breaths, I decided I was ready to face Ned's

194

increasingly unsubtle hostility and Eileen's increasingly sensitive feelings.

Once I was settled on the couch with my own glass of wine, I listened to Ned drone on with his opinions about the Yankees and his thoughts on the various players' strengths and weaknesses and how the team might better serve their fans. Then he talked about a trip he'd taken to San Francisco six years ago, trying to drag me into his memories. Or possibly prying into the details of my past. "Eileen said you lived in San Francisco. For a year or so?"

"Yes."

"Did you like it?"

"I did."

"Why did you leave?"

"Work."

"You're not in a very talkative mood."

I shrugged.

"It's a great city. One of my favorites. I want to get your perspective on it, if that's not too much trouble."

I smiled. "Why don't you tell me yours."

We talked in circles, Ned telling me about all the touristy things he'd done in San Francisco, me talking about the restaurants I liked, him not having heard of any of them. Finally, Eileen told us dinner was ready. It felt like we raced each other to the table, both glad to escape the other's company and our parallel experiences of San Francisco.

Over dinner, he started up again, commenting that I seemed to move around a lot, change jobs a lot.

"I want to experience *a lot*. Isn't that how most people are when they're young?" I looked pointedly at the side of his head, where his hair was almost entirely gray.

"There's experience, and there's running away."

I picked up my taco and took a large bite. I chewed slowly, looking him in the eye. He held my gaze with equal intensity, and I knew that the moment I swallowed, he would repeat the comment, believing he could force me into responding. But he didn't know me as well as he thought he did.

I took a sip of wine.

"Are you running away from someone, Alex? Eileen tells me you have a violent ex."

"I don't want to talk about it."

"Is it painful? Maybe I can help."

"You can't."

"I'm a very sympathetic guy."

I took another bite of my taco.

"Or are you running from yourself? Many people who can't settle are actually running from themselves, afraid to look in the mirror. They're terrified to think about what their lives mean or where they're headed."

I stood and filled a glass with water from the faucet. "Does anyone else want water?"

Neither of them did, so I returned to the table.

"You're even running from my questions. Do you find them uncomfortable?"

"I didn't hear any questions. Just a few internet psychology bullet points."

"I asked if you're running from yourself?"

"No. Are you?"

He laughed. "I've lived in New York City for more years than I can count."

"Good for you."

"Do you move from man to man as often as you change jobs and homes?"

"I haven't kept track. Like I said, I'm young, and I want to experience everything I can."

"You don't travel much, for someone seeking experiences."

"I can't always afford it."

"I imagine you make a pretty good salary."

"That's none of your business." I began filling another tortilla with chicken and tomatoes, and avocado. After I piled in lettuce and cheese, I drenched it in pico de gallo, folded it in half, and took a bite.

"You're my girlfriend's roommate. I'd like to know you better. I'm really making an effort here, but you don't seem to want to do the same."

"It feels more like an interrogation, or an attempt to label me with your amateur psychological theories."

"Don't be offended."

"These tacos are awesome," I said.

"Thanks." Eileen poured more wine into my glass.

Ned kept probing into my life as if he were throwing darts at a wall of balloons, hoping that if he threw enough and his darts were sharp enough, eventually, one of the balloons would pop.

I ate a third taco and finished another glass of wine. I stood and began putting the plates in the dishwasher and the leftover food in containers. I poured myself a healthy glass of wine and turned to face them. "I don't mean to be rude. I know you're sensitive to that, Ned, but I'm tired. I'm going to relax in my room. It was a long day, and I'm all talked out."

"Absolutely." Ned raised his glass toward me and grinned like he'd won a debate contest.

I went to my room and closed the door behind me. I leaned against it and took a sip of wine.

Since the wine was more than cold enough, I decided to take a shower to wash the irritation of Ned and the grit of the day off my skin. I shampooed my hair, shaved my legs, and blew my hair dry. When I was finished, dressed in yoga clothes, I picked up my glass off the dresser. The wine was still pleasantly cool and quite good.

I leaned my ear against the door. It sounded like Eileen's favorite baking show playing on the TV. That was strange. Ned did not like the baking show that Eileen was addicted to. I took another sip of wine and slowly opened my door a few inches. It was definitely the baking show.

Moving carefully, I inched out of my room and toward the living room, trying to stay out of sight. Eileen sat alone on the couch. All the lights were off, and there was no light coming from the direction of her bedroom or the hall bathroom. I stepped into the living room and moved closer until she saw me.

She paused the show. "Want to watch it with me?"

"Where's Ned?"

"He went home. He had a headache."

"Is that why he stood you up last weekend? A headache?"

She looked startled.

"You thought I wouldn't bring it up again?"

"It's over. It's not a big—"

"You were a mess."

"I was upset at the time, but he—"

"You thought he was dead. He ignored your messages for hours. And now everything is perfectly fine?"

"He ran into someone, and they got into a deep conversation, I guess."

"And he couldn't reply to a text message? It was too difficult to type, *I'm okay?*"

"They were talking. You know how that is."

I didn't know how that was at all. It sounded like a weak lie coming from anyone.

"They were talking and went for a drink, which turned into two drinks, and he lost track of time."

"That sounds like a lie."

"Don't say that."

"That's what I think, so I'm saying it."

"How can you think that? He's not a liar."

"Because people don't lose track of time when they have plans, especially with someone important to them."

"It happens all the time."

"If you say so. Have you ever forgotten a date?"

"Do you want to watch the baking show or not?"

"Sure. Do you want more wine?"

She nodded. I took her glass and went to the kitchen. She'd already opened another bottle. I poured each of us half a glass, filled a small bowl with salted cashews, and managed to carry all of it back to the living room.

We ate nuts and drank our wine and watched the show. I decided it was best to stop trying to figure out why Ned was lying to Eileen. Instead, I returned to considering the problem of James while the bakers chattered and made plans in the background.

CHAPTER 34

*A*lexandra was the most unusual girl Hunter had ever met. Nothing he said made her react in a predictable way. She didn't appear to get embarrassed or upset about anything. After their date, she'd invited herself back to his apartment as if they'd agreed to it ahead of time. Not that he'd minded. She didn't seem to care one way or another if he even sent her a text message after they'd hooked up. He hadn't texted her immediately. She'd started it all by tracking him down like a stalker, and he'd needed some time to figure out how he felt about the situation. She downed three martinis and hardly seemed to show the effects.

She scared him. At the same time, he wanted to be around her all the time. He felt as if he was addicted to her. One dinner. One night in bed. Half a night. A *quarter* of a night, and he felt like he needed to know every single detail about her. He wanted to know every inch of her body and every thought that passed through her head. He'd never felt that way in his life, and he wasn't sure if it meant he was in love or just obsessed and a little out of his mind because the sex was so good it was making him crazy. Maybe his animal brain was thinking if he knew everything about her, he could control her. She wouldn't have such a hold over him. He liked the hold, and at the same time, he didn't like it.

So, he'd decided to invite her out for a picnic. There was nothing less threatening than a picnic on a blanket in a park on a summer evening.

Besides, eating in a restaurant was designed for interruptions. If you were on a first date, constant interruptions were welcomed—a stranger stopping by to talk about food if the conversation was dragging. But he didn't want interruptions. He wanted something casual. He also didn't want her to be able to get away too easily. Maybe. So maybe he *was* trying to control her.

He sent her a text.

It's excellent picnic weather. How about Central Park? Wednesday evening? Near the Lake.

She didn't respond for over two hours.

With other girls, he would assume it was a calculated move. With Alexandra, he was almost certain it was the same, but on a whole other level. As if she knew he'd assume it was calculated, and so she had another calculation on top of the usual, don't look too eager, calculation. Maybe he was reading into it. There was just something incredibly unique about her, and he felt like he was engaged in some type of strategic game. He had no idea what the purpose was or what his role was.

Maybe he was imagining that, too.

When her answer came, he was further mystified.

How about a wine bar or maybe Vietnamese?

I exist inside air-conditioned walls all day, every day. I want to get out and enjoy the city. Don't you?

I go running.

What's not to like about a picnic? A blanket. Lying down after you eat? Watching the stars come out.

He put a winking face to let her know that lying down might be more exciting than simple star gazing.

Ants. Flies. Beetles.

Take a risk.

I take plenty.

I love picnics.

I prefer restaurants. And sitting in a chair while I'm eating.

Mix it up.

What kind of food?

Sandwiches. Obviously.

Is it? Obvious?

He felt the pressure of a headache starting on the right side of his skull. He wasn't sure if she was flirting and giving him a hard time or she really hated picnics this much, and the specifics of the menu were a deal breaker.

We could order pizza at your place if you want to LIE DOWN.

He stared at his phone. Did she just want to eat and have sex? Now he was completely off balance. What was up with her? It was like she was a guy in a woman's body. Or something. He didn't think he was making a stereotypical assumption. Lots of women loved sex. He knew that. Most of the women he'd known loved sex. And some of those women wanted sex without strings just as much as a lot of guys did. It wasn't as common, but it happened. Was that what she was saying? But what woman didn't want to have a picnic and talk?

He tapped out a reply without thinking. *Total honesty. I thought we could get to know each other better.*

We will.

Okay.

It's NYC. There are a million awesome restaurants. Who comes to NYC for the picnics?

You really hate picnics that much?

I don't like eating on the ground. I don't like bugs.

Got it. No picnic.

He had no idea what to say next. He wanted to get to know her, but for some reason, he really did not want to go to a restaurant and have a flirty, superficial conversation. After all this, he wanted it even less. She was interesting and different, and he wanted to *talk*. He wanted more time. That was another thing about restaurants—it wasn't as if you could extend the meal for five hours. He'd thought she was really into him, but now he was confused. He didn't like it, and he didn't like that she was making a few ants, and eating a sandwich on the ground sound like medieval torture. He tossed his phone on the couch. He saw the screen light up, but he wasn't in the mood.

He grabbed a beer, twisted off the cap, and took a long swallow. He went onto the fire escape and felt the warm, still air settle over him like a blanket. It was nice. He liked the heat of the city in the summer. He didn't mind the resulting sweat. He liked being outside. He liked the press of too many people. Sitting around the park was one of his favorite things to do when it was hot. He couldn't imagine not spending time in the park every weekend.

Who didn't like picnics? As far as he was concerned, it was the same as not liking chocolate chip cookies. Maybe she didn't like those either. He leaned on the railing and sipped his beer, trying to get her out of his head. It was a futile effort. Their weird conversation crawled through the nerves in his brain like a thousand ants scurrying without any clear direction. And now, wondering what she'd texted back was poking at the back of his brain.

He still didn't want to look. Asking someone to go on a picnic should not be so exhausting. He was waiting for her to apologize, making a calculated move of his own. But he knew without even thinking about it that she was not the type of person who was going to apologize, not about this, and probably not about anything, ever.

When the beer bottle was empty, he went inside. He set it on the kitchen counter in the line where he kept all his empties. It was his way of keeping track each week of how many he was consuming. It was as good a trick as any to make sure he didn't overdo it, as long as he made sure to leave empty spots for the drinks he had when he went out.

He picked up his phone and looked at the message.

How about somewhere in Little Italy?

He let the screen fade to dark. He was going to concede. He could feel it. Did she just want him to spend money on her? But then why the suggestion of pizza and sex? It couldn't just be about the bugs and eating on the ground. Did she think he was moving too fast? Did she somehow view a picnic as a fourth or seventh-date activity? But she'd wanted sex the minute they'd walked out the doors of the restaurant, so it wasn't as if she had some kind of rule about what she would allow on a second date. All the normal rules did not apply here, and he wasn't sure if there were any rules at all.

He texted back: *Sure. Sounds good.*

Don't sulk.

I'm not.

You sound sulky.

How can a text message sound like anything?

It's a tone.

There's no tone.

If you don't want to go to Little Italy, suggest something else.

I did.

Is this our first fight?

What the actual hell was going on here? Now he had a splitting headache. At the same time, he felt excited and insanely anxious to see her. He was tempted to invite her over right that minute. He shoved the phone between the couch cushions. He went to the bedroom, took off his shirt, and got down on the floor. He did twenty-seven pushups, making himself move as slowly as possible, forcing his muscles to work harder than usual, forcing himself to concentrate on feeling them burn until he couldn't think of anything else.

When he was finished, he got his phone and texted back that she should pick a good restaurant and text him the name. He would meet her there the following Saturday evening at six. After the unsettling exchange, he needed some time to get his equilibrium back. She replied with two emojis—a plate of pasta and a glass of wine.

CHAPTER 35

*I*t was obvious Hunter was upset that I didn't want to go on a picnic with him. I couldn't understand why he was so worked up about it. Eating sandwiches on the ground wasn't that exciting. I didn't like the idea of sitting around on a blanket with rocks poking my bones, and possibly lying down wrapped around each other with satisfied stomachs and drifting to sleep. Even if you dressed it up with fried chicken and potato salad and beer, I didn't want to eat on a blanket, holding my food in one hand and flicking away bugs with the other. In some ways, nicer food made it worse as you hunched over trying to get the food to your mouth without making a mess. I never understood the appeal.

And there was another reason.

It wasn't as if people were walking around the city who knew the things I'd done and my life was at risk, forcing me to worry about public exposure, but there was something about it that suggested it wouldn't be very smart. There's something about sleeping in public that announces—come take advantage of me. There's something about eating on a blanket, without walls around me, that screams: unnecessary exposure.

I figured I could soothe him over dinner. But now he was sulking, proving it by pushing our date to the weekend.

I also thought he was eager to *get to know me*. Of course, I wanted the same with him. I wanted to learn all about him, every tiny little thing, but the reverse of that was something I had to take slowly, consider carefully. When you make up a lot of stories, life can get tricky. I didn't want to start filling his ears with too many complicated lies that I had to keep organized.

There should be an app for that. Why hasn't anyone thought of that?

I wanted to have fun. I wanted to have sex and talk and laugh and find out his thoughts on everything. But most people, when they say they want to *get to know you better,* want to know things you've done in your life. That is dangerous ground.

Now, I was enjoying the freedom of having the apartment to myself on a Sunday afternoon. Eileen had spent the night at Ned's and wasn't planning to return until after dinner. I felt like I could breathe for the first time in weeks. Maybe for the first time since I'd moved in with her, which made me wonder for the hundredth time if moving in with her had been a dangerous mistake. And now, I was trapped—by the fact that it wasn't exactly easy to find an affordable place in New York, by my own desire for comfort that was so much more satisfied in this apartment.

This turned my thoughts to considering whether I needed to leave New York. I loved it here, but it was expensive. All large cities that offer breathtaking architecture and mouth-watering restaurants are expensive—the places that offer endless choices in art galleries and museums, with large enough populations to be hospitable to bookstores and art movie theaters. I love large, exciting cities. It was a conundrum for sure.

I was lying on the couch with an iced latte on the coffee table, a dish of M&Ms beside it, and a baseball game on TV. Watching sports on TV was not something I liked or understood. I would rather throw a ball back and forth with another person, catching it half the time, missing it the other half, for hours on end than watch people who were paid to do it and did it far more often and with far more skill than I did. But they were *paid*. Where was the fun in that?

I was hoping I would learn something about baseball that would help me talk to Ned, catching him off guard the next time words started dribbling out of his mouth. So far, I'd learned nothing but a few players' names and what the announcer thought of their abilities. Why would I care what that guy thought? Why did anyone care what he thought? It made no sense to me.

I muted the sound and picked up my phone, hoping for something more interesting to distract me. Hoping for noise and sounds and tidbits of news and witty comments and funny memes and snippets of music. Anything but that pompous voice feeding me the useless information of his opinions.

I got up and turned off the TV. I could hear Ned making a remark about that move.

As I held my phone, expecting to be rescued from my boredom, a message flashed across the screen. Pauline Herrera. The message commanded me to give her a call when I had time. I had the time. I took a sip of my latte and tapped her number.

She answered right away. "I thought you'd be out enjoying the summer day."

"I'm watching baseball."

"Who's winning?"

"I'm not sure."

She laughed. "How can you not be sure?"

"I'm not a baseball fan."

"Then why are you watching?"

"Trying to learn."

She didn't comment. Maybe it confused her. "I found a job for your friend."

"Cool."

"It's nothing fancy. It's for a hostess at a French restaurant. I'll be straight with you. They like that she's beautiful."

At the word, hostess, I felt a coolness on my skin. With her final words, I was decidedly cold. I wondered how that would play out. A job was a job, but ... I wasn't naïve enough to think that hostesses were hired for much more than how they looked and the charm of their smiles. But still. I sighed. Quite loudly.

"I know it's a step down. But they do tip pooling, so she'll get something."

"It's a start." I sounded like a motivational speaker.

"Unfortunately, this is all I can offer. I'm sorry if you're disappointed. You do understand I'm running a multi-million dollar modeling agency. I can't be—"

"I know. And I appreciate it. I'm sure she will too."

She told me she would text me the details. We talked about the weather and a TV show she was addicted to and then hung up. The text arrived immediately. I put my phone on the table and settled back on the couch. I closed my eyes. I wondered what Rada would say. I was pretty sure she wasn't going to be at all excited.

I pictured Rada standing in my living room. Young, with a near-perfect body and spectacular hair. Eyes that looked at you as if she wanted to pour her soul into yours. Of course, she hadn't been giving James or me those kinds of looks when she was serving our lunch, but she'd certainly given them to me when her eyes were full of tears, and she told me about the near-death state of her bank account.

It was terrible to be hired for the thickness of your hair and the shape and length of your legs. Would she care? She already knew that about her career. She was well aware she had to dress to look good but not so good the patrons wanted her more than they desired the food.

I thought about Pauline and her models, who didn't get to hide behind platters of food or hostess stations. All that mattered was the way their flesh fit around their bones. Of course, they were paid quite a lot more, but still ...

When Diana started talking to Pauline about her career, about why she felt stagnant, about why she missed modeling itself, would any of this come out? Why did a woman want to be a model to begin with? I really should ask Eileen that question.

I opened my eyes and stared at the ceiling. I should text Rada the news immediately. It was what she was waiting for. She was being rescued. Her knight had come for her. She was being given a job where she could start to rebuild her reputation. Maybe. Of course, that potential bad reference was going to trail after her for a while, but she would have money coming in, and she could take a little breath to figure out what she would do next. She could sleep at night.

Maybe once she calmed down, she could talk to her former supervisor herself instead of relying upon James to do it for her. Maybe if she was calm, if they'd had enough time to cool off, if she took a former co-worker with her to help provide perspective, there was a way to show them how wrong it was that James had been able to sabotage her career with a single, unjustified complaint.

Maybe.

CHAPTER 36

*A*fter my iced latte and the M&Ms were gone. After I'd done an hour of yoga on the living room floor. After I took my camera to the lobby and sat near a potted plant where I was mostly hidden and took candid shots of people coming into the building, I sent a message to Rada.

I invited her to dinner at a place called All & Sundry. I thought a cool place, made cool by their dedicated martini menu and savory bar snacks, would soften the blow of a job offer that was a definite demotion. During all those stalling activities, even when I was supposed to be focusing my thoughts on my breathing through various poses, my mind was drilling into the certainty that this job offer was going to make her feel she was sinking in quicksand.

She was envisioning a new job that would make the humiliation and anxiety seem like a fair price to pay. She hadn't said this, but I could feel it in the way she begged for updates and her unsteady grip on her emotions. She wanted something that she could point to and say—*It turns out, what I suffered was worth it. If I hadn't been mistreated and lost my job and been scared of running out of money, then maybe this amazing job wouldn't have appeared on the horizon.*

Instead, she was going to make less money and have less control over the hours she worked. She could no longer go out of her way to give customers a great experience to increase her tips. They would be a token pat on the back, scraped off the tips of others. Pocket change that would take more time to accumulate into something useful.

Looking at Rada now, the last image that came to mind was a candidate for hostess in a Manhattan restaurant. She wasn't wearing any makeup, and her hair looked like she hadn't washed it for two days. She was so pretty, it kind of blurred the edges of all her defeat, but she was definitely not in a good place. She would not make the cut against other women hired to look inviting. I couldn't believe that a series of vicious words from James had caused so much damage.

Why was she so fragile? I'd asked myself that question before about a lot of women. It was never clear to me why some women grew up fighting to secure their places in the world, and some collapsed under the weight of difficult or horrid circumstances. And not just women. Men, too. But I think about women more. Or maybe I just see a reflection that's closer to my own in other women. I look at that reflection and wonder how she can look like me and think like me in many ways, and yet be entirely different at her core.

I decided not to heap more disrespect on Rada by pretending I thought Pauline's job offer was something that would light up her world. Once we were settled with drinks and plates of fried olives and cheese sticks, I took a sip of my vodka martini without offering a toast. It would sound like a charade after the fact.

"The woman I've been talking to has a friend who has a position available for you, if you want it."

"You don't sound very excited."

"It's not exciting. But it's something. And it's yours. No interview. You can start Thursday with two days of orientation. It's in a French restaurant. They want someone with a classy appearance, like you. It's for their weekday dinner hostess."

She stared at me.

"The servers give a share of their tips to the bus and hostess staff."

"I can't live on that. More than seventy-five percent of my income was from tips."

"Like I said, *if* you want it. And no references ..."

"I barely got by before. I'd be stuck like that for years." Her lips seemed to lose their color.

"I thought it would be better," I said.

"I knew all that shit about women helping each other was just words. She has hers, why should she help me? She doesn't even know me. Some stupid waitress ..." She stopped talking and turned her gaze away from mine. "I wanted to go to college." Her voice dropped to a whisper. "I wanted to study biology because I ..." She picked up her drink and took a few sips. "It doesn't matter." Her bottom lip trembled as she spoke.

We ate our snacks, sipped our drinks, and watched the people around us, neither of us saying anything for a few minutes. I glanced at my glass, still half full. Rada's was empty. Without asking if she wanted a second manhattan martini, I ordered her one. It annoyed me to order fruity drinks and call them martinis, but it's not a topic that anyone can be persuaded to change their mind about. I've tried. Whenever I insist a martini is only made from gin or vodka and vermouth, end of story, bartenders and servers, dates and strangers, and other women look at me as if I have some kind of disorder that compels me to sort my food and beverages into obscure categories before I can eat.

"This is what my father said would happen to me."

"What do you mean?"

"He said girls aren't supposed to live in apartments with other girls. He predicted I would end up on the street."

"Why can't you live with other girls? Because—"

"He means I should be married. He doesn't think women should be single."

She looked at me as if she expected me to laugh. She probably thought I'd never heard something like that before, but of course, I had. It made me want to ask if her parents were involved in the same type of church that had enveloped and taken control of my family, but I didn't. It was clear she wanted to talk, not to listen to the stories of my distorted childhood.

"That must have been something when you moved out," I said.

"There was a boy I was supposed to marry. The son of my father's best friend. I've known him all my life. And I've known since I was six that I was supposed to marry him. It was so embarrassing. At every family picnic or festive dinner, we were made to sit beside each other. We were told to take walks together. Alone."

"Even when you were children?"

"He's four years older. So yes, pretty much."

"That's disgusting."

"I was supposed to study and get good grades so my intended husband wouldn't be ashamed of me. So that my father would look good for producing a smart girl. But I was also supposed to be a smart girl who didn't shoot her mouth off. That's what my dad always said—no one likes a girl who shoots her mouth off."

I ate an olive off my stir stick. Rada's second drink was delivered. I ordered another plate of fried olives, finished my martini, and ordered a second for myself. "What does your mother think?"

"Exactly what my father said."

"Exactly?"

"If she ever had a thought that differed from his by even a single word, I never heard it. Girls are supposed to be beautiful and smart, quiet and kind. They should make their husbands feel like kings. They should..."

"I know the script," I said.

"Is that how your family was?"

"Let's talk about you."

She didn't object. "He said I would run out of money. He said I would turn into an old hag serving food to a bunch of lechers who

214

would put their filthy hands on me and try to get me to go home with them, or just take me out to the alley and treat me like a stray cat. I guess he was absolutely right on every point." Her eyes filled with tears.

"It doesn't have to be that way."

"How can it be different? I'm trapped. I can't afford to go to school. Now I can't even hope to get a job making more money so I can save up to take a few classes at a time. I'm stuck forever."

"You're so young. Maybe there are other ways."

"Like what?"

"I don't know. I'm not a career counselor, but—"

"That's almost exactly what you are."

"I take photographs."

"You must know a little about it."

"We don't really help people at your ... we ..."

She took a long swallow of her drink. "You don't have to explain. I get it. I can move back home. But then it will be on his terms. I'll marry Arin. Have kids. And spend my life making Arin feel like a king. What can I do for you today, your royal highness?" She giggled. Her giggle turned hysterical, then grew louder.

The two guys at the table beside us turned. At first, they smiled. As her laughter continued, they looked slightly uneasy. They turned away and searched the room frantically as if they hoped to be rescued.

Rada stopped laughing. "My father thinks the world is for men, careers are for men, sports are for men, government is for men. And, women are for men. That's it. That's how things are supposed to work. All the problems we have in the world are because women are trying to be men."

I felt as if the colored globes of the lights were falling on me, hundreds of balls raining down like giant hailstones. She was indeed trapped, but without the resources of someone like Pauline, I was in no position to help her. I felt equally trapped.

CHAPTER 37

Sitting in Pauline's lobby without an appointment on Tuesday morning, I felt like I was close to entrapping myself as surely as Rada was trapped in her tiny, choice-less world. I'd managed to convince myself I had a different story to tell Pauline now, but I wasn't sure if I was massively delusional or there was actually something in what Rada had said that would set fire to Pauline.

It wasn't as if I was now in the business of telling other people how to spend their money, but I just didn't get it. She was someone who admitted she was bored with her career because she'd achieved everything she wanted. She was successful beyond what most people imagined. Hadn't it occurred to her that it might give her some new energy to take on a project like Rada's career advancement? I was sure Rada wouldn't be thrilled at being called a project, but it was the only word I could come up with.

If I could engineer a meeting between them, maybe Pauline would feel a connection. Even if she didn't want to or couldn't help Rada with her long-term dreams, she might offer her a chance to leapfrog others into the modeling business. Not that this would give her freedom from being a commodity or inspected and labeled like a steak, but it *would* give her money. And money was freedom. Money was power. There had to be something Pauline could do.

Rada's father sounded like a noble from the middle ages, selling his daughter off to the lord of the neighboring fiefdom in some deal they made before the heirs were even born.

I stared at the same eighteen-foot photograph I'd gazed at the other day. The model wore a long white dress that clung to her thin body and dragged on the ground, exposing one bare foot without toenail polish. It was a radical statement in a pedicured world.

The photograph reminded me, because I had stared at it for so long during my previous wait, that I still hadn't worked out how I was going to address the challenge of James. But I needed to leave that for another time. First, I needed Rada out of my head. James required one hundred percent focus if I was going to do it right.

Pauline had turned down meeting at a coffee shop. She'd turned down going for a run with me or joining me as a guest at my gym. She'd said no thanks to getting together for a drink that evening. Clearly, she knew what I wanted, but strangely enough, she'd said yes to my coming to her office.

This time, I hoped not to run into Hunter.

Focus.

Rada.

I needed all my thoughts directed toward untangling myself from the details of her life that had snarled around me before I realized what I was doing.

Pauline came out to greet me herself, another surprise.

I walked beside her to her office. She chatted about her weekend on a friend's sailboat. I imagined this sailboat, large enough to accommodate Pauline and what sounded like ten or twelve friends for a three-day weekend. I thought about all that water surrounding the boat as it drifted out there alone, other boats nothing but white specks on the horizon. I shivered.

"Is the AC too much?"

"It's fine, just a random chill."

In her office, she gestured toward the two sofas facing each other. On the table between them was a pewter coffee pot, a smaller pewter teapot, and a ceramic container with tea bags. Two white cups sat on saucers that were so close to the size of the cups they might as well not have been there.

"Coffee? Or tea?"

"Coffee."

She filled both cups. I added cream to mine.

"I don't have to ask why you're here," she said.

I smiled.

"It was nice of you to go to all this trouble to offer a personal thank you. A text would have been fine. I truly was happy to help."

I picked up my cup and took several quick sips, burning my lips, tongue, and throat despite the cream. I tried not to think about the huge leap I now had to make—from her expectation of what I'd come for to my expanded request.

After a pause and a few more sips of coffee, I spoke. "When I photographed you the first time, you said you wanted to hire us to explore your next steps because you felt uneasy about your career, and your life, even though you'd achieved everything you wanted."

She gave me a puzzled look.

"You mentioned that you were a little bored."

"I'm not sure why you're bringing that up. Diana said we'll be getting to that. I appreciate you stopping by to thank me, but I wasn't prepared to work on those issues this morning." She glanced at her watch.

"Diana will work on it with you. Absolutely. I wasn't trying to step into her place. I was just thinking about what you'd said … and about Rada."

Her face wrinkled like a crumpled piece of paper. Her eyes darted from mine to her coffee to the windows, back to her watch.

"I won't stay too long. I should get right to the point."

"Please."

"I really appreciate what you did for her, and so does Rada.

Obviously. What you did is life-saving. But she has so much potential, and working as a hostess will trap her for years. She'll spend the best part of her life paying for something a petulant man did to her. And she has zero choices."

Barely pausing for a breath and leaving my coffee alone, so there was no opportunity for Pauline to graciously interrupt, I told her about Rada's father. I reminded her about her own childhood, how she'd described the freedom she'd had to dream about being whatever she wanted, about pursuing anything that interested her. I told her that having passion for a career, or any desire of her own, was an unknown concept in the house where Rada grew up. I even mentioned my own father. Not much, just enough to give her a general idea. And strangely, that was what changed everything.

She got up and came over to sit beside me. She put her arm around me and told me how strong I was. She told me I was remarkable. She told me I was a good person to stand up for Rada.

All of this made me feel slightly short of breath. It was hard not to laugh as she described the person she believed I was, a person who was a figment of her imagination. This person was completely unrecognizable to me.

I straightened my back. I inched away from her and went for broke. "What Rada really wants is to go to college. She wants to study biology. I wonder if there's any way to set up a scholarship through some of your connections or get her in touch with resources who could help to make that happen."

"I get it," Pauline said. "And I honestly don't know why I didn't see it before. I guess I'm so focused on my ennui that I didn't think about looking outside my profession or doing something that wasn't about making more money. It sounds so simplistic when I say it."

"Lots of things do."

"You're very wise."

"Not really. I'm just stating the obvious. And I know what it's like to be locked in a virtual cage."

"I suppose I was really lucky," she said. "I never wondered if I could do what I wanted. And I know I made a fortune in a superficial profession. But I never saw it that way. I loved the clothes, and I loved creating a look and a mood. I loved the makeup. I still do love all those things. And no one ever told me I couldn't have any of that. Certainly, no one ever told me they would choose who I married." She shivered. "I can't imagine. It's appalling. What if you ..." She shuddered more violently. "Will you arrange a time for Rada and I to meet?"

"Absolutely." I smiled and stood. My head felt clear. As I shook her hand and turned to leave, an image of James, a mocking grin spread across his face, consumed my thoughts.

CHAPTER 38

 ortland, Oregon

* * *

The day after he pretended to take us for a treat, we didn't see Mr. Caruthers for the entire morning. Lexy didn't say a word to our parents about him or what had happened the night before. She acted as if nothing was wrong, and I did the same. We didn't even mention him to each other.

I felt the air as it brushed across my skin and the hairs on my head as if each strand were trying to break free. Icy needles ran down my spine, telling me he was somewhere close by. He could show up any minute. I wondered if he was watching us, waiting to see what we would do. Still, we didn't see *him*.

After a while, always looking around, wondering where he might be, made me tired.

He was not going to allow us to keep lying to him. Since I was the big sister, I should have made Lexy tell him she'd found the thing he was looking for, but I wouldn't do that to her. She was absolutely certain he had no right to know what she'd found.

I told her we should sneak up to his car and hide it under the seat. Maybe he would find it later and think it had been there the whole time. She shook her head. She looked at me, staring into my eyes as if she knew my thoughts. It seemed as if she was disappointed in me for even thinking about doing that. It seemed as if she wasn't quite sure she could count on me.

After that, I let my scalp hum as much as it wanted, and my spine turn into an icicle, knowing I would stay by her side no matter what. I also knew Mr. Caruthers was going to punish us.

Normal children would have told their parents. But I wasn't a normal child, and I think I knew that Lexy wasn't all that normal either. Our parents definitely weren't normal but in a different way. Although maybe we were very alike in one way—we were all stubborn.

Telling my parents would have brought more trouble, and I knew this clearly at the age of five. I'd heard it in my father's voice when he spoke to *that man* the night before, with the crackle of the sparks from the campfire punctuating his words. My mother would follow wherever my father led.

I wasn't sure why Lexy wasn't normal. Was there something in my parents that made us this way? Had she been imprinted with some piece of me after sharing my bedroom since she was a tiny baby, learning from the earliest days of her life how I interacted with the world? Had she adopted my attitude for herself because she had no choice, because there are no choices when you're in a crib and your thoughts are fed to you by the people around you?

These are questions I'll never know the answers to. And since I can't know the answers, I prefer to think about it differently. I prefer to think Lexy was born the way she was. She had her own thoughts and her own wants, and she was not going to allow the world to make her into someone else, just like me.

So we were on our own. Two small girls who thought they could do anything. Two little girls who knew there weren't any adults who were truly on their side.

All day my scalp prickled, and my spine felt like ice. All day long, Lexy walked with her hand in her pocket, cupping the sour-smelling cap that she'd made into a make-believe friend.

I asked her if she felt funny, and she stared at me.

I touched the top of her head. "Does it feel funny here?"

She nodded. "My hair hurts, like it's trying to grow-ed and it can't."

We did our crafts. We ate hot dogs for lunch. We rested in our tent during the quiet time required for all children under the age of eight. While we rested, our mother sat outside the zippered flap to make sure we were truly quiet. We went on a hike and learned that the spongy bark on redwood trees protects them from forest fires and parasites. We went wading in the creek, where we collected pebbles before returning to our campsite for dinner.

By the time the sun was setting, and we were putting on warmer clothes for the campfire, I felt as if insects had crept inside my body and made their home there.

"Why are you so squirmy?" my mother asked.

"I don't want to go to the campfire."

"Why in heaven's name not?"

"I just don't."

"That's not an answer."

I thought it was, but I could see she'd already decided it was not.

"What's the matter?" she asked.

"Nothing."

She looked at Lexy. "You're both fidgety."

Lexy blinked several times, but said nothing.

"Is there something going on I should know about?"

We shook our heads.

"We're going to the campfire. You need to put smiles on your faces and think about how blessed we are to enjoy this beautiful place."

My brothers were as excited as always about the fire. They wanted to sit in the front row. We were early enough that there was plenty of space in the first ring of log benches. My father sat on one end, my oldest brother on the other. My mother sat between Lexy and me. Probably because we were so fidgety.

I wondered if that man was behind us, staring at us. I wondered if he'd been watching us at our tent, if he'd followed us to the campfire. I wondered if he'd chosen a seat where he could hear if Lexy or I said something. I wanted to turn and look, but I didn't want him to know I was thinking about him.

The songs were the same ones we'd sung every night. The prayers and the things the minister said also seemed mostly the same, but maybe that's because I hardly listened. Instead, I tried to imagine what Mr. Caruthers was planning.

It seemed as if the moment the minister said, *Amen*, Mr. Caruthers was standing beside my father. It felt as if he'd dropped from the top of one of the massive redwood trees, fallen right beside us like an angel descending from heaven.

"What a beautiful family you have," Mr. Caruthers said.

"Thank you." My father nodded his head several times.

"I'd like to take your two charming daughters out for a treat again. They're such bright lights. Shining examples."

My father's eyebrows twitched, but he got them under control quickly. "Sure. They enjoyed themselves last evening. There's something about walking in the darkness that makes us trust in our Heavenly Father, isn't that right girls?" When we didn't answer, my father laughed as if it was the funniest thing he'd ever heard. I wondered if the heavenly father he wanted us to trust thought it was funny. "My girls don't even use nightlights. I encouraged them not to, of course, but I'm proud of them for that. Trust. It's what we're all about."

I didn't like having a nightlight because I could feel the brightness poking through my eyelids, and I couldn't sleep. It had nothing to do with trust, and I wasn't even sure what he meant, but I didn't say anything. I did not want to go on a walk. There was no treat waiting for us. And I did not want to be with that man. I was sure my father knew that. If he didn't, he should have known from the way my mother was making strange shapes with her mouth and little jerks of her head, like she was trying to get his attention, wanting to talk to him without Mr. Caruthers hearing. My father ignored her.

We left on our walk.

This walk didn't take nearly as long because we went very fast. I had to take really long steps, and Lexy had to run to keep up with Mr. Caruthers.

"I don't want to go on a walk," I said.

"Tough shit."

"That's a bad word."

"No talking."

When we stopped, Mr. Caruthers shone his huge flashlight right in our eyes. "Okay. I've had enough of your lying." He moved the light so it was on Lexy's face. "The only reason your sister is here is because I can't understand your babbling. For a girl that acts like a little whore, you talk like a baby. Now tell me what you did with the thing you found in my car."

Lexy pouted. Her lips looked bright red, and her skin utterly pale under the bright light shining on her face.

"I took my car to be detailed. A three-and-a-half-hour round trip, which I do not appreciate. It's a waste of the Lord's resources. Gasoline. My time. My leadership and guidance required for this camping trip. They found nothing. The item I'm looking for was in my car, and you were the only one in there. I asked you to find it. I trusted you to do something for me. I'm an elder for this church body, and it's an honor to be of service to me. I trusted you to be truthful, and you are a lying little bitch." He swung the beam of light onto my face. "Don't give me that outraged expression. Whorish behavior has to be dug out at a young age, and I see that it's already putting down roots in the two of you."

"You told Daddy we—"

"I'm talking. I'm the adult. I'm the elder. I've been given

authority by Almighty God. Children listen. Children obey. Adults talk. That's how the world is organized, and you need to learn that."

"She told you she doesn't have it," I said.

"She's lying."

"Mr. Caruthers?" A woman's voice spoke out of the surrounding darkness.

He swung the flashlight wildly. His eyes widened so the white made him look like a cartoon character who was panicking, ready for his legs to start cycling madly, trying to run away. "Hello?" His voice was completely different. It was deep and smooth, like it usually was. He sounded like he wanted to be friendly and nice, pretending he hadn't just said all those bad words.

"Who's there?" His voice was still as calm as if he were opening his front door to the man across the street.

The woman spoke again. "I heard your voice, and you sounded upset. Where are you?"

Mr. Caruthers put his finger to his lips. Then, he looked right at me, holding the flashlight up so I could see clearly. He dragged his finger across his neck as if he were cutting his throat. A five-year-old girl with three older brothers knows what that means. He took Lexy's hand and began walking toward the voice.

I heard them talking, but his voice, and the other person's voice, were so low, I couldn't understand the words. As I stood there, the voices got softer and softer, and I realized they were walking away from me.

I started following them as fast as I could, barely able to hear them now. I wasn't sure if the sounds I heard were the branches moving above me in the wind or their voices, still talking. I tried to think and listen at the same time, trying to decide what I should do.

If I told my father that Mr. Caruthers left me alone in the woods, what would he say? Would he do anything at all? Was Mr. Caruthers bringing Lexy back to our campsite? Why did he leave me alone in the woods? The questions ran through my head, tripping over each other as I hurried after the soft sounds of the trees and maybe animals scurrying away from me in the darkness.

When I was close to our campsite, I saw the lantern on our picnic table. My parents and brothers were sitting around the table eating the brownies Lexy and I had helped my mother bake before the camping trip. Lexy wasn't with them. I stood watching, wondering what my family would be like without Lexy and me. They looked a little tired and not very interesting.

I turned and ran back the way I'd come, my eyes adjusted to the dark after all that time walking without the help of a flashlight. I was also helped by the brilliant half-moon.

I knew I should get my parents. But they wouldn't run, they would walk. First, they would waste time getting the right shoes and jackets and giving instructions to my brothers. I knew they would tell me to settle down. They would tell me Lexy was fine. God was watching over her. I needed to trust she was safe in his hands. They might even say we should wait until Mr. Caruthers came back.

But no one at our church ever said the words he'd said. I only knew about those bad words because I'd heard older kids on our street say them. I heard my oldest brother, Eric, say one of them once, and I saw what happened to him. Afterward, my father talked all the way through dinner about bad words. He talked non-stop about how they made god so upset. They showed you had a wicked heart and an evil mind.

Mr. Caruthers didn't have to say those words for me to know he had an evil mind. And if I told my father he said those words, he wouldn't believe me anyway. I would end up with a big bar of the bad-smelling soap we used when we went camping shoved into my mouth and scraped on my teeth.

I ran to the picnic table where we did crafts and found the plastic tubs where they kept the supplies. There was a tarp over them for the night. I pulled it off and dug around until I found a flashlight. As fast as I could, I ran all the way toward the grove of trees where Mr. Caruthers had first taken us.

My insides felt like they were turning into oatmeal. I thought my dinner, and probably my lunch and breakfast, were going to come pouring out of me if I didn't find Mr. Caruthers waiting in that spot. I called Lexy's name, but the only one who answered was an owl.

The light from my flashlight was ripping across the trees and over the ground, racing everywhere, as fast as my thoughts flew through my head, trying to think where he would have taken my sister. Then, I remembered what he'd said about bad girls getting stones thrown at them. I remembered all the rocks in one place beside the river where we'd gone wading after our hike.

I ran there, my breath getting hotter with every step, burning inside my chest. I tripped over a tree root and fell on my face. Pine needles and dirt filled my mouth. I spit them out. I pushed myself up and started running again.

Finally, I reached a ledge just above the river. I waved my flashlight over the rocks below. They looked wet. The river sounded peaceful, gurgling past, rippling over the stones that were under the water. I couldn't get down there in the dark because even with the flashlight, it was hard to see the cutout spaces of earth where you could put your feet.

I walked to the edge and squatted. I held the flashlight close to my shoulder. I moved it more slowly.

And then, I saw Lexy.

She was lying on her face. Her hair was spread out around her. The rocks were wet, and it wasn't water. All around her was blood. So much wet, red blood. Even in the dark, the brightness of the flashlight beam showed me it was bright red blood.

And then, everything in my head went dark.

CHAPTER 39

N *ew York*

* * *

I was sitting at my desk with my office door closed. It was always closed since my lunch with James. Looking at the back of the door, I recalled how many times I'd shut Stephanie out of my office and wanted to laugh at how much worse it was to endure James invading my space. How had I managed to find a job that was so satisfying and provided such a nice income but drew highly unpleasant people into my life?

And why was it that the people I worked for were absolutely great, more or less, and one or two of the ones I worked beside were intolerable? I'd thought my job would be pure bliss with Diana in charge and Stephanie dead or living in another realm, if her beliefs turned out to be true. Instead, something more sinister had sprouted in the place she'd left vacant.

I moved the mouse across the pad and clicked to open the first file of new photographs. Again, I was behind on organizing the shots I'd taken. Probably because I'd been focused on everything but my job lately. Or maybe not lately, maybe most of the time.

There was a knock on the door. I recalled what Rada had said about being a prisoner. If I didn't figure out a way to get rid of James soon, I was going to have to find another job. I refused to sit in an office like a woman in solitary confinement, only going out for meals and a run around the exercise yard.

A second knock followed the first.

"It's open," I said, hoping it was Diana. Or Fallon. Maybe even a client, although that was so rare, it was absurd to consider it a possibility.

The door opened, and Rada was standing there. I felt my shoulders relax. "Hey. How did you get in here?"

"The person at the reception desk was super friendly." She smiled.

"Come on in."

She stepped inside slowly and glanced over her shoulder.

"Close the door."

She settled herself in the chair facing my desk. She looked so much better. She looked like the woman I'd seen that day in the restaurant. She was wearing a white T-shirt, white jeans, a gold belt, and red flip-flops.

"What's up?" I asked.

"I felt bad that I kind of lost it the other day. Not kind of … I did lose it. I was really ungrateful. I just wanted to thank you for trying so hard to help me. You don't owe me anything, and I wanted you to know I really appreciate how you went out of your way."

"No worries."

"This is a nice office." She looked around, gazing at my sleek computer and the uncluttered desk, turning to look at the framed photographs on the wall behind her. She stood and went to the window. "Do you look out every day and feel lucky that you work here?"

"No."

"Why not?"

"Good question."

She turned. "Anyway, I just wanted to come by in person. I decided I'm going to call about the hostess job. I need to do something. So …" She shrugged.

"Pauline wants to meet you."

"Why?"

"I told her about your father. The marriage thing."

"What does she want?"

"I'm not sure, but I think she realized …" I cut myself off. I'd already tossed out enough suggestions that she had taken as promises. Rada was planning to call about the hostess job. Was it really a good idea to suggest Pauline had something better in mind after all? Rada was smiling. She seemed calm. "I shouldn't try to guess what she's thinking. Who ever knows what another person thinks?"

"Right?" She laughed. "Why do we do that—imagine that we can guess?"

I shrugged.

There was a knock on the door. I ignored it, knowing that neither Diana nor James would give up, eventually opening the door without an invitation.

"Should you …?" Rada asked.

"I'm busy."

She stared at me as if ignoring a knock was the most outrageous act she'd witnessed. She wiggled in her chair, about to stand up. "I only came to say thanks. So, I should probably go. I'm sure you have work—"

There was another sharp rap, and the door opened. "Oh," Diana said. "You have a guest."

Rada turned toward her. "Hi."

"James said you haven't finished organizing all the photos from the last three client sessions," Diana said.

"I'm working on them now."

"Are you?" She looked pointedly at Rada.

"She just stopped by for a minute."

"A friend of yours?" Diana took a few steps toward Rada. "Diana Clarke."

"I'm Rada." She didn't give her last name. "Alex is helping me with my job situation."

"How nice of her," Diana said.

"Thanks again." Rada stood.

"Send me a few dates and times that work for you," I said.

She nodded and hurried to the door. Diana's cool gaze followed Rada as she left, then she walked to the door and closed it. She turned to face me, folding her arms. "What are you doing?"

"Rada told you."

"During business hours?"

"I'm not an hourly employee. She was here for ten minutes. Not even that."

"It seems like you're a little obsessed with this person. James mentioned she's been hanging around outside the building. I guess she made quite a scene the other day."

"He *mentioned* that?"

"What's going on? Is there something I need to know about?"

"No."

"I feel like there's some kind of drama going on behind my back, something between you and James and this waitress. And you've dragged one of our clients into it. I don't like it."

"Nothing's going on." Now that I'd made a firm decision to be rid of James, I needed Diana to forget all about this. I needed her to think things were professional and cordial between us. I did not need James telling her about Rada's supposed failures or giving any hint that he and I were not getting along.

"Can you get it resolved? It seems like you're not focused, whatever it is."

"I am focused. Why are you treating me like a child?"

"You're acting like one."

"You're so different now that you're running the organization. It's a little surprising. It's hard to get used to."

"I have a vision I'm trying to execute on. It's a lot of responsibility. Of course I'm different."

"You can still have fun."

"I will have fun. When you stop slacking off and stirring up petty fights with James."

"There aren't any petty fights."

"I hope not." She opened the door. "Please get the photographs organized today. And talk to Fallon about your schedule because there are six new clients that we need to set up for their initial meetings."

"I will."

She stepped out and closed the door.

I returned my attention to my computer. It was so easy to put off stuff like this. I hated working on the computer. I got bored organizing the photographs, and it was worse when I let them pile up. The endless repetition of it made my brain feel like it was melting.

It was much more interesting to try to think about how I was going to get James alone without anyone knowing where he'd gone. It was challenging and exciting trying to figure out how I was going to get him to trust me, and how I was going to disable him and remove him from my life forever.

CHAPTER 40

*B*efore I knew it, my thoughts had drifted away from my files filled with hundreds of photographs once again. I was thinking about James and what kind of person he was. I was trying to figure out if I'd shown my loathing to him so clearly that he would never fall for a fake flirtation. How swollen was his ego? It seemed quite large. Was it big enough that he would forget everything I'd said to him, every disparaging glance, every sharp, cutting word, and believe that I found him wildly attractive instead of offensive and repulsive?

Maybe it was still possible to soften my attitude around the edges. I could convince him I'd changed. I could become the woman he wanted to work with—fun and sassy. I could become the woman he believed all women were. If I could do that, it would be easier to take care of everything else.

I closed my eyes and tried to remember if he'd told me anything about his living situation. Nothing came to mind. Instead, a slowly emerging image appeared behind my eyelids—James with his own eyes closed, his breath still, his body motionless, and me slipping out of an anonymous hotel room, clothed in something unmemorable.

The light in the room changed. I opened my eyes to see my computer screen had gone to sleep.

I stood and stretched. I went to the window and looked down on the street below, watching cars move past like beetles, pedestrians scurrying like ants. I pressed my forehead against the glass. I had to get those photographs organized, or Diana was going to get even more annoyed with me.

A cup of coffee was what I needed. Preferably a nice drink from a coffee shop, but that would just be more time spent not getting the photographs done. I crossed the hall to the break room. I took the pot off the stand and poured the contents down the drain.

Suddenly, James was standing behind me. "Why did you dump that? I made it less than half an hour ago."

"I wanted fresh."

"It was fresh."

"Fresh is when it just finished brewing. Not turning stale on a burner for thirty minutes."

"It's wasteful."

I began washing the carafe.

"Let me do that for you."

"I can take care of it, but thanks."

"I saw that skanky waitress was here."

"Don't use words like that."

He laughed.

"Is that funny?"

"Are you my mother?"

"It's inappropriate, especially in the workplace."

"Is there a list?"

"A list of what?"

"Of forbidden words?"

I dried the carafe and filled it with fresh water. I added grounds to the receptacle and switched the machine on, then leaned against the counter, turning my shoulder toward him, so I didn't have to look at his face. He was standing too close. His expression was leering and vicious as if he wanted to touch me but also wanted to fight with me. I felt like he wanted me to lose my temper, so he had an excuse for a fight. I wasn't sure if that was so he could get me in trouble with Diana, if he wanted to feel he had power over me, or if it just excited him to see a woman upset.

I was leaning toward the last one. I took a deep breath and reminded myself of my end game.

"Is there a list?" he repeated.

"You should ask Diana. I'm sure she'll have a harassment policy soon if she doesn't yet."

"Am I harassing you?"

I opened the cabinet, looking for the heaviest mug I could find. I ached to bash it into his forehead, but forced myself to be content imagining it filled with coffee and the pleasure of recalling that image later while I sipped the hot liquid and clicked on photographs.

"Am I?" he asked.

"Do you want a cup of coffee?"

"Sure. So what did the waitress want?"

I took out a second mug and placed it on the counter. "She just stopped by to say hi."

"I doubt that. I get the impression she's stalking you."

"Why would she do that?"

"You're her savior."

"I doubt that."

"Then what are you?"

"Just a friend."

"You should keep away from her. If you want my advice."

I literally bit my tongue. I could not say a single word to him, or he would twist the conversation into an un-winnable argument. Unwinnable in that I needed him to think I liked him. I had to concentrate one hundred percent on my plans for him. Arguing was a waste of breath and would only get me into a difficult situation with Diana. But it was tempting. Unbearably tempting. Eve, looking at that juicy red apple, would have had no idea what I was up against.

I poured coffee into both mugs and handed one to him. I picked up the other and stepped around him.

"Where are you going?"

"Back to work. I heard you were in a hurry for the photographs I haven't organized yet."

"I'm never in a hurry."

I smiled and blew on the surface of my coffee.

"How did the waitress get into the building? Did she schedule an appointment with you?"

"What does it matter?"

"Just ..." He waited for several seconds, keeping his eyes locked on mine. I'm sure he hoped I would beg him to finish his thought. "I'm concerned she might be dangerous."

"Are you good at recognizing when a woman is dangerous? Or a man?"

"Of course. Look at my profession. I could recognize a killer, given the opportunity."

"I hadn't thought of that." I gave him an admiring gaze. "I bet you could."

"She shouldn't be loitering around our building. And I'm not sure how she got up to our floor unless she had an appointment. And I can't think how she would have one. Do you have business with her?"

"I need to get to work, James. None of this has anything to do with you."

"It does if she's a threat to our workplace."

"She's not a threat."

"I think I'm a better judge of that."

"She's loitering because you ruined her livelihood over some petty wound to your ego. You're so pathetically insecure you couldn't tolerate a woman not responding to your creepy, predatory behavior," I said, knowing with each word that it was not what I should be saying. I had abandoned ultimate success for immediate satisfaction, and it was going to take a lot of effort to recover.

The first look that passed over his face, not that I knew how to read micro-expressions, but there was nothing micro about it, was fear. He hid it quickly, replaced by anger. "I bet that tongue has gotten you into trouble. A lot of trouble. You'd better watch it, or you might end up like your waitress."

"Don't threaten me."

"It's not a threat. Diana was clear we should treat each other with respect."

"And don't call her *my* waitress. She's not a toy. She's a human being." I took a long swallow of coffee so it wouldn't splash out of the mug. I walked quickly out of the room.

"Typical female." His voice rose. "Has to have the last word. Stomp out of the room when she's upset instead of finishing a conversation. Temper, temper." He laughed.

He was still chortling as I closed my office door, more loudly than I should have.

I put down the coffee. I sat at my desk and stuffed my earbuds into my ears. I put on a Rachmaninoff playlist, and turned up the volume. I worked on the photographs until it was dark outside. But when I locked my computer screen and stood up, they were finished.

The following day, I left work the moment I heard James start his trek down the hall to say goodnight to Diana. I waited on one of the lobby benches, seated so that an artificial tree blocked anyone going from the elevator to the doors couldn't see me. When James passed by, I waited a moment, and then followed him out of the building.

I trailed behind him to the subway and down the stairs, jumping onto his car just as the doors closed. Eight blocks later, I followed him off the subway. He walked around the corner to a small bar and went in.

While he was inside, I lingered on the sidewalk, longing for the days when I enjoyed cigarettes. They were the key to loitering without looking awkward. To calm myself, I spent a few minutes thinking about how much farther I ran without them. But I stood there for over an hour and a half, so my mind returned repeatedly to the cigarettes. I guessed James probably had two drinks at a steady pace. What I couldn't know was whether he'd met anyone inside or if he drank alone. Maybe he harassed any unlucky woman who happened to sit near him, or a female bartender.

When he finally emerged, I followed him to his apartment.

This would become my evening diversion for the next week or so. While I'd been waiting for him to drink, I'd texted Eileen and told her I would be eating dinner late. If she wanted to wait for me, she could, but I didn't mind eating alone. There would be plenty to occupy my thoughts during a solitary meal.

CHAPTER 41

*P*auline was available for breakfast on Saturday morning at six-thirty, so that's when she met Rada for the first time. Instead of suggesting a coffee shop or a brunch buffet, Pauline invited us to a catered breakfast in her conference room.

It was eerie, being the only three people occupying the entire floor of a skyscraper. It felt as if the whole building was devoid of human life. We saw the security guard in the lobby, and one person had obviously taken the elevator up before us, because the numbered lights told us one of the cars was on the eighth floor. Surely, people were working on the weekend, and some were surely there at sunrise, but their lack of visibility to us made it feel like a ghost town—a ghost town in a glass and steel tower in the middle of Manhattan.

Pauline met us in her lobby and escorted us to the conference room.

The feast laid out for us included two ice buckets with opened champagne bottles. Six-thirty in the morning was a little early for champagne, but once I'd eaten a few of the freshest, ripest strawberries I'd ever tasted, I changed my mind.

The long oval table had been moved to the side and covered with a white cloth where the food and beverages were displayed on platters worthy of one of the best restaurants in the city. The glassware sparkled, and the ultra-modern utensils looked brand new.

We were served bacon, avocado toast, quiche, fruit that tasted like it had come straight from the orchard, and freshly ground coffee.

A man filled three flutes with champagne, and Pauline raised hers to Rada. "To getting what you deserve," she said.

We all drank to that.

We sat at a smaller table, also covered in a white cloth, beautifully set, with a vase of white tulips in the center. After a few more sips of champagne, Pauline told Rada about her change of heart.

"I don't know if it's because Alexandra was so persistent, or rather … pushy." She looked at me and winked. "Or, if it's because my head was suddenly in a different place, but your story was an absolute epiphany for me."

Rada sipped nervously at her champagne.

"Your father's plans for your life sounded like something out of the middle ages."

"The middle ages haven't died out," I said.

"It's easy to ignore that reality when you experience a different kind of life. Maybe I needed to be shocked out of my complacency. I've been getting my photograph taken and taking tests and writing essays, trying to poke through my psyche to figure out why I don't feel the same enthusiasm for my career that I'm used to. I've become the clichéd poster child for privilege. I have absolutely everything I desired in terms of career success and money. So many people achieve the kind of success I have and start looking for ways to give back, but that thought never crossed my mind. I don't know why, but there it is. I guess it's my less flattering side that I've hidden from the camera."

"You're not the only successful person who isn't oriented toward giving back," I said. "It's an entirely different mindset from the drive you need to be so successful." I was sure if I were in her position, I'd likely fit that category. I couldn't see myself settling in and saying I had plenty. I wasn't even sure what plenty was. There's something about money that feels like a type of insulation. But I could see how the more you had, the more you might want, thinking that you could wrap this big comfortable bubble around your life and your psyche, keeping yourself safe from anything that might ever have the potential to hurt you. And the more you had, the more insulation you might need.

Or maybe you just wanted more because acquiring more was a kind of game.

It made me think of Eileen. In the grand scale of New Yorkers with serious money, she had a very small amount, but she had some. A lot more than most. I wondered if she was already craving more. If, now that she had an incredibly comfortable nest egg, it looked slightly inadequate. I might ask her that question.

"Your story was like a ..." Pauline hesitated, gazing into her champagne glass. She spoke in a soft voice. "I almost feel like I had a vision of some kind." She laughed, and the sound turned to a giggle as if the champagne bubbles were floating out from her throat into the cool, sweet-smelling air of the conference room.

Rada sipped nervously at her own champagne.

I wanted to roll my eyes, but instead, I also took a sip of champagne, then ate a strawberry, drank some coffee, and managed to keep what I hoped was a neutral expression on my face.

"I feel a little foolish. It makes me feel ill, actually," Pauline said. "Offering you that job. I know it would barely cover your rent, a job that was a step down from what you were doing before. Now, I want to do something life-changing. Go big or go home, right?"

"What?" Rada asked.

"It's a truism. Go big or go home."

Rada nodded. Clearly, she understood the concept, she just didn't know how it was going to apply to her.

"Don't bother if you aren't going to give it every single thing you've got, if you aren't going to make a magnificent splash, or do something really important," Pauline said.

"Uh huh," Rada said.

Pauline stood and walked toward the back of the room. She reached into her purse and pulled out a thick, cream-colored envelope. It looked like a wedding invitation. She returned to the table and handed it to Rada. "Alex said you were working as a server because you were saving money for college. I think we can fast-track that. You're young. You should be in school now, not in ten years."

Rada put down the champagne glass that she'd been pinching between her fingertips. She pulled the flap out of the envelope and removed a cream-colored greeting card with an embossed tulip on the front. She opened it. Her gasp was so loud it sounded like she was choking. "Oh my god. I can't … you can't give this to me. I … this is too much." She shoved the card back into the envelope, licked the flap, sealed it, and handed it to Pauline.

"It's yours. For your education. We'll just need to make an appointment at my bank to set up your account."

Rada shook her head furiously. "No. It's embarrassing. My father would be furious. He would say—"

"Your father has nothing to do with this."

"He would find out. He wouldn't allow it. He would say it was wrong. He would say I—"

"He doesn't need to know," Pauline said.

I wanted to know what she'd written on that card. And now the envelope was sealed. There was no way for me to see. I tried to imagine how much. I assumed, given Rada's shock, it must be enough for her to complete a four-year degree. The question was— at any school in the country? I couldn't fathom how much money must be sitting in a bank, waiting to be moved into an account with Rada's name on it.

I took a sip of champagne and considered my own unfinished education. But I hadn't left it unfinished because there was no money or willingness on my father's part to pay for it. I didn't want to fill in all the tedious pieces required to get that piece of paper that ended up framed, wrapped in tissue paper inside a box, on the top shelf of a closet until you were dead.

Still …

Pauline picked up the envelope and handed it to Rada. "I want you to take it. I'm sure it seems like an enormous amount of money. Probably more than you've ever thought about, and I know it's more than you've held in your hand or earned so far in your life. But in my world, it's not like that. It's easy for me to part with, and I won't even notice it's gone."

"No," Rada said.

"You have to trust me. I want to do this. You won't have another opportunity like this. Ever. Not without strings. You're young, and you don't know how life can take sudden, unexpected turns. You can't shake your head and say, I'm not going that way. You have to jump when the train slows, and you have a chance to change tracks."

Rada looked terrified. "What if you change your mind and want it back? I'll never be able to pay it back, and then my life will be over."

"My attorney is working on an agreement to cover that. I want to be sure you feel comfortable in every way. I want you to know it's yours. There is absolutely no obligation."

"My father—"

"You have to stop listening to your father. If you can't do that, then marry the guy he's chosen for you," I said. "He's already angry you're working and living in an apartment and not marrying that guy. So what difference does it make if he has one more thing to be angry about?"

Rada stared at me. She pushed the champagne glass away from her and picked up the envelope. She pressed it close to her chest and closed her eyes. "I don't know what to say."

"Thank you, is more than enough," Pauline said. "I hope you'll be the first of many."

Rada smiled, her eyes like wet stones.

"I guess there is one string," Pauline said. "I would love you to keep in touch and let me know what you're studying, how it's going. I'm not checking in ... I don't care about grades. You don't have to prove anything. But I just want to hear how you're doing ... if you need anything."

"I'll never need anything again," Rada said.

Pauline and I laughed at the same time, then we all clinked our glasses together, and Pauline said, "To always needing more."

CHAPTER 42

*C*hen I returned from breakfast, I was tipsy with champagne. Eileen was sitting on the couch in her robe, drinking coffee. There was a plate with two pieces of toast and half a peach on the coffee table. She was watching videos on her tablet about applying makeup, the volume so loud I heard the makeup artist shouting at me about the shape of my brow line the minute I opened the door.

Eileen tapped the screen to pause it. "I thought you went for a run." She eyed my high heels and short pink dress. She cocked her head and studied the shape of my brow line as if I had something to offer she hadn't seen in the video.

"Breakfast," I said.

"How fun. With the new guy?"

"No."

"Who?"

"A client."

"That's unusual, isn't it?"

"I suppose." I sat down and kicked off my shoes. I should have considered this. I didn't want to talk about Rada or what Pauline had done for her, or any of it. I needed Eileen to forget anything

246

negative I'd ever said about James. I needed her to forget I didn't like him. I needed her to think I had no opinion about him one way or the other. I needed her to forget I'd said more than three words about him. How was I going to manage that?

And for what must have been the hundredth time already, I wondered—*Why* had I thought having a roommate was a good idea?

I needed more money of my own. A lot more. I had to stop requiring other people to improve my living environment. It was starting to look like I was sliding backward in my life rather than climbing higher. Not that I'd ever planned an upward climb, but I certainly hadn't planned to have people scrutinizing my habits in exchange for a decent couch and windows that closed all the way. Not to mention a state-of-the-art television and chic cookware and utensils.

"Were you taking photographs?"

"Not this time. Just exploring her plans." I needed to start talking fast, pouring out words to distract her, making it sound like I was sharing real and useful information. "It was a fantastic breakfast. In a skyscraper, with the whole floor to ourselves. It was catered. The food was incredible—the fruit tasted like it had just been picked. And champagne."

"No wonder you're so smiley. And chatty."

"Am I?" I smiled.

"A little. What did you talk about?"

"It was Pauline. From the modeling agency. So I probably shouldn't say too much since it's your industry."

"I wouldn't tell."

"She just wants to do more—now that she's reached the top. I think she wants to give back, so that's a little different from most of our clients."

"That's nice."

I picked up my shoes and headed toward my bedroom.

She called after me—"What should we do today?"

"I'm ready for a nap, after all that champagne."

"That's no fun. Shopping?"

"Ugh. I really can't."

"Then we can have a slug day. Eat junk food and hang out here."

"Maybe."

"Why are we roommates if you never want to hang out?"

"I do. I'm just sleepy from the champagne."

"I've never seen you get sleepy. You can drink martinis all night, and you don't get tired."

"Champagne for breakfast is different."

"Do you want to hang out after your nap or not?"

I turned and gave her a cheerful smile. "Sure."

"You take a little nap. I'll go out and get some snacks."

When I woke, it was lunchtime. I took a shower and wandered out to the living room wearing shorts and a tank top. Eileen had arranged bowls of chips and nuts and crackers on the kitchen table. There was beer and wine and containers of dip, tapenade, olives, and marinated mushrooms in the fridge.

"This looks delicious," I said.

We settled on the couch, the TV tuned to a station playing hits from the nineties.

"Tell me what's going on with work," she said.

"Isn't that a little boring? It's the weekend."

"Well, you won't talk about the super secret new guy, so I figured you must have something interesting with all the fascinating new clients you've been so busy with, or gossip about the people you're hiring."

"Not really."

"Are you loving having a female boss?"

"I've worked for women before."

"I mean this female boss. Diana."

"She's okay. She's changed."

"I guess you'd expect that."

"Yeah. She said it's a lot of responsibility, but it's like a complete personality change."

We talked for nearly two hours. Her job, my job. I managed to say a lot about our clients without saying anything at all, and I did my best to talk up James and Fallon. She talked for a long time about how great Ned was, and I gave her some sketchy details about Hunter. Not because I didn't want to tell her, but because all I had were sketchy details. It would have been fun to complain about James. It really would have, but then she would know. And if anyone ever asked any questions about my relationship with him or whether there was any conflict between us or a hundred other things, she might wonder, and they might wonder.

She couldn't know I found him despicable. She couldn't know about Rada. She couldn't know about the college education Pauline was funding. There were so many things she couldn't know, I felt them piling up around me, threatening to come crashing down on top of me, smothering me as I searched my mind for things to say that wouldn't lead to any of those topics.

I didn't like considering every word. I didn't like watching what came out of my mouth. I'd never had to be so careful because I'd never talked much about my life to anyone. My conversations were mostly superficial or theoretical.

I was going to have to give serious thought to how I was going to get myself out of this beautiful apartment I'd just spent a fair amount of time getting myself into. I could not continue removing disturbing men, and women, from the world while living with a person who wanted an intimate relationship involving constant conversation about my daily thoughts and activities.

As I stared at her wounded expression, it came to me. Maybe the answer was sitting right there in her probing questions and her concern that we weren't close, her feeling that I was withholding things from her. Maybe if I fed that feeling, she would become upset with me and leave to spend a few days staying with Ned. Then, I would have the freedom to take care of James without someone clocking every time my key entered the lock, every time I uncorked a bottle of wine, every time I flushed the toilet. I would just have to be careful with the timing. More careful than ever before.

Our chatter only ended when it was time for me to get ready for dinner with Hunter. Eileen was all smiles about that, telling me I had to promise to tell her all the details later. I didn't promise, obviously.

250

CHAPTER 43

*T*he Italian place Alexandra had texted Hunter to meet for dinner was new to him, even though he thought he'd eaten at nearly every restaurant in Little Italy. When he arrived, she was already seated at the table with a martini in front of her.

"I was early," she said.

He told the server he'd have the same and slid into the booth across from her. She looked even better than he remembered. All the pissed-off feelings that had been stuck inside his gut dissolved when she looked at him, holding his gaze for so long he felt as if she had some kind of physical grip on his eyeballs. But even with that, he was not going to give up on getting her to the park for a summer sunset. He refused to live all through July and August in New York City and not hang out at the park.

While they ate bread slathered in butter, he asked questions, and she dodged them. He'd never encountered someone who avoided questions as blatantly as she did. It was almost funny. He wasn't sure if she was being coy or he should view it as a red flag.

"Where did you grow up?" he asked.

"Portland."

"Maine or Oregon?"

"Oregon."

"Did you have a big family?"

"Define big."

He laughed. "I don't know. No one has ever asked me to define a big family before. It's kind of understood, don't you think? I guess … more than four kids."

She took several sips of her drink and said, "Does a big family make you different from kids who grow up in small families?"

"Sometimes."

"Was yours big?"

"You haven't answered me."

"I like talking about what's happening now."

"So … not a great family experience?" he asked.

"There were some good moments."

"But overall, no?"

"Why do people want to talk about the past so much?"

"Because it helps explain who we are."

"How many kids are in your family?"

"My brother and me." He reached for another piece of bread.

"Do you like him?"

"You sort of have to, right?"

"No."

He laughed. "Maybe you fight. And okay, maybe sometimes you hate your sibling, but you still love them underneath it all."

"It's not required."

"Do you hate your siblings?"

"My siblings are awesome. But I'm not required to think that."

"You have a strange way of looking at things," he said.

"So do you."

They ordered salads and pasta and a bottle of red wine. They finished their martinis, and Alex put her hand on his leg. She leaned closer. "Where did you grow up?"

"New Jersey."

"How long have you lived in Manhattan?"

"Since college. I came to NYU and never looked back."

"Do you think you'll stay here forever?"

"No one can know anything forever," he said.

"It seems like a lot of people who live in New York, who love New York, can't imagine ever leaving. My boss already has her grave picked out here."

"That's extreme," he said. "I'm not into picking out my grave." He wondered what kind of person her boss was, whether she was morbid or just a planner. "I do know what you mean though, some people act like they're glued to the pavement here. I like to keep my options open."

"I agree," she said.

"So forget death and forget birth. Tell me about your exes," he said.

She laughed. "Really? What's the point of that?"

"Context."

"I don't think so. Clean slate."

"It's interesting to know. I'm not jealous, just curious."

"I'm not. So next topic."

"You have a lot of subjects that are off limits," he said.

"There are a million things that two human beings can talk about. At any moment of any day, think about all the events taking place all around the planet—natural events, crimes, sports, concerts, plays, movies, accidents, funny experiences, new discoveries, scandals—I think we'll manage to find something to talk about."

"You want to talk about hurricanes? Wildfires? Or the Yankees?"

"Either would be fine, as long as we find a way to make it interesting."

Their meal came, and they ended up talking about a guy who had found a cat on the subway. He managed to find its owner after a lot of persistence. Then they talked about all the unusual animals people adopted as pets. That led to a discussion of all the weird animals they'd ever heard of. Next, they talked about all the clever and funny things they'd seen animals doing on YouTube.

He realized she was absolutely right, and he wondered if she was on to something. Maybe the human race spent far too much time talking about themselves and their own life histories.

Then, as if to prove his new theory utterly absurd, she said, "Tell me the worst thing you've ever done."

"How did you come up with that idea?" he asked.

"I was thinking about that guy you told me about who was trying to care for the alligator in his bathtub. And I started thinking about people who have done things outside the law and never gotten caught."

She was giving him a playful look. It was the strangest question he'd ever been asked, full stop. Not just by a gorgeous girl on a date. It made him feel somewhat lightheaded because he felt as if she knew something about him that no one else knew. Or at least that he thought no one else knew.

He was overcome by a rush of paranoia. He'd thought she came onto him because she was interested. She'd literally chased him into the building and asked him out, and he'd assumed it was all about being hot for him. Now, he looked at those events in a new light. Did she know something about him? Was she trying to get to know him because someone had told her to?

"You first," he said.

"I asked the question."

"It's too broad."

"Is it?"

He took a sip of wine. He stabbed a piece of sausage that was immersed in creamy tomato sauce but didn't lift it to his mouth. He took another sip of wine.

"It must be pretty bad if it's taking this long," she said.

"I just have no idea how to answer."

"Because you've done so many despicable things in your life?"

"No, because I don't know if you're referring to pranks, crimes, general shittiness to other human beings, lying ... Like I said, it's a very broad topic. You can't weigh all those things and call one of them the worst."

"What's the best thing you've ever done?" she asked.

Again, she was making him feel tired. How could she be so much fun and so exhausting at the same time? She couldn't answer a simple question about the size of her family, which she still hadn't answered, but she wanted to ask these other questions that no one ever, anywhere, that he'd ever met, talked about. Was she disturbed? Could there be a very twisted mind behind that absolutely beautiful face?

"Just have fun." She rubbed her hand on his leg. She leaned closer and gently bit his earlobe. That he liked. He relaxed into her and looked at the food left on his plate. "The best thing I've ever done was agree to have dinner with you."

She laughed. She moved away from him and continued laughing, the sound of it growing louder. People at the surrounding tables turned to look.

"That's funny," she said.

"Was that what you were hoping I'd say?"

"No. And I don't believe you."

"Why not?"

"Because it's too convenient and cliché."

"Well, right now, it's all I can think of, so for right now, it's the truth."

"Fair enough," she said.

They finished eating. They finished the bottle of wine. They ordered dessert and then took an Uber to his apartment. And he didn't think either one of them learned a single thing about the other, except that he was from Jersey and she was from Portland, Oregon. Oh, and that he had a brother.

CHAPTER 44

I didn't know why I'd asked Hunter to tell me the worst thing he'd ever done. The question came into my head for the first time in my life. I absolutely did not ever want to answer that question myself, and I was aware of that even as I was speaking the words. I knew he would ask me the same question, so why had I done it?

Was there something about this guy that had driven me to expose myself in a way I'd never done before? In an insanely risky way? Did some part of me want to tell him things I shouldn't? The thought was very disturbing. And I was even more drawn to him after the way he turned the conversation away from that question and then took the opposite end of it and made it into something we could laugh about. From there, the date became sort of normal, if there is any such thing as a normal date for me.

Maybe I asked him that question because I wanted to know what he would think of me if, at some point in time, a long way down the road, he really did get to know me, since he was so determined to *get to know me.* Maybe it was some strange psychological eruption in my subconscious mind.

That night, I stayed at his apartment until two in the morning.

I'd told him I would leave before morning, but I don't think he believed me, so I wrote a note on his bathroom mirror, which I thought he would think was funny in a kitschy way. I took an Uber back to Eileen's apartment that no longer felt like it was half mine. It probably never was.

On Sunday, Eileen went off to brunch with Ned after knocking on my bedroom door to say goodbye. I didn't open the door. I didn't think it was necessary to say goodbye every time we went out. I definitely didn't want to start the habit of knocking on each other's doors every time one of us left the apartment. I took a deep breath and tried to notice whether the oxygen seemed as if it was going to every cell in my lungs. It seemed as if they were slightly pinched. Maybe I was being slowly suffocated, cell by cell.

When I got out of the shower, there were three text messages from Tess.

I'm back!

Landed two days ago.

Can you meet for brunch in an hour?

I texted back that I could meet for brunch and stripped off my jeans.

An hour later, we were sitting in the restaurant of the Conrad Hotel with small plates in front of us. Each of us had a croissant, a ceramic cup of whipped butter, sliced strawberries, kiwi, and blueberries.

Tess's hair was cut short and shaggy, which made her face look thinner. She wore the same dark, heavy eye makeup as always, but her skin was tanned, which made her look healthier. She also looked slightly less American, although that was probably my imagination because I couldn't figure out why I thought that.

Despite the changes in her hair and skin, her eyes had the same mesmerizing gaze, the same dark depths that forced you to pay attention to her, that kept you locked into whatever she was saying. They even kept your attention on her when she paused, waiting for what came next.

I felt as if it had only been a few days since I'd last sat across the table from her, listening to the confident tone of her voice, a tone that was contradicted by her bouts of self-analysis and indecision. Now, she told me with a bold smile that she wanted *everything* in her life to be different. It was ironic because that was the one thing that was always the same about Tess—wanting things to be different.

She said she was tired of working in marketing. Once and for all, she was absolutely sick of the vaporous quality of it, sometimes giving her the feeling that nothing she produced was real.

"I can understand that," I said.

"I don't know if you can. It's been my entire career. Sometimes it feels like it's all I've thought about. Over fifteen years. I don't think it compares to your two or three years, if that." She laughed and sipped her champagne.

"Maybe I'm smarter," I said. "I figured out it was vapor in a fraction of the time."

"But I made a lot more money." She lifted her glass. "To your brains and my financial success."

We laughed, clicked our glasses, and sipped our champagne.

She told me about Marcus, the love of her life. She told me about his company that had something to do with cyber security.

"I thought you were going to be the chief marketing officer for his company. Didn't you tell me that three weeks ago?"

"Things changed."

"Why?"

She glanced around the room. "Where's our server?"

"You should be more subtle if you're trying to avoid the question."

"I'm hungry."

"I'm sure he'll be back. He probably noticed we haven't taken more than two bites of our fruit. You haven't touched your croissant."

"Maybe." She picked up her croissant and took a bite. She glanced around again.

"So what changed so fast?"

"I'm just really so tired of it. I can't explain how completely over it I am."

"What are you going to do? Be a socialite? Raise money for charities and throw fancy parties? I think you'll get tired of that a lot faster."

"Possibly."

"Then what?"

Finally, she met my gaze. "We're going to have a baby." She grinned. "Don't laugh."

"I'm not. Congratulations. But no more champagne for you."

"Not yet." She sipped her champagne eagerly.

"So you're not pregnant?"

"After we're married."

"You're just going to sit around waiting to get pregnant?"

"It takes more than sitting around." She winked.

"Obviously. Then why not be the CMO while you're waiting? It can take a while, I've heard."

She shrugged. "I don't need the stress. Or the boredom."

Our server appeared, and we ordered brunch—omelets for both of us.

"It's hard to see you chasing a small unsocialized human being around a playground," I said.

"I'm up for it."

"I'm sure you are." I had no doubt she was capable, I just couldn't form the picture in my mind.

"Well, that's my news. Buy a house in California ... actually ..." She took another sip of champagne, "We're looking at buying a vineyard. That will keep me busy as well." She smiled and took another bite of croissant.

"What do you know about making wine? Or even growing grapes?"

"I love wine."

I laughed.

"And I'll learn."

Of course, she was more than capable. She was capable of anything she decided to do. She was smart, she was driven. It was just … I couldn't keep up with her fast-moving train.

"So first the house, then—"

"The vineyard," I said.

She smiled. "Yes, the vineyard, a fabulous wedding, an adorable baby."

"Happily ever after." I clicked my glass against hers.

Our food arrived. We pushed our plates of fruit and half-eaten croissants to the side to make room for the perfectly cooked omelets garnished with mango salsa. Tess ordered mimosas for both of us. While we ate, I told her everything, but also nothing, about Hunter. For example, I didn't tell her that he'd taken possession of my thoughts. And I didn't tell her that he might, possibly, have the potential to contribute to my living happily ever after, if there was such a thing.

If he didn't destroy me first.

CHAPTER 45

 ortland, Oregon

* * *

Supposedly the members of Pure Truth Tabernacle weren't bound by the laws written in the old testament section of the bible. That was supposed to be the point of the *new* testament. That's what our minister said almost every time he opened his mouth. That's what my parents said. But they also talked a lot about stories and rules from the old testament and all the lessons we needed to learn from those stories. Some of those rules mattered, some didn't, and no one really explained how you could tell the difference. But even when I was five, I knew throwing rocks at someone was not one of the rules we were supposed to follow.

Mr. Caruthers had his own ideas. He acted as if he'd written the bible himself.

He stoned Lexy to death. No one ever admitted that, but I knew.

He did it alone in the dark. I wonder what he said to her. I wonder if she knew what was going to happen. I wonder if she was scared. I know she didn't even understand the words from the book of Deuteronomy that he'd shouted at us. I hadn't understood them. Not then. Except the part about the stones.

If someone has a stubborn and rebellious son who does not obey his father and mother and will not listen to them when they discipline him, his father and mother shall take hold of him and bring him to the elders at the gate of his town. They shall say to the elders, "This son of ours is stubborn and rebellious. He will not obey us. He is a glutton and a drunkard." Then all the men of his town are to stone him to death. You must purge the evil from among you.

The bible was filled with gruesome, bloody stories. I never understood what we were supposed to learn from those stories and rules.

When I found my sister's tiny, broken, bloody body, I lay beside her. I spent the whole night holding her close. I held onto her as tightly as I could. I hoped she knew I was there.

Throughout the night, I heard them calling our names, but we didn't answer.

Of course, Mr. Caruthers joined the search for the two missing girls. But he couldn't lead them to the spot where he knew Lexy's body was. That would make the others wonder why he found us so easily. They might see him as the monster he was. The devil he was. The devil they were all so afraid of. The devil they thought was whispering in our hearts and tempting us to disobey. The devil who was leading us to do bad things was actually standing at the front of the church every Sunday morning with a shit-eating grin on his face. He was holding out baskets, collecting money. He was entrusted with children, no questions asked.

The devil was sneaking drinks from a fancy bottle of whiskey in his car, but he'd lost the bottle cap, and he needed to make sure he corked the bottle so it didn't spill. If it spilled, there would be a powerful odor, shouting to the world that he was the drunkard. And drunkards deserved stoning, if you believed the book of Deuteronomy.

My eleven-year-old brother, Eric, was the one who found us.

Me, I guess. He only found me, because Lexy was gone. Just her cold body was left behind. By morning, not even the heat from my arms and legs could keep her warm.

When I heard Eric's footsteps on the rocks, I poked my fingers in Lexy's pocket to look for the cap with the cork attached. It wasn't there.

Eric had to peel my arms away from Lexy's shoulders and waist.

He carried me back to our tent. He told my parents and the others what he'd found.

After that, everything happened like it was a movie.

I felt as if I was sitting in a chair, way up in the balcony section of an old-fashioned theater. I was watching the adults do things and say things. They didn't seem to notice I was there as if they also thought I was in the audience, and they were on the screen, so they couldn't even see me.

The camping trip ended that day. Everyone packed up their tents and the crafts and the food. By the time it started to get warm, most of the people had left.

My father and the minister and Mr. Caruthers had lots of serious conversations, but I couldn't hear very much of what they said. They talked about the *police* and *keeping a lid on things* and *dealing with the situation*. They whispered a lot, and then their voices got louder. When they looked at me and noticed I was listening, they would start to whisper again.

My father was crying, but it was just tears on his face, not the kind of crying that made sounds. My mother cried and wailed like she was in the worst pain she'd ever experienced in her life. It sounded as if someone had stuck thorns in her body. She hugged me and cried, she hugged my brothers and cried, she went inside our tent and fell on the sleeping bags and curled herself into a ball and cried. She refused to eat, and she couldn't talk in a way that anyone could understand.

The mom from another family packed our things. She drove my mother and my brothers and me home in our car.

No one ever said what happened after we left.

A few days later, when my mother wasn't crying so hard, I told her Mr. Caruthers said Lexy was bad. I told her that he said she lied. I told her he was the one who lied! He lied about giving us treats. I told her that he yelled at us, and he made her search his car. I told her what he said about stoning children who were bad.

She cried even harder. She told me not to upset myself with such terrible thoughts. She said Lexy hit her head on a rock. It wasn't what I said. It made her heart hurt when I said awful things like that. It wasn't good to dwell on remembering how my sister died. She said not to think about the details of how it happened. She said Lexy fell a long way, and a lot of rocks hit her body when she was falling down to the side of the riverbank, but I had to stop thinking about that part of it. I should think about Lexy floating around in heaven. I should remember that she would be happy and safe for all of eternity.

Lexy's funeral was ten days after our camping trip. I counted them because every day for a hundred days, I counted the days I woke up in the morning and knew that Lexy's bed underneath mine was empty.

The church was filled with so many people it seemed like they must be people we didn't know because I didn't remember ever talking to that many grownups in my whole life. The Mallory family sat in the front row, but we weren't really the Mallory family because one of us was in an ugly white box on the steps leading up to the pulpit. There were roses on it, and it was shiny white with gold handles to try to make it look pretty, but it was ugly.

If we were the Mallory family, the other person in our family would have been sitting in the chair beside me. So we weren't a family even though my father kept saying our family had to keep each other strong.

I didn't cry at Lexy's funeral. My mother kept squeezing my hand and telling me it was okay to cry, but no tears came out of my eyes. She whispered that she was worried about me. Even before the funeral, I heard her talking to my father about me. After she talked to him, she told me it wasn't good to hold things inside. I said I wasn't holding things inside. I asked questions about the stoning and told her what Mr. Caruthers said.

She said those things wouldn't bring Lexy back. I said crying wouldn't bring her back either.

She asked if I missed Lexy, and I said I didn't want to talk about that. I wanted to talk about the stones, and why didn't *she* want to talk about *that*? I said god was a bad man if he said it was okay to throw stones at a person, especially someone so little. My mother said it was a very complicated thing to understand parts of the bible and the wisdom of god, and I should wait until I was older and the spirit would reveal it to me.

After a while, I think she was tired of talking to me, and she just squeezed my hand and cried even more.

Maybe she thought she had to cry for me, too.

They sang a lot of songs. When I didn't sing, my mother poked me a few times and whispered for me to sing, but then she gave up. They prayed a lot. They read bible verses about living forever and little children being precious. They didn't read any verses about stoning or drunkards.

Then, my father got up to say a few words. That's what the minister said. *Brother Mallory would like to say a few words on behalf of the family at this difficult time.*

It seemed like my brothers and I all took a deep breath at the same time and then held onto it.

My brothers and I had already whispered to each other just like the adults kept whispering. We whispered that there was a big hole in our family without Lexy. We talked about how much fun she was and how smart she was. We told stories about her, and we imagined how she would be if she got to live until she was older. We imagined her riding a horse, which she always wanted to do.

I don't think my brothers liked that my father was going to talk for all of us any more than I did. But they would never let a little girl like me stand up and talk about her dead sister. Not ever. And especially not if I told them about the cap named Miss Dinky Dinko and not at all if I talked about stoning. They wouldn't let my brothers talk either.

My father talked about Lexy, but he didn't call her that. He called her Alexandra. He didn't mention how smart she was. He talked about how beautiful she was and how pure her heart was. He didn't say anything about how funny she was. She always made me and our brothers laugh. He said she was obedient and liked Sunday School.

He probably said a lot of things I forgot. He might have said things I didn't understand because I was five. But at the end, he said something I always remembered. I didn't like it at all. I also didn't completely understand it, but I knew I didn't like it. And I remembered it. When I got older, I understood it perfectly.

My father took a deep breath and said in a quiet voice that boomed through the microphone that it was an honor to have daughters. It was his mission to raise godly women. There weren't enough godly females for the godly men in the world. Because Lexy had been taken to heaven, he was sad that his mission was smaller.

"I will still honor that mission with my older daughter." He looked at me, but it was clear that the tears in his eyes made him blind, so he couldn't see me at all. It seemed like he was more sad about his mission getting spoiled than he was about missing Lexy.

After her funeral, I asked my mother about the rocks over and over. Each time, she got more upset. She told me to stop making her cry. She told me to stop thinking terrible thoughts. She told me I would never feel better if I kept thinking about it. She said I had to let Lexy go to heaven, and if I kept talking about how she died and imagining gory details, and if I wouldn't let go of my desire to have her with me, she wouldn't be able to go. I didn't see how that could possibly be true, because she was already gone. She'd been gone when I saw her in the dark. She was gone when I held her all night, trying to keep her warm. But my mother said she wasn't really gone, and I had to stop trying to capture her and hang onto her. She said I was selfish, wanting to make my own self feel better, thinking only of how upset I was and not how much I needed to let Lexy live free in heaven with the angels, not keep tying her down to the earth.

After a while, I realized my mother was never going to answer my questions. She was never going to talk to Mr. Caruthers or tell anyone what I said, not even my father.

CHAPTER 46

$\mathcal{N}$ew York

* * *

After brunch with Tess, sitting on the subway, I saw a text from Diana telling me she had a few things to discuss with me. She wanted me in her office at eight o'clock Monday morning. Because she'd been out with clients all day Friday, I was pretty sure this meeting was the result of James' nightly tattletale the Thursday before. I could imagine him feeding my words to Diana, one by one, as if he were handing biscuits to a dog—*pathetically insecure* and *creepy, predatory behavior*. It was probably the *pathetically insecure* that hit him the hardest, since he had zero concern about being a predator.

I arrived at my office at seven-fifteen on Monday, looked over the list of clients who required photographs that week, reviewed their bios, and then went out to get coffee.

I bought two lattes and two slices of banana bread. I was standing outside Diana's office door at ten minutes to eight.

She gave me a grim smile that I took to mean she did not appreciate my attempt to bribe her with a breakfast treat. I wasn't really. I wanted a latte. And, I was hungry because all I'd eaten before I left my apartment was a small container of blueberry yogurt.

"Please give me a few minutes to get settled," she said.

"Sure." I carried the coffees and bread to my office and placed them on my desk. I looked at my phone, started a game, then heard the main door open and the voices of James and Fallon. Now I would have to parade my coffees past James and his sensitive ego. It was not the best set-up for a meeting in which I would be chastised for piercing that ego.

I picked up the cardboard container of coffees and the bread, which was no longer nicely warmed and started back toward Diana's office. As if he'd smelled the unfamiliar brew through the walls, James popped out of the break room.

"Why are you so impatient? I'm making coffee right now."

"I was in early."

"That looks like you just bought it."

"Actually, no." I continued moving toward Diana's office.

"I always make a cup for Diana first thing."

"Not today."

"Private meeting?"

I remembered my vow to make him think I was a transformed woman, someone who had forgotten and forgiven all. Otherwise, I would never be able to lure him where I needed to take him. I gave him a winning smile. "Just catching up on my responsibilities. I didn't think you'd have time to make coffee before we started. I'm sure we'll both have one of your delicious cups later this morning."

He looked like I'd slapped him. I had a lot of work to do in a very short time. I went into Diana's office and nudged the door closed with my hip.

I'd barely seated myself and crossed my legs before she started talking.

"There are two critical things we need to discuss." She moved the latte and slice of banana bread to the side. She didn't thank me, which I suppose would have made her feel she owed me something, and she was not in the frame of mind to consider any sort of give and take.

"First, I asked you weeks ago, when we originally talked about staffing, to get me some candidates for another photographer."

I sipped my coffee.

"Have you done anything on that?"

She knew I hadn't. "Not yet."

"Why not?"

"I've been busy, but I'll get to it this—"

"You have not been that busy. The workload is normal."

"Which is why we're not in a rush for a backup photographer."

"Don't fight me on this. I don't have time, and I don't have the patience. We need another photographer. I want five resumés by the end of the week."

"Sure."

"Repeat it."

"What?"

"I want to be clear. Tell me you'll have five resumés delivered to my inbox by Friday."

"Are you serious?"

"Yes."

I laughed. "You'll have five resumés delivered to your inbox by Friday."

"Thank you." She didn't even smile. I wasn't sure if she was trying to get control of me or she was just being petty to try to show me she already had control over me. It was strange to see how things between us had changed so completely. I couldn't figure it out, but every time I asked, she talked about the weight of her responsibility, and that made me wonder if she didn't even realize how ridiculous she was being. Or maybe, she'd never felt all that friendly toward me. Maybe gossiping and going hiking with me had been a game, even part of her strategy, because she'd always hoped Trystan might move on and she would end up with an opportunity to take over. Maybe she liked to manipulate people as much as I did, but she just wasn't as smooth about it. At least, I hoped I was more adept than she was.

"The other thing is more serious," she said.

I took a bite of banana bread. I chewed it quickly and took another bite right away, guessing that I might not get any more for several minutes.

She scowled. "James was upset because you said some pretty degrading things to him last week. Bordering on harassment."

It was not the right reaction, but it happened too fast. I laughed so hard, bits of banana bread flew out of my mouth. "Excuse me." I grabbed the napkin, still laughing, trying to stop, but failing, and wiped my lips. Luckily I had a spare, and I used that to clean up the edge of her desk. "I'll get some cleanser and do this—" I started to push my chair back.

"Leave it," she said. "I really want you on my team. You're a terrific photographer. Clients respond well to you, and you have a lot of energy. But you are not a team player. Your antagonism toward colleagues and your pettiness has to stop, or it's just not worth it. No matter how good you are. Do you not get that?"

"I don't think I'm petty."

"Name-calling is always petty."

"It wasn't name-calling. He ..." I was going down the wrong track. Again. She didn't need to understand what he'd done. The less she knew the better. I had to stop defending and explaining my point of view. Especially with James. "It won't happen again."

"I need you to apologize. Sincerely. And with a promise to change your attitude toward him."

"I can do that."

"Can you?"

"Absolutely. It would be my pleasure."

"Don't mock me."

"I'm not."

"Do you want to work here?"

"Yes."

"Can we stop having these conversations? Can you figure out a way to cooperate as part of a team or not?"

"I can."

"He's extremely talented and experienced. He might have some flaws, we all do. He might occasionally be clumsy in his personal interactions, but he has incredible insight into people. And he's top in the field of micro-expressions."

"Have you known him a long time?"

"Since college."

"I didn't realize that."

"I'm sure I told you."

She had definitely not told me. She'd made it sound as if she'd met him a few times at conferences. "I guess I forgot."

She gave me a puzzled look but said nothing.

"Are you close?"

"That's a ..." She glanced toward the window. "He helped me through ..." She sighed. "He was really there for me when my mom died."

I couldn't imagine him being the sort of person who would be at all helpful in a situation like that, but what did I know? I wasn't the sort of person who relied on others in situations like that. I gave her a sympathetic smile.

Her face twisted into a strange expression, something I couldn't read at all. She picked up the coffee cup and took a sip. Her hand trembled slightly, and she put it down quickly. "So ... anyway. I'm not saying any of this because it's personal. That was a long time ago, and I didn't hire him because we have ... had a rel ... he's top in the field. That's all."

Now, I had a creeping feeling I knew what that odd, possibly embarrassed twist to her lips was. I was pretty sure that *there* for her involved having sex. Maybe it was only once, probably it was only once, but something happened that wasn't just him patting her shoulder while she cried for her mother.

Diana went on to ask me, made me vow, actually, not to focus on that. I vowed to keep it to myself because she *regretted sharing too much*. I vowed to *go out of my way* to work on my relationship with James and to show him *the respect he deserved*.

My final vow was sincere. I would show him the respect he deserved. What she didn't know, of course, was that the respect he deserved was absolutely none.

First, I had to start laying the groundwork with Eileen so that I could have some breathing room. I planned to take my first step that evening by picking a fight that would cause things between us to deteriorate to the point that she would demand some space to herself. I needed her to leave for at least two or three nights. Unless she and Ned were safely out of the way, I couldn't set it all up, get all the things I needed and stash them in my room, kill James, and take some time to unwind. Ideally, I would be rid of her for a week, but that was extremely unlikely. Three days would be good.

So the fight needed to be significant. But it also needed to be something we could recover from. Despite my claustrophobia, I wasn't ready to start over with a new apartment already.

Fighting about Ned was off-limits because that could escalate into something too difficult to control. Also too risky was anything to do with the two of us spending endless hours together, or sharing stories about our lives. The topic I'd decided on was food. We hadn't argued about it, and there was nothing about the subject that might spiral out of control and cause permanent damage. I hoped.

Instead of following James to his after-work hangout and then to his apartment, as I'd been doing most evenings after work, I went directly home.

I found Eileen in the kitchen. She was cooking a pork stir fry. She'd made an impressive-looking Chinese chicken salad that was sitting in a glass bowl in the center of the table.

"Oh, I timed it perfectly," she said. "The stir fry will be done in two minutes."

"I'm not eating."

"But I made dinner."

I shrugged. "I'm just here to change into workout clothes."

"You said you'd be here for dinner."

"I changed my mind."

"Why didn't you text me?"

I shrugged again. "I need to—"

"God, Alex." She shut off the gas, turned, and crossed her arms. She looked like my mother, wearing an apron with a bib top, her arms across her ribs. "That's so rude. I made all this food, and now it will go to waste."

"You can save it."

"It's not as good left over."

"I'm sure it will be fine." I lifted my foot and pulled off one high heel, then the other. "I need to get—"

"I was really looking forward to having dinner with you."

"I told you a hundred times, I need space. I can't always—"

"I know that, but that's not at all the same as changing your mind without telling me. It's just so rude. And honestly, really hurtful."

"Okay. I get it. But it can't be helped."

"Yes, it can!" Her voice rose. "You can stop treating me like your housekeeper or chef or whatever you think I am. You can—"

"I don't think you're any of those things. Don't get so wound up. I really need to go for a run. So let's talk about this another time."

"That's so cowardly to just walk out."

I picked up my shoes and walked out.

She wouldn't run to Ned's on that minor provocation, but it was a start, and I was certain I could carefully turn up the heat from there.

CHAPTER 47

*T*he Italian dinner and the night Hunter had spent with Alexandra had dissolved his irritation from fighting over eating outdoors on a blanket. If that were her thing, he would find a way to deal with it. Maybe he could even live without picnics. Maybe ... she was right about eating on the ground.

He couldn't remember a dinner with a girl where he'd had such a good time just talking. Of course, it wasn't just talking. There had been the energy surrounding them. Throughout the entire meal, his body had been on fire, looking at her, thinking about what might, what *would* happen next.

He hadn't wasted any time, texting her immediately Monday night to suggest a movie and pizza on Tuesday. She agreed, and he'd left work at three to make sure the apartment was cleaned up and looking good for her arrival, even though it wouldn't be until seven that evening.

This would be the first time she was in his apartment during daylight, and he expected a lot of curiosity. In his experience, most girls were bleeding curiosity, and although Alex was very different from anyone he'd fallen for in the past, she was still female, and he figured the curiosity thing would be the same. And really, it wasn't exclusive to women. Everyone was curious about the place where a new friend lived. It's as if everyone was an amateur anthropologist, wanting to do a quick study, eager to draw a few conclusions about people they were inviting into their lives. He'd done it himself. Even guys who didn't give a shit about decorating or looking at someone else's photographs would check out an apartment to find out what another person collected or what they kept in the fridge.

The buzzer rang a few minutes before seven, and he let her up. He opened the door, and she stepped inside. Her hair was twisted up on top of her head, strands falling around her face, which looked really good and made him want to kiss her, but he decided to wait to see what she would do. That was something he liked about her. She made him want to play around. Not like they were playing games to manipulate each other, but just having fun.

She was wearing a black dress with no back and black tennis shoes with no laces. She dropped the large leather bag she always carried on the armchair near the door. She walked to the kitchen and opened the fridge. "Do you have any beer? I'm dying of thirst."

He followed her into the kitchen, ready to open two beers, but she was already holding two. She twisted off the caps and handed one to him. "Cheers." She raised her bottle and took a swallow. "I should probably have water, but I had a sudden craving." She grinned, took another swallow, then licked foam off her lip.

He felt himself slipping under her spell.

She returned to the living room and walked around. She studied the contents of his bookcases, gazed at the framed photographs of his trips to Europe, then went out onto the fire escape. When she didn't come back inside, he followed her out there. She was leaning on the rail. "I wish I had one of these."

"It's nice to get outside."

"My old apartment had couches and potted plants on the roof. But this is cool because it's all yours. My new place is bigger and has better AC and heating and no roaches, but I miss that roof garden."

"More info than I've gotten from you in two entire dates."

She laughed. She took a sip of beer and looked down at the street.

"Where's your new place?" he asked.

"We probably won't go there, so it's not important."

"Why not?"

"I have a roommate who will want to have dinner as a foursome all the time."

"What's wrong with that?"

She laughed.

"You don't like dinner as a foursome? Or you don't like the guy your roommate is with? Or ...?"

"Sometimes." She turned to face him. "What movie are we watching?"

He stared at her, and considered the non-answer to his questions. He spoke slowly, not sure he wanted to let it go. "I thought you could choose."

"From every film ever, or is there a curated list?"

He grinned. "Not every film ever, just what's available from my subscriptions. I do have a DVD player, believe it or not. And a collection of DVDs."

"Why?"

"My parents bought me a bunch of DVDs when I was growing up. They gave me their player when I was in high school, and it still works, so why not?"

A look crossed over her face that he couldn't read. She seemed shocked, maybe. Or was it incomprehension? Did she not understand why someone would keep such an ancient piece of technology? Or was it something to do with his parents? She hadn't talked about her family. In fact, she'd somewhat clumsily forced the conversation away from even revealing how many siblings she had.

Was there something terribly wrong in her family that kept her from wanting to discuss it at all? Did that explain her somewhat unusual behavior, making her unique among the women he'd known? He wasn't sure, and he also wasn't sure how hard to push,

CATHRYN GRANT

trying to find out why she had worked so hard to avoid telling him even the simplest detail.

"You never had one?" he asked.

"What?"

"You looked shocked that I would have a DVD player. Or that my parents gave me theirs, or something."

"Did I?"

"Yes."

"I don't think I would be shocked about something like that."

"You definitely looked shocked."

"I think you misread me. I'm *definitely not* shocked. I think it's cute." She lifted the beer to her beautiful mouth and took a long, seductive swallow. She slowly moved the bottle away and smiled. "Should we choose our movie?"

"It seems like you want to avoid answering me sometimes."

She started to go back inside the apartment. "I'm not. But let's not get bogged down with DVD players."

"Did you have a bad experience growing up?"

"You're really into digging around in the past, aren't you?"

"It's kind of important."

"It's kind of not."

"At some point, it is."

"At some point?"

He'd walked right into it. This was too soon. It wasn't time to be talking about a relationship or understanding each other, or wounds or anything like that. He wasn't sure why he'd let things take that turn. Probably because she was so obvious about it. If she thought she was being coy or clever, she was so wrong. But he didn't think she was. She was blunt. She wasn't going to talk about it, and she didn't really care what he thought about her refusal or her motive.

"Did you already order the pizza?" she asked.

"No." They went inside, and Hunter turned on the TV. He handed the remote to her so she could scroll through the offerings.

He didn't mention the DVD player or point out the collection, although he realized she'd looked at the collection when she'd surveyed the living room earlier.

Leaving her to the movie offerings, he went into the kitchen and opened a bottle of Malbec. He got out two wine glasses and plates for the pizza. They wouldn't be eating out of the box like he did when his friends came over to watch a baseball game.

Staring at the wine bottle, he felt antsy. He considered whether he should take a sip before filling both glasses. He didn't want to leave things hanging. She didn't seem to think anything was left open-ended, but he felt like there was an unfinished conversation. Several, in fact. He didn't like it. He liked tossing words around with her, shooting smart, snappy comments back and forth, but he also liked to be serious. He didn't want it to always be this way.

And there it was again. *At some point. Always.* As if he were planning the future. A very long future.

Maybe that was why she was behaving this way, not wanting to let him get closer. Maybe he was moving too fast, and she sensed it.

He poured a bit of wine into each glass and carried them to the living room.

"Picked one yet?" he asked.

"No, but I think I'm getting close." She didn't turn to look at him.

He sat beside her and handed a glass to her. She put down the remote and looked at him. She smiled, and he tapped his glass against hers. "You know, if there's something in your past that you don't want to talk about, I didn't mean to push. I can be patient."

She smiled in a way that he absolutely could not read, and he didn't have a single guess about how to interpret it. They both sipped their wine. She put down her glass and picked up the remote.

CHAPTER 48

J could not stay away from Hunter. If he'd asked me over to his apartment every night of the week, I might have said yes.

Although maybe I would have said no just to keep control of the situation.

Maybe, in that situation, I absolutely *should* say no. The problem was, he also gave me shivers in a bad way. It seemed as if he could see inside me. It was becoming clear that he wasn't going to let me simply be whoever I felt like being any day of the week, any hour of the day. He was going to keep asking questions and looking puzzled when he didn't think the answers made sense.

It was not going to be very easy to lie to him. Or distract him whenever I felt like it.

I wondered if I should think of some things we could do together that did not involve talking. But all the things would have sex at the end, and that always ended up including some talking, so I was trapped.

The next morning when I went into the kitchen to grab a piece of toast before heading to work, Eileen was sitting at the table with a cup of tea in front of her. It was only six-thirty. I never saw her that early in the day. Her eyes were dark, with shadows above and below, and her lips had almost no color. Her hair was tucked behind her ears, and she was wearing a long T-shirt with a hoodie over it. Her feet were bare, and her toes were freshly painted dark red.

The words rushed out of her before I could even ask why she was awake. "I'm really sorry about the other night. I wanted to make sure I got to talk to you before you went to work. So I've been up since four." She laughed. "I must look awful." She picked up her mug and took a sip of tea.

This was not what I'd expected from her and was not the next part of how I wanted things to play out in my effort to force her to leave me alone for a few days. I dropped two slices of whole-grain bread into the toaster slots and pressed the button. I got out a plate, knife, and the butter.

"Do you want some tea?" she asked.

"I don't have time."

"It's early."

"I'm taking my toast on the subway."

"That's messy."

"I have a lot to do."

"What about coffee?"

"James makes coffee."

She nodded. "The guy you don't like?"

"Actually, we're getting along really well now."

"Oh. That's good." She took a sip of tea. "Well, I'm really sorry. I've been thinking a lot about how you want these really clear boundaries. And how you try so hard not to get close to people. And I've—"

"Are you psychoanalyzing me?"

"Just a little." She grinned.

"Please don't."

"Don't be mad. I just … I've been thinking. And I'm sorry if I'm smothering you or trying to control you."

"Thanks." I wasn't sure where she was headed with this, but it was clear she wasn't done. And it was also clear that I was not going to be able to set up the disagreement I'd been hoping to manufacture. Now I'd be forced to find another way to get her out of the apartment.

"You seem so strong. So confident," she said. "I keep forgetting about your ex ... that he was abusive, or you implied that he was. And even though it's impossible to picture you in that situation. I mean, it *is* impossible. But I can't imagine how that must have affected you. So I'm sorry if I'm making you feel like you're in another controlling relationship. Even if it's not romantic." She laughed. "Obviously it's different, but I think things can feel the same with controlling people, whether it's romantic or not. So I'm going to try harder not to have expectations about dinner together and schedules and things like that. Okay?"

The toast popped up. I pulled it out and started spreading butter across the surface. It had seemed so easy to imply a guy was stalking me. It seemed like such a throwaway lie. The kind of thing that millions of women deal with. I shouldn't have used that. I shouldn't have let her think it was an ex-boyfriend. Now she was going to walk around me like she had to take care of me and worry about all kinds of supposed trauma.

She thought she had me figured out, and she was going to operate from that mindset.

I would have to find a way to correct that problem another time. The more important thing was to come up with a new way to get her out of the apartment while I took care of James. Now that Diana had given me an ultimatum, I had a very short time to be rid of him. I was juggling a lot of things, and while I was halfway enjoying the adrenaline rush of it all, I was also concerned that I was going to make a mistake.

It looked like I was already making tiny miscalculations, and the more time I spent correcting mistakes, the less time I had to focus on what was important. Maybe the best thing to do with Hunter was to take a little break from him. His curiosity might be the thing that pushed me until I got myself into trouble that I couldn't find my way out of.

I slid my buttered toast into a plastic container and sealed the lid. I put the knife and plate in the dishwasher.

"Does that sound good?" Eileen asked.

"Other people don't control me," I said.

"That's what I mean." She sipped her tea. "I don't want to put you in that position ever again."

"I haven't been in that position. The stalking was something else."

"Oh. You never—"

"I need to get going."

She nodded. "We can talk about it later." She gave me a nervous smile. "If you want. We don't have to. And we don't have to eat dinner together all the time. I just thought it would be fun. And I know how you love to eat." She laughed, again with a nervous, anxious edge to it. "And we both need to eat. I'm sorry if Ned's here a lot. If you want to plan certain nights when he's not here, we could do that."

I moved toward the doorway. "I don't like to plan everything. We'll just see what happens, okay?"

"Okay."

"See you later." I felt like I was running for my life when I left our apartment. All the way down in the elevator, during the entire subway ride, while I gobbled down my toast, during the walk from the subway to work, and up the elevator to my office, I thought about how I could remove Eileen from the apartment long enough to focus all my attention on James.

I finally decided there was no failsafe way to do that. As much as I hated doing it, I was going to have to consider suggesting Eileen invite Ned to dinner on the same night I planned to set up James. Before I left to meet James, I might be forced to drop roofies into Ned and Eileen's wine glasses.

It would be the riskiest thing I'd ever done. And the chances of one of them being aware the following morning that they'd been drugged was huge. I didn't like my plan, and I hoped something better would come into my mind before it was too late.

CHAPTER 49

 ortland, Oregon

* * *

With Lexy's empty bed beneath mine, I continued to whisper to her at night as I always had, pretending she could still hear me.

My mother didn't like it. She said the empty bed broke her heart. It reminded her that Lexy was gone, that she was never coming back. I thought that was the stupidest thing I'd ever heard in my life. Not that my life was very long, but what she said made no sense.

Everything reminded me that Lexy was gone. How was the bunk bed different? When I opened my eyes, I remembered Lexy was gone. When I ate cereal, I remembered she was gone. When I washed my face and went to school and sat in church and brushed my teeth and played in the backyard, I remembered she was gone. There wasn't a single thing that did not remind me she was never coming back. The birds, the sky, our house, our car, her toys, her chair, the front door, the living room couch, other kids, TV shows, books, music, trees, and every person I saw reminded me Lexy wasn't there anymore.

I liked having her empty bed beneath me. It made me remember how she would wake in the night and say my name. It made me think about how we liked sleeping with me on top of her, as if I were protecting her and that someday, she wanted to try the top bunk. I liked remembering how it was when we first got our bunk beds and how excited we were.

I counted the one hundred days that Lexy's bunk bed was empty beneath mine because that was the highest I'd learned to count so far. My brother Jake had told me that after one hundred, it was easy because the numbers started over again. I would have done that, but on Saturday morning, the day after I reached one hundred, my father came into our room before I got up. He said they were taking apart the bunk beds because they were upsetting for my mother.

I said it wasn't fair. It was my room, and the beds were supposed to go together. He said it was their house, and they were the ones who decided what furniture would go in each room. When my mother came into the room, her eyes were red from crying. I said I liked to think about Lexy underneath me. She let out a little scream and ran out of the room.

My father got busy with his tools. He told me to stop arguing, or I would not have the opportunity to talk at all because I would find myself eating dinner by myself, all alone at the kitchen table, while the rest of the family ate together in the dining room.

I went out to the backyard and sat on the swing because I didn't want to watch him break our beds apart. After a while, I heard his voice through the open window, shouting for Eric and Jake to come help him lift my bed off Lexy's bed.

In the months after that, it seemed as if I had turned into a ghost in my house.

We weren't supposed to talk about ghosts because they weren't real. And if they were real, they were from the devil. I wasn't sure which it was, if they were make-believe or real evil spirits, but I knew about ghosts from kids at school who dressed up for

Halloween and from the ghost stories our teacher read during October.

I felt like my body was cloudy and misty, almost invisible. My mother was sad. She didn't talk much, and she cried all the time. She sat in her favorite armchair with her legs curled up and stared out the window. My father was sad too, but in a different way. He was sad, but he didn't think sad feelings should be *indulged* because that meant we weren't trusting god's plan.

My mother cried when he said that Lexy dying was god's plan. I heard her on the phone talking to her friends. She didn't believe god was so cruel he would take a sweet little girl like Lexy. She said it wasn't fair, and it seemed to her that there was no plan.

At dinner, she tried to talk about Lexy, but my father said it was better to talk about Lexy's purpose in the world, and why god wanted her to have the short life she did. My mother nodded and changed the subject to other things that had nothing to do with Lexy. My father didn't seem to notice she was doing that. He went along, and before I knew it, no one was saying a word about her.

I could tell my mother wanted to talk about her more, to remember things about her, but she stopped mentioning her at all when my father was around. When we went on family outings, she stopped telling stories about the cute things Lexy used to say and do. For a long time after that, the things my mother did say only sounded like a very quiet echo of everything my father said.

When I was older, that changed. But only a little.

But by then, no one talked about Lexy at all.

It was okay with me that my father didn't want to talk about Lexy, because everything he said was wrong. Even the stories my mother was trying to tell weren't really the truth. They sounded like stories about an imaginary girl. The girl they described was nothing but a shadow of Lexy. They weren't the real Lexy. They weren't the girl that looked at me and smiled or giggled, or climbed into my bed and asked me to tell her a story. They weren't about the girl who collected stones and feathers and acorns and liked to look at books with pictures of animals. They weren't about the girl that made me laugh. They weren't about the girl who whispered secrets in my ear and drew pictures of trees for my brothers. They weren't about the girl who didn't give in to the most awful man in the world. The things my parents said had nothing to do with the actual person who lived in the same bedroom with me for longer than I could even remember. Until she disappeared, and I never heard her voice again.

CHAPTER 50

*N*ew York

* * *

It was going to be my greatest performance in a long time, maybe ever—convincing James that I wanted to spend an evening with him when all I'd done was point out his failures and deficiencies in agonizing detail.

I used a flat iron to make my hair sleek and sharp. I put on more than my usual makeup, a short black skirt, ballerina flats, and a tight black T-shirt. I stuffed a black sweater into my bag just in case the air-conditioned bar veered too close to an arctic winter, as they often did.

It was the perfect day for approaching James because I had three photo sessions, and I wouldn't be going to the office at all. At the final session of the day, I was taking photographs of Pauline while she gave an inspirational talk to the models represented by her agency. Although it was late in the process to still be taking photos, because she'd already had two brainstorming sessions with Diana to analyze the results of her tests and photographs, it was something we'd planned, and Diana wanted it done for thoroughness.

When I finished, I took my camera equipment back to the apartment, touched up my hair and makeup, and headed out to the bar James loved so dearly he spent every weekday evening drinking there. I was confident that if he had drinking buddies, male or female, they weren't particularly close because every time I'd seen him, he entered alone and left alone.

Inside, I sat at the bar, ordered a martini, ate an olive, and waited.

Promptly at six-twenty, James walked through the doorway, which I could observe easily, thanks to the mirror behind the bar. I saw him glance at my back, not recognizing me because I was careful to keep my head slightly forward, my hair covering the sides of my face. I watched as he checked out another woman at the bar, gazed around the room at the tables, mostly occupied by groups of after-work colleagues, then took a seat about eight stools down from me at the bar. There were two men between us.

I sipped my drink and considered my next move.

It was only a few minutes before James had a drink in front of him—a shot of whiskey that he didn't immediately taste. He sat staring into the glass, which surprised me. I would have expected him to be looking for ways to start a conversation with someone seated nearby. He might be a regular, but it didn't appear that he had regular acquaintances. Maybe they hadn't arrived yet.

I slid off my stool, picked up my drink, and walked over to him.

"James! You're the last person I expected to see here."

He turned and looked at me, almost as if he couldn't place me for a moment. A smile spread across his face. "Are you following me?"

I laughed. "Would you like that?"

As he stared, a twitch developed at the corner of his lips. Was it really going to be this easy?

"Are you seriously flirting with me?" he asked. "After being a bitch since the day I met you?"

"I owe you an apology for that."

"Diana forced you into it, did she?" He picked up his glass and swallowed some of the dark liquid. He nodded toward my drink. "You like the strong stuff. I should have guessed."

"Why is that?"

"Because you're very aggressive."

I took a sip of my drink. "Mind if I join you?"

"There are plenty of seats."

I settled beside him and put my glass on the bar. I ate an olive.

"Why so friendly all of a sudden?" he asked.

"I told you, I owe you an apology."

"I haven't heard it."

"I'm very sorry for not making more of an effort to get along, to show you the respect you deserve."

"Why don't I believe you?"

"Are my micro-expressions suggesting I'm lying?"

"Actually, no." He finished his drink and signaled the bartender for a refill. "Do you want another?"

"I've barely started."

"So why did you happen to show up here of all places? *Are* you following me?"

"Maybe." I laughed. "I like to try different bars around the city. Just like I make it a habit to constantly try new restaurants."

"Seems like a big coincidence," he said.

"It's a small city, when you get right down to it."

"That's what everyone says, but it's not true."

"Well, here I am. We don't need to analyze why. I just want to start over," I said.

"If you say so."

I took a long, slow sip of my drink.

He smirked. "You'll be ready for another before you know it."

"I can't stay long."

"Of course not." He smirked again.

"Why are you smirking?"

"Because you're playing some game. I don't know what it is, but it's a game. You're a piece of work, and I follow one principle."

"What's that?"

"When someone shows you who they are, believe them the first time."

I took a more cautious sip of my drink. "That's a good principle."

"I think so."

I took another healthy sip, leaving not very much in my glass. I needed a slight buzz of alcohol for my next move. I put down the glass and placed my hand on his wrist. "I am genuinely sorry that I was so argumentative. Rada, our server, reminded me of someone I used to know, and I overreacted."

I knew that most of what was in my mind never made its way to my face, but I wondered if that was the case in this situation. Surely James must pick up on something in my tone of voice. A hint of phoniness? A verbal smirk of my own?

Apparently not. Because I felt the muscle in his forearm relax slightly.

I was pleased with myself to know that nothing in my mind was leaking out anywhere that he could see it, even though his instinct was still telling him something wasn't right. The conflict between what he was experiencing and what his gut was shouting was driving him insane, I could see that clearly in his eyes.

"Another good principle is there's always an exception that proves the rule," I said. "Maybe this is it. I hope you'll give me a second chance. I wanted to invite you out to dinner. My treat. We won't have the pressure of needing to get back to the office. We can enjoy a bottle of wine and really get to know each other." I mentally thanked Hunter for putting that popular social terminology at the top of my thoughts.

James hadn't moved his arm away from beneath my hand. He studied my fingers and then returned his gaze to my face, letting his eyes meet mine. Slowly, I loosened my light grip on his arm and picked up my glass. I finished my drink.

"Sure. Why not?" He finished his drink and signaled for another.

I was glad to be leaving if he was already racing into his third shot in less than thirty minutes. "Saturday night?" I asked. "Seven-thirty?"

"On the weekend?"

I shrugged. "Diana really wants us to get along. We should work things out sooner rather than later, don't you think?"

"Yeah. Sure."

I suggested a steak house, to which he nodded somewhat eagerly. I ate my last olive, slid off the bar stool, and said goodbye.

I wasn't deluding myself that he believed I genuinely wanted to start over. I still had a steep uphill climb to make the dinner work out in a such way that I could get him to a hotel room. I also still had to figure out how I would change my appearance without arousing his suspicion, but that was a project for the following day. At least I'd made it over the first hurdle.

He'd said yes.

CHAPTER 51

There was so much work to do I was forced to make a list. When I was setting out to kill someone, I'd never written anything down. It made my skin crawl, thinking about putting even the smallest, most cryptic detail on the most unimportant-looking scrap of paper, and I didn't like that I was doing it now.

I chose the back of a receipt from a coffee shop. I wrote in black ink and used only what was needed, such as a D with a thick circle to indicate duct tape. Still, I didn't like it.

Everything on my list had been purchased before, but when something is done regularly, it's easy for the small details to slip out of your mind simply because they're familiar. And this time, those familiar things were buried under a deluge of the unfamiliar and the risky.

Friday morning I went into the office, then left for an afternoon photography session. On my way to the session, I texted the client and rescheduled for Monday, pleading a migraine. I set a reminder to send a similar message to Diana in a few hours. I wanted to be sure she didn't casually mention the headache to James before the end of the day.

I took Ubers rather than the subway to save time. My first stop was a hotel in midtown where I rented two rooms, forced to use a credit card, but I'd finally come up with a plan in which they would never connect James to either of those rooms. The first was a room on the third floor where I would take James, and the other was on the tenth floor. I spent the next three hours buying plastic bags, scissors, duct tape, and cleaning products. I usually had roofies on hand, and I'd brought them with me. My last stop was a sporting goods store where I used cash to purchase a surfboard cover, three duffel bags, and twelve oversized beach towels.

After thinking about the long, branching lists of ways things could go wrong if I tried to give Eileen and Ned a deep and undisturbed night's sleep with a roofie in their wine, I'd decided against it. I would simply tell Eileen I was spending a few nights at Hunter's place. I would have to end up sleeping at the hotel before I was ready to go back and face the rest of my life, which was the reason for the extra room. This would be an expensive job, but every other solution I'd considered presented unacceptable risks.

Trying to get an invite to James's apartment opened the door for him to tell Diana and a bunch of people I didn't even know existed that I was coming over. Returning to my apartment or even sleeping at Hunter's for real was too much exposure. I was always careful, always went above and beyond to make sure there were no mistakes. I wasn't going to let added expenses stop me from doing the same this time.

When all my supplies were properly stashed at the hotel, I went shopping for new clothes. Even that would be money down the drain because I wouldn't be able to keep any of my new things. I bought a red, calf-length dress and red high heels. I also bought a black dress with long sleeves and a zipper down the front.

I left the clothes in the tenth-story room at the hotel then took the elevator to the basement. I wandered around the service area for a few minutes, studying the layout. I was stopped by a housekeeper who told me I didn't belong there. I smiled and asked for extra towels, handing her a twenty. She piled them into my arms, smiled at the tip, and left me alone. After a few minutes, I found a closet that held the extra uniforms the bellhops wore. I grabbed the matching top and pants and folded them inside my stack of towels. I carried everything up to the third-floor room and put them on the closet shelf, tucking the uniform beneath the extra blanket and pillows.

The last thing I did before getting dressed was to make reservations at two restaurants. One for six-thirty, the other, at the restaurant where I'd arranged to meet James, for seven-thirty.

It was almost five o'clock when I took an Uber back to my apartment. I indulged in a longish shower, dried my hair, and packed a small suitcase with yoga pants, T-shirt, running shoes, and a navy hoodie. I threw in my brush and other hair stuff, makeup, and a few extra pairs of shoes. At five-thirty, I was eager for Eileen to get home so I could make my escape. If she didn't show up in the next five minutes, I would text her, but I preferred to do it face-to-face.

I wheeled my suitcase into the entryway, and just as I was about to send her a text, the door opened.

She looked at my bag, then at me, her face full of questions.

"I'm spending the weekend at Hunter's," I said.

Her mouth opened slightly as she stared at me. "That was … fast."

"I know." I grinned. "It's a little soon, but he wouldn't take no for an answer."

"That sounds aggressive."

"It's all good."

"I hope so. What are you going to do?"

"What do you think?" I grabbed the suitcase handle and extended it, stepping around her.

She laughed. "I meant, are you—"

"I know what you meant. Mostly just hang out. Go to a few restaurants. Probably go dancing."

"Maybe Ned and I will run into you."

Her eager smile sent a chill down my spine. It was something I'd never considered. With all my list-making and the two hotel rooms and the carefully planned restaurant reservations, the thought of seeing someone I knew had not entered my mind. Of course, it was unlikely, but once the thought was there, it was hard to be rid of it. "You never know, but probably not," I said.

"Have fun."

I left quickly. I did not like this. It was too much extra work, and too much extra planning and too many things to think about.

CHAPTER 52

$\mathcal{I}$n the tenth-floor room of the hotel, I changed into the red dress and high heels. I put on fresh makeup, curled my hair, and piled it lavishly on top of my head, with a few seductive strands hanging down around the sides of my face.

I took a cab to the restaurant where I'd made the six-thirty reservation for two. I was seated when I told the host my dinner date would be there any minute. I sipped the water that was offered. I declined a cocktail and a glass of wine. Starting at six-forty, I looked anxiously at the entrance every two or three minutes. In between door checks, I tapped my phone as if hoping for a message.

The server stopped by several more times, asking if I was sure I didn't want a glass of wine. I smiled sadly and said, *no thank you, I don't want to be rude.*

At seven, I stood, holding my chin up as if I were trying to look proud and unwilling to succumb to shame. I picked up my purse. The server rushed to my side.

"It looks like he's not coming," I said.

"May I call you a cab?" he asked.

I shook my head meekly. I scurried to the door and left. I walked a block and slid into my waiting Uber. Back at the hotel, I rode to the tenth floor and swapped the red dress for the black with black heels. I let my hair down, leaving it wavy and tousled. I was only five minutes late to the restaurant with the seven-thirty reservation. James was also late. I ordered a bottle of expensive cabernet and asked the server to open it so it could breathe.

I also needed to do some breathing.

Waiting at the decoy restaurant might have been unnecessary, but I thought it provided a bit of solid ground for my story if James had mentioned our dinner to Diana. Not that Diana would check up on me when I told her that story. Just in case the police had any interest in me when James turned up dead, I would be remembered as the woman who sat waiting for a man who never showed up. Just in case. In the extreme chance James had mentioned the name of the restaurant, both were steak houses. I figured I could convince Diana she had misremembered. She wouldn't believe me, but there would be a thread of doubt. And how could she prove me wrong? The police would have the slightly sad and dramatic story of the woman in the red dress.

When James arrived, we ordered an appetizer and toasted the success of Fly Higher. Then, I listened to him go on for nearly twenty minutes about the conferences where he'd given lectures on micro-expressions to ballrooms packed with fascinated colleagues. I couldn't fault him for giving me all that detail. I'd asked the question. I asked follow-up questions. Then, I asked more questions. I'd asked so many questions, I thought maybe I was going too far, pushing my interest to the point of a farce, but he was eager to talk and didn't appear to notice anything farcical about it.

By the time we were ready for our main courses, the wine bottle was nearly empty. Most of it had gone down his throat due to my careful and repeated refills of his glass with only occasional, very small dribbles into my own.

"Should we order another bottle?" I asked.

"That's a lot of wine."

"It is, but we're having this nice meal, and I hate to not have wine with our steaks."

"I feel the same."

I gave him a charming, thrilled smile. "I think we have so much more in common than we originally thought."

"Maybe we do, now that you've calmed down," he said.

"Then let's order another."

He signaled the server, and we placed our order.

I excused myself for the restroom, using the privacy of the stall to move the zipper on the front of my dress significantly lower. I arranged my hair over the front of my dress. I didn't want to end up calling too much attention to myself at this restaurant. Here, I wanted to be forgettable.

When I was settled again at our table, I raised my wine glass for another toast. "To good food, good wine, good company."

"Cheers," James said.

When our steaks came, I moved my hair away from the front of my dress. I saw his gaze flick quickly from his plate to my dress. He didn't look away. His neck grew slightly red before he finally forced his attention to his dinner plate.

"It's funny that we started off fighting with each other," I said. "It reminds me of those movies where a man and woman hate each other, then they suddenly realize the sparks are flying because they're secretly attracted to each other."

"Huh." He put a piece of steak in his mouth and chewed slowly, trying not to look at the pull for my zipper.

I could see from the way he chewed that he was feeling the wine, his mouth moving slowly and sloppily as if he wasn't aware of what he was doing. I poured wine into his glass.

When his attention turned to the tops of my breasts, it remained longer each time. He seemed less and less concerned that I might react badly, if he'd ever had a single concerning thought about a woman reacting badly to anything he did.

"That's an awfully inviting dress you have." He put down his knife and picked up his wineglass. "It's a little unclear what message it's trying to send."

"Do dresses send messages?" I asked.

He laughed. "You know what I mean."

I reminded myself to be agreeable at all times, and gave him an inviting smile.

"Why did you want to have dinner on the weekend? It seems ... out of bounds," he said.

I laughed. "Out of bounds?"

"Blurring the lines."

"Are there lines?"

He put down his glass with a slight thump. "Okay. Now I really ... I'm not sure ..."

I touched the zipper pull as if I might drag it lower.

"What's going on here?" he asked.

"We're having an amazing dinner. Fabulous wine. Getting to know each other."

"Are you trying to trap me, so you can report me to Diana for harassment?"

I laughed.

He looked triumphant, absolutely certain he'd found me out.

"We're not at work," I said. "*I* invited *you*. I'm the one who suggested the second bottle of wine. I don't see where any rational person could see even a hint of harassment in this scenario."

"Neither do I, but some people think everything is harassment now. If you smile at a girl, it's harassment. I've had the definite impression you're one of those types. It's almost like people don't want men and women to be together anymore."

"That would be awful."

"You're always giving the vibe of trying to get away from me. And why were you so pissed off about that waitress?"

"I felt sorry for her because she was trying to work, and you were distracting her. If she liked you, she couldn't be flirting with you while she was *working*. Right? That would have gotten her in trouble too. But let's forget about her, she's landed on her feet and moving on. We can too."

"Good." He picked up his utensils and began eating.

"I'm stuffed." I poured more wine into his glass. I filled my own and took a long swallow. I pushed my plate aside and leaned my arms on the table to show I wasn't trying to get away from him.

He stared at my breasts that were now spilling out slightly. "You're killing me. If we didn't work together …"

"What does that have to do with anything? We're peers. *I* don't report to you. And I'm not *your* boss."

"Hmm."

I smiled and sat up straight. I picked up my glass and gazed at him over the top.

"You're a complicated person," he said.

"Thank you."

He smirked. "What did you mean about movies where two people hate each other and then realize they're attracted?"

"It happens all the time. It's a cliché. But it's a cliché *because* it's so common. Love and hate are very close to each other—both are at the top of the passion scale, right?"

He narrowed his eyes slightly.

"I guess you're going to leave it to me to make the first move," I said.

He took a sip of wine.

I laughed. "You're still worried about harassment?"

He stared at my breasts, and I could see he was having trouble focusing on what I was saying. I could imagine the blood pounding in his ears, the wine blurring his thoughts and his reason.

"I needed a break from my annoying roommate," I said. "So I booked a hotel room in midtown for the night. How about an after-dinner drink in my room?"

I thought he might want a little more back and forth. I thought he might question my motives again. I thought he might want to finish his steak. I thought he would look shocked. I thought he might wonder if I was trying to trap him in some way he hadn't figured out. But I was wrong about all of that. He signaled for the waiter and handed over his credit card without asking for the bill or looking at me for a card to share the expense.

Before I knew it, we were in the back seat of an Uber, and then we were walking into the hotel lobby, and then we were in the elevator.

In the room, I used the bathroom, taking the opportunity to close my zipper slightly. I returned to the room and mixed martinis from the supplies I'd left earlier, including a roofie for James, using the elegant glasses I'd purchased when I was buying my dresses. I wanted it to seem high-class because I thought that would increase his trust in me, but maybe we were past that point. Maybe he no longer cared.

At my suggestion, he took off his shoes and sat in one of the armchairs. The simple suggestion to remove his shoes made him appear giddy with anticipation. I placed the drinks on the table between the armchairs and sat beside him. He reached across the space and ran his finger along the side of my breast. I squelched the revulsion in my stomach and made a toast to evenings with surprising outcomes. He liked that. Following my lead, he took several long swallows of his drink.

As we continued sipping our drinks, his gaze was fixed almost permanently on my zipper pull. I was sure he noticed it had changed position, but it seemed he didn't quite have the chutzpah to ask about it. Or maybe he was becoming aware of how much alcohol was circulating in his body, and he thought the fact that I was no longer seated at a table made it appear different. I'll never know what he was thinking, and not knowing will never trouble me.

It took less than thirty minutes for his speech, which was already rambling and somewhat incoherent, to develop a distinct slur. Only a few minutes after that, he put the glass down hard on the table, causing what little remained of the vodka and vermouth to splash out onto the back of his hand.

I was glad I didn't have to drink too much. I had a long night ahead of me.

Once he was passed out, I changed into comfortable clothes and put my dress and the martini glasses in a plastic bag in my suitcase for later disposal. I braided my hair and secured it inside a shower cap. Then I put on surgical gloves.

Next, I dragged him onto the floor. I placed a plastic garbage bag over his head, sealed it around his neck with duct tape, and took my phone into the bathroom. I closed the door and distracted myself with YouTube videos for an appropriate amount of time. When I returned, he was dead. I removed the bag and tape, keeping my eyes averted from his face as much as possible. I wadded up the tape and plastic and put it in a clean garbage bag.

It took me quite a while to stuff his body into the surfboard cover. It was tricky zipping it closed past his shoulders, but I finally managed to squish him into place. The duffel bags were already plump with their beach towel contents. I spent the next hour using cleanser to wipe down everything I'd touched in the room and bathroom. I used duct tape on every inch of the carpet and chairs to pick up any loose hairs or skin cells I'd shed with the effort of concealing his body. I changed into the bellhop uniform and my black running shoes. I removed the shower cap and gloves and used a hotel towel to open the door.

The hallway was empty. I took the elevator to the basement. At that time of night, the housekeeping supply room was dark and locked. But the luggage racks were lined up near the elevators. I wheeled one to the elevator and took it up to the third-floor room. I loaded James's body onto the cart, then piled the duffel bags on top of the lumpy-looking surfboard cover that looked sort of like a very large, collapsed duffel bag. My back was damp with sweat. I stood for a few moments to steady my breathing. When my heart rate had returned to normal, I wheeled the cart down the hall to the elevator and rode to the basement again, leaving the cart beside the others.

I returned to the room, finished cleaning, and left.

When I collapsed into bed on the tenth floor, it was three-fifteen in the morning.

I woke to my alarm at nine-thirty on Saturday. I went to the lobby and checked out of the third-floor room. Then I returned to the tenth floor and ordered an omelet, bacon, and toast from room service. I spent the rest of the day relaxing.

Apparently, James had been wrong. He was unable to recognize a killer, or a dangerous woman, for that matter.

I went to bed at nine that night, knowing the world was a better place, fairly certain I'd remembered every detail. For the first time ever, the police were not my biggest concern. Diana was.

CHAPTER 53

The only fallout from my lie to Eileen was that the moment I walked in the door on Sunday afternoon, she asked me when she was going to meet Hunter. I told her I needed to clear my head and was going for a run, which I did. When I returned from running, I faced the same question, asked with an even more enthusiastic smile.

I mirrored her grin and told her that I wasn't ready for that, it was too much *pressure*. But I would be sure to let her know. She rubbed my arm and told me to take my time.

On Monday morning, the first thing Diana said to me was—"How was your dinner with James?"

"I waited for half an hour," I said. "But he never showed."

"That doesn't sound like him. Did you text him? Or call?"

"No."

"Why not?"

This was one of the weak points in my plan, but there was no way to make it work, so I figured I would have to rely on Diana thinking I was rude or petty or whatever else she wanted to think. As long as she didn't think I was a killer.

"I assumed he would text if he couldn't make it or forgot the restaurant. I didn't hear from him, so I assumed something came up, or he changed his mind."

"You should never assume."

"Probably not, but I did. I invited him to dinner. I'm not going to beg. Getting along is a two-way street."

"It doesn't sound like you're trying as hard as you could," she said.

"I asked him to dinner. I told him I'd pay. I let him choose the restaurant. I got dressed up and waited for half an hour. I think that's quite a lot of effort."

"Maybe he didn't think your invitation sounded genuine."

"If you don't think I was genuine, ask him. It sounded like he was looking forward to it."

"You've been unbelievably petty," she said. "I think he's justifiably uncertain about your motives. You must realize that."

"Maybe. Once or twice, and so has he. But my invitation was absolutely genuine. If you don't trust me enough to believe that, then I have nothing else to say."

I could see her recoil ever so slightly. She finally sighed. "It's odd that he's not in yet." She glanced at her watch. "I'll call him now." She went into her office and closed the door.

Diana didn't call the police to report him missing until the following day. I think she wanted to, but had convinced herself there had to be a reasonable explanation.

It turned out by the time she did call, his body had already been found, but we didn't know that until much later. It was another day before the police came to the Fly Higher offices to talk to us about his work relationships and to ask when we'd last seen him, what his mood had been like, and whether we were aware of any issues in his personal life.

The police were almost gleeful when I mentioned the broken dinner date because it helped with their *timeline* to pinpoint when James might have gone missing. I liked knowing I could help the police, and it seemed to divert Diana's attention.

However, her attention would not be diverted permanently. I expected that over the coming weeks, we would hear from the police again. Even if we didn't, she would not allow the bizarre circumstances of her friend and employee's murder to be written off as one of those things that can never be explained. It would nag at her. That nagging would make her continue to sift through the pieces of his life that she knew about, looking for clues.

She would want to talk about it, and my animosity toward him would return to her thoughts and unsettle her. But I was confident I would be able to strike the right note in my responses. Confident that eventually, over time, she would have to choose to let it go, because the only alternative would be to drive herself insane. She wouldn't want that, so she *would* let it go. Eventually.

Since James wasn't there to analyze the micro-expressions in the photographs from Pauline's inspirational talk to the models she represented, Diana took that on herself. Because she relished the team atmosphere of brainstorming about our clients, she invited me to share my thoughts. But instead of actually wanting to hear my thoughts, she mostly wanted to review every comment James had made on previous photos I'd taken of Pauline. She wanted to marvel over his insight into human nature. She wanted to discuss his profound sensitivity and awareness of every crease and muscle shift in the human face. She wanted to be sure that her coaching to Pauline reflected the things James had determined about the state of her career and her innermost, unrecognized desires and feelings.

She didn't want to *brainstorm*. She wanted me to agree with what James had said. She wanted me to be the echo chamber for her belief that his recommendations and perceptions were brilliant and accurate.

I could do that.

CHAPTER 54

*I*ronically, two weeks after I killed James, Eileen and Ned went away for the weekend to a B&B in Vermont. I wished they'd told me. At the same time, maybe I couldn't have waited that long.

Alone in the apartment, I was making a roast beef sandwich on dark rye bread, debating my choice of bread the moment I'd smeared mayo across one slice and stone ground mustard on the other. Sourdough might have been a better choice with roast beef.

The buzzer went off announcing someone was in our lobby wanting to come up. I answered and heard Tess's voice.

"Hey, it's me. Tess. Sorry for the unannounced visit. Can I come up?"

When she knocked on the apartment door a few minutes later, I opened it ready to offer her a sandwich. Before I could speak, I was interrupted by the raucous voice of her cockatoo.

G'day. Chardonnay time!

I laughed, hearing that he still liked to announce it was time for a glass of wine, even when it wasn't. I wasn't surprised to hear he'd picked up a piece of Aussie slang.

I put my face close to the cage. "Hello, Damien. I didn't know you were in New York."

He laughed with that slightly mocking tone he had.

That bird. It always seemed as if it were possible to carry on a meaningful conversation with him. It was an eery sensation, with one part of my mind insisting he was simply repeating learned phrases, while another part of me was stunned that he seemed to respond to specific things I said.

Tess walked inside and placed his travel cage on the floor of the entryway.

"Why did you bring Damien?"

"I just picked him up from quarantine."

"And you came directly here?"

"I know how much you like him, and it's been ages since you've seen him."

It had been ages, and he was entertaining, but it was strange that she was so eager to organize a play date for us, or whatever she wanted to call it. "Do you want a roast beef sandwich?"

"Sure."

Delicious mango!

I shivered slightly as he once again proved he seemed to know at least the context of what we were saying. I got busy putting together another sandwich, adding thinly sliced onion and dill pickles, tomatoes and alfalfa sprouts. I pulled out two bottles of lime-flavored sparkling water and filled two glasses with ice. We sat at the kitchen table. Tess talked about her wedding plans, although they were still rather vague at the moment. The wedding would take place on this marvelous vineyard she and Marcus were purchasing, but had not yet made an offer on. She hadn't even seen it except in photographs, so the plans mostly revolved around the style of dress she wanted, the food, and music.

After we ate, she wanted a tour of my apartment, which took approximately ninety seconds.

"It's really nice," she said. "You have great taste, but I already knew that."

"A lot of it's Eileen."

"I'm a little shocked you have a roommate, to be honest."

"So am I, to be honest."

She laughed.

We talked about roommates, and she talked about marriage. The entire time, Damien nibbled on sunflower seeds, since there was no mango, and muttered to himself. Every so often, I picked up a coherent word.

"Barry's already in California," Tess said. "He's really anxious for me to see the vineyard."

"I still can't imagine you running a vineyard. Where do you even start?"

"There are people who know what to do. It's not like I have to pick the grapes myself."

I laughed. "I know that, but it's so ... different."

"I don't want to do the same thing my whole life. I started looking around at people who are ten or fifteen years older than I am, and it looks like they're on a speeding train toward retirement, making short little stops to take bucket list trips, but never really changing their lives much at all. Living in the same place with their career set in stone, locked into—"

"Married to one guy forever."

"That's different. You can have wild adventures together."

"If you have money."

"I know I'm lucky. I'm fully aware. But since I am lucky, and have worked hard, by the way, I want to make the most of the opportunities I have."

She made me wonder if my life wasn't quite as free and full of choices as I'd imagined, drifting from one situation to the next. Maybe it was growing stale. I might be drifting right into a concrete wall. Maybe there was something to be said for planning things out a bit, planning changes.

Chardonnay time! Damien shouted.

Tess laughed. "Should we?"

"Sure." I went to the wine cooler Eileen had purchased the weekend I was busy with James. It was well stocked with reds and whites and a few bottles of champagne. I pulled out a Chardonnay. It wasn't quite as chilled as it would be in the fridge, but cool enough to do it justice. I opened it and poured some for each of us. I carried the glasses to the living room.

Chardonnay time. Damien's tone was calmer as if he were relieved to see we'd followed his directive. The yellow crown on top of his head was relaxed slightly, making him look less frantic than he had when he'd first arrived.

"He seems content here," Tess said.

It should have been obvious the moment she walked in with him, but I'd been startled by his presence, so I hadn't thought past her explanation of quarantine. Now it was obvious that she had a reason for putting him in an Uber and bringing him directly to my apartment. And it wasn't simply that the hotel where she was staying wouldn't allow him.

"I have a favor to ask." She took a sip of wine. "It's huge, I know, but I also know how you adore him."

That comment was going a long way in projecting her own feelings onto me. I was charmed by Damien, entertained by him, slightly unsettled by him. But I would never say I adored him. It wasn't a word I used for myself.

"He's been through so much, and I don't know what my immediate situation will be in California. Not for a few weeks. And I was hoping he could stay with you."

I took a sip of wine.

Dangerous woman, Damien said, using a slight monotone, which wasn't like him.

I stared at him. How did he know? *Did* he know? Of course, he didn't *know*. He was a bird. A bird does not possess that kind of intelligence. They may remember faces and locations. They may be able to do simple tasks, but they do not have intuition, and they do not understand the nature of consciousness. *Do* they?

That's what we of reportedly higher intelligence believe. And yet, the way he was looking at me ... I took a long swallow of wine.

I knew with every cell in my brain that he did not know. It was a phrase he'd learned, and he repeated it at random. It had nothing to do with me whatsoever.

"Would you?" Tess asked.

"I don't know if the apartment—"

"If they require a deposit, I'll pay it, of course. But for a few weeks, they probably wouldn't even know."

"Eileen ..." I hesitated. It wasn't just Eileen. This would fence me in even more. Responsibility for a large bird? It was like having a child. How could I possibly escape for any length of time? Although was that really necessary in the next few weeks?

Eileen might hate him. Ned would definitely be unsettled by him. Even if Damien never said a word, Ned would be uncomfortable with a large cockatoo in the living room. Maybe he would come over less frequently. Damien might change the whole dynamic in our apartment. He might add a bit of fun.

"Why not. But there's obviously no space for him to have his own room like he's used to."

"I was going to buy a much larger cage. He'll be okay with that for a while, as long as he gets time outside of it every day."

I pictured bird droppings on Ned's stocking feet. I smiled.

"Why are you smiling?" She grinned. "You're excited, aren't you? I knew you were crazy about him."

"If it doesn't work out, you have to come back and get him."

"Absolutely." She sipped her wine. "But I can't imagine why it wouldn't work out."

I couldn't think of a reason, although I did think about his eating schedule and how it would interfere with my effort to disrupt the routine with Eileen. But I also thought about how eager she was to strengthen our connection. Surely she wouldn't mind giving him

CATHRYN GRANT

some fruit and seeds for his evening meal a few times a week. I took a sip of wine and smiled to myself, imagining Ned's introduction to Damien.

Damien's crown rose straight up. *Dangerous woman!* His crown slowly returned to a position indicating more calm. *Delicious mango. Delicious mango. Dangerous woman.*

Tess went into the kitchen for more wine. I stared at Damien, and he stared back. He dipped his upper body toward me, and I raised my glass to him.

CHAPTER 55

*D*amien was settled into his new five-foot-high, three-by-four-foot cage. He didn't look particularly thrilled. His crown stood at a ninety-degree angle, and his eyes had a slight glare to them, but perhaps I was projecting a microexpression that wasn't there.

When she brought the cage, Tess had also handed over a bag filled with mangos, an enormous package of raw sunflower seeds, pellets made from a variety of seeds to be sure he got a good mix instead of picking out his favorites, a container of strawberries, and several apples.

His parting words to Tess were, *bad girl*, but the minute she was out the door, he began shouting *wine country!* I texted a recording of that to her. She replied with about twenty happy emojis, so I suppose it was hard for her to leave him, and she took his new mantra to mean he was wishing her well.

I imagined that when that bird settled in California, he would have a palatial home. She'd talked about building an aviary for him and wondered if it would be possible to introduce a few companions into his environment. I wondered what the responsibilities of a child, a vintner, and an aviary filled with exotic birds would do to the thrilling, constantly changing, unpredictable life she was mapping out in her imagination. But maybe those few large changes would be enough for her.

After Damien had something to eat, I waited an appropriate amount of time for him to relieve himself and then let him out of the cage. He strutted around the living room, repeating his favorite phrases, mostly ignoring me. I mostly ignored him as well, spending the time playing a game on my tablet, drinking sparkling water, and thinking that I wanted to go for a run but knowing I couldn't leave him alone while he was still getting acclimated.

At least I had his introduction to Ned and Eileen to look forward to. Still, my muscles and nerves were jumpy. I got my yoga mat from my bedroom, rolled it out in the living room, and spent twenty minutes doing some of the most challenging poses I could think of. It helped, but it also involved a lot of falling. The bird kept walking around me, coming quite close, twisting his head upside down and peering up at me, his face and that deadly-looking beak inches from mine.

An hour later, when Damien was back in his cage, Eileen entered the apartment. Before she even saw him, Damien greeted her enthusiastically. *Bad girl! G'Day!*

I laughed.

"What is *that*?"

Ned was close behind her. He pulled their suitcases inside and closed the door.

G'day! G'day! G'day!

Ned let go of the suitcase handles and walked directly to the cage, almost as if he'd known it would be there. He studied Damien for several seconds. "I sure hope this doesn't belong to you. Are you aware you have to disclose it on your lease if you're going to have a pet? And the—"

"He's not mine. I'm bird sitting."

Ned was still staring at Damien, who was staring back at him with equal interest. "Without checking first?"

"It's only for a few weeks."

"A few *weeks?*" Eileen said. "I don't know. He's so ... big. And the mess. Does it smell?" She sniffed several times, turning her head from side to side, raising her face toward the ceiling as if she was sure to detect something if she tried long enough.

"Not if I keep his cage clean."

"I wish you'd asked. I don't want to lose our lease," she said.

"And you could." Ned turned. "This is so thoughtless ... and selfish."

"Selfish? I'm helping a friend."

"Your first responsibility is to Eileen," he said.

"It's just a bird. It's only for a few weeks. If you want to ask the property manager and pay the deposit for a pet, Tess is happy to cover it."

"I don't know if they allow exotic birds," Eileen said. "He seems like he could be loud."

As if to make my life more difficult, Damien let out a screech that made Eileen shudder. It was rare for him to do that. Tess had told me when I first met Damien that they shrieked if they were bored. She kept him well-supplied with toys and tried to make getting his food challenging as often as possible, hiding it so he had to hunt, although when she was in a hurry, it was served like he was sitting down to dine in a restaurant.

"The neighbors are going to hear that," Eileen said.

"He rarely squawks. He might be picking up on your antagonism," I said.

Eileen flopped on the couch. "I really wish you'd asked. Is there any way she can find someone else? If we lose our lease ..."

"They mostly squawk like that in the wild. That's how they communicate. It won't be a problem." I didn't mention the boredom. They would jump all over that. Maybe Damien and I were cut from the same cloth because I had the same desire to shriek when I was bored. "You'll get to like him. He's very funny."

Dangerous woman, Damien said. *Delicious mango.*

"How is that funny?" Ned asked. "He's just repeating phrases by rote."

I shrugged. "I think he's entertaining."

"He shouldn't be caged."

"Maybe not. But in Australia, I saw wild cockatoos that were sick. They couldn't stand their ground with the others when they were getting food, so there are tradeoffs."

"Are there?" He glared at the bird.

Tradeoffs, Damien said. *Tradeoffs*.

I saw a smirk on Ned's face that he quickly got rid of. I hoped Damien had some more choice words for Ned in the future. If I couldn't put him in his place, maybe the bird would do it for me.

CHAPTER 56

 ortland, Oregon

* * *

My sister will always be in the shadows of my life. She's part of me. I'll never stop thinking about her and dreaming about her. Even though she never became an adult, never even a schoolgirl or a teenager, that doesn't stop me from imagining her life continuing on in a spectacular way. In my mind, I give her all kinds of fabulous experiences that make her smile and laugh.

I know they're not real. And I'm not so arrogant to think it means anything, or to pretend I know how things might have turned out for her. I don't know what she would have liked or chosen for her life. All I know is that it would have been amazing.

There were pictures of her on the walls of our house, even though no one talked about her much. It truly was better that way— the silence that surrounded her memory. Maybe the real her was more complete inside our heads, without trying to explain her. Maybe telling stories about her, or wondering out loud what she might be doing at any point in time, or saying anything at all about her would have shaped her into something small and imperfect—a shadow of who she really was.

The family portraits looked damaged when there were only six of us in the frame instead of seven, but my parents kept making us pose for them every single year. They finally gave up when I was sixteen.

Mr. Caruthers died of a heart attack when he was fifty-two.

Since he remained a church elder until the day he keeled over, I don't think anyone ever found out he liked to sneak sips of alcohol. If Lexy had given that whisky cork to anyone at our church and told them where she found it, he would have been shamed and shunned.

I desperately wish I could have rid the earth of him myself, but I never had the opportunity.

If anyone knew what I do in my spare time now, they might try to explain it as some sort of vengeance worked out over and over. They might suggest I see Mr. Caruthers in every monstrous man, my little sister in every woman who is dominated and mistreated and abused by a misogynistic male.

Maybe they would be right.

But they'll never find out what I do, so it's not worth considering.

Explaining why any of us do what we do isn't so simple.

I was different from the day I was born. My parents recognized that. They didn't think twice about taking my middle name and giving it to my sister. In the end, it was the best thing they ever did. I was glad she could have it, and I'm glad she has it now. I'm glad her tombstone says *Alexandra Laura Mallory* because it means we're connected in life and in death.

Or, it could mean nothing except that my parents had incredibly bizarre ideas and habits. I prefer to think it means Lexy and I are connected.

My father spent the rest of my childhood trying to make me into the godly female he'd decided it was his job to create. As if he thought he was Pygmalion and he could sculpt a false woman in his image or whatever nonsense he believes. His relentless, daily battle to break me into a thousand pieces didn't fracture a single part of me. I also failed to break him. We both remained standing at the end, bloody and certain we were the victor.

I suppose that story is not yet finished.

This is why I have two passports.

My parents took away Lexy's bed, but in their grief, they forgot about her passport. I took that for myself.

When I was twelve, without even knowing myself why I wanted it, I convinced my oldest brother, Eric, to help me renew it. I used a photograph of myself in which I'd cut thick bangs that covered my eyebrows. My parents hated those bangs and made me use hairclips to sweep them off my face until they grew out, but not before I'd asked Eric to take me to get the passport picture taken. Eric thought I was weird. He worried I was exhibiting some sort of deeply repressed grief. But he did it anyway because I pestered him relentlessly for weeks. I told him it made me feel as if Lexy would be able to travel with me anywhere I went.

Later, the two documents felt like they added an extra layer of protection around me, like a mother swaddling her infant tightly to make the child feel safe. I've never used the other passport, and I honestly am not sure where I got the idea that having two made me safer. The names are essentially the same.

However, there are two documents, with two different numbers, and I'm almost certain they track people via the number more than the name. Hopefully, my belief is accurate on this point. It might give me a brief window of safety if I ever need to leave the country permanently, although it wouldn't be an entirely new identity.

I've come to know there really is no security at all. Still, I like having two passports.

And I like knowing Lexy's cells are indeed living inside my body.

CHAPTER 57

*N*ew York

* * *

After their romantic weekend in Vermont, it seemed as if Ned came to dinner every single night of the week. It probably wasn't every night, because I wasn't there every night, but when I was, so was he. I suppose Eileen wanted the company, and since she couldn't count on me, she opened the door and pulled out a chair at the table for him. It was also possible I hadn't considered how accustomed she'd become to constant companionship after living with her mother for most of her adult life. Eileen rarely talked about her mother, knowing what I thought of Stephanie, but she'd only been gone a few months. I'd never stopped to consider that Eileen's instability might have been the result of Stephanie's death. I realized I was a little obtuse for not having seen that earlier.

Maybe the trauma of how Stephanie had ended her life had increased Eileen's neediness. Was it possible, a tiny, barely noticed part of Eileen believed that I might have pushed Stephanie so hard, she broke? Did Eileen blame me on some level she wasn't aware of?

So when Ned started again on his quest to find out more about me, I wondered whether she was actually completely okay with his intrusive questions and suspicious nature. Maybe she tried to smooth it over with me by saying she didn't want to believe she had to watch her back, but maybe the truth was she was a little bit afraid of me.

Ned handed me the salad bowl. "You're really into that bird. I wouldn't have guessed that."

"I think he's clever."

"You seem to like him more than you like people."

"He's more intelligent than some people I've known, that's for sure."

"That's not accurate."

"How would you know?"

"It's biologically impossible for a bird to have a higher IQ than a human being."

"If you say so."

"I don't say so, science does."

I placed my napkin on my lap and picked up my fork. I eyed the back of his hand, too close to my plate for my comfort. I tried to imagine what would happen if I stabbed my fork into his hand.

"You act as if he understands you," he said.

"Maybe he does."

"I wonder if you talk to him when we're not around. If you do, you'd better be careful. He might spill your secrets."

"We have an understanding." I stabbed half a grape tomato and a slice of red onion. I put my fork into my mouth with a sense of having avoided an unplanned moment of violence.

Eileen laughed. "He repeats everything."

Ned coughed slightly and leaned back in his chair. "I think I should clear the air about something."

I could feel the intensity in his words, and I braced myself, my mind turning over the possibilities of where he was headed—making a wild accusation that Hunter was a figment of my imagination, embarrassing Eileen again with the suggestion I might creep into her bedroom when they were having sex, or perhaps insisting Damien move out. Maybe something I couldn't foresee. Some complaint Eileen didn't have the courage to confront me about, or something entirely out of left field.

"I know Eileen was very upset when I didn't show up for our date a few weeks ago."

That hadn't been on my list. But it seemed like a topic for clearing the air with Eileen, not me.

"I've sensed that you're holding that incident against me."

"That's between you and Eileen," I said.

"I wasn't completely truthful about what happened that evening. I ran into your old neighbor."

My muscles froze as Victoria flashed through my mind. Rafe. Another unsolved murder in New York City. Another tidy, antiseptically clean murder, but still ...

"You two had a weird relationship. He said all you wanted was sex."

Kent. I was relieved. And I should have realized Ned wouldn't have known Victoria. A chance meeting that allowed him to uncover that she used to live across the hall from me would have been quite long and involved and filled with unexpected turns. But Kent. I thought I'd left him far behind. I'd left my apartment and moved in with Eileen to be rid of him. I'd given up my solitude to be rid of him. How on earth ...

"It wasn't entirely casual, in case you're wondering how I could possibly run into your old neighbor. Rather your old boyfriend, if you could even call him that, which I would not. Drinking, food, and sex. Lots of it, according to Kent."

"He was happy. I was happy."

"Was he? Did you ever ask him?"

"How is this any of your business?" I asked.

"He had an interesting perspective on you, that's all I'm saying.

We had quite a long talk, and it was so absorbing, I honestly lost complete track of the time and forgot about my plans with Eileen."

"You don't need to explain it to me," I said.

"You seemed to think my forgetting wasn't genuine and interpreted that to mean I don't love her."

"As I already said, it's between you and Eileen. It has nothing to do with me." I wanted to know what Kent had said. I couldn't imagine he had anything that interesting to reveal about my personality or any important details of my life. But had all the seemingly innocuous but relentless questions Kent had asked me about Rafe and Victoria come up when he was talking to Ned? Had he wondered out loud to Ned about my relationship with them? Had Kent's curiosity over Rafe's abrupt departure come up? That would not be good.

It seemed as if Ned was focused on my *relationship* with Kent because it didn't meet his approval. But what if it wasn't that at all? There was no way to find out what they'd talked about without letting Ned see that I was concerned, that I had things I didn't want him to be curious about.

"Don't you want to know what we talked about?"

"No."

"That's very unusual. I don't think I know a single person who wouldn't be curious what their ex had to say about them."

"I would say it's pathetic to care what your ex says about you. It's not a good idea to be invested in what anyone says about you. That can make you into an avatar."

"I have no idea what you're talking about," he said. "How does curiosity about the impression you make turn you into an avatar?"

"Choosing bits and pieces to create a self based on suggestions offered up by others. All you end up with is a cartoon figure."

"That's really interesting," Eileen said.

Ned picked up a chicken drumstick and peeled off the skin with his teeth. "It's a little twisted."

"It's not," Eileen said. "It makes sense."

"Well, I think the air is as clear as it's going to get." I refilled my wineglass. "Would anyone like more?" I raised the bottle over the center of the table. They both nodded, and I refilled their glasses.

"His parting words were the most interesting," he said.

I sipped my wine.

"You're not even curious about that?"

"No."

"I think you're lying."

"Why do you think that?"

"Because all women care what guys think about them. Especially the guys they had relationships with."

I took another sip of wine. I wanted him to give me useful information, but I wasn't hopeful. I also knew that my answer wasn't a lie. I wasn't curious because I cared what Kent thought about me. I was only curious about one thing—I wanted to know if there was anyone, anywhere on the planet, that thought I had an unexplained interaction with a dead man. That was my only concern.

"It turns out my instinct about you was spot-on, Alexandra." He put his hand on Eileen's wrist. "You're a fascinating and entertaining person, and I imagine you're a fabulous roommate in some ways. If someone wants to party, go shopping, or find the best restaurants and clubs. I can see why Eileen is drawn to you."

I glanced at Eileen to see how she was taking his condescension. She didn't look pleased, but she said nothing.

"Kent thought you were someone around whom it was a good idea to watch my back. He agreed you have a stealthy quality about you."

I took a sip of wine.

"Isn't that fascinating? He repeated exactly what I suggested to Eileen."

"It's really rude," Eileen said.

"He repeated what I said just like that parrot."

"He's a cockatoo," I said.

"Anyway ..." Ned raised his glass. "Cheers. Just know I'll be keeping my eye on you."

It made me wonder if he was going to move in, or install cameras. Obviously, he couldn't keep an eye on me twenty-four-seven. But I felt a tightness in my chest that was unfamiliar and unpleasant.

CHAPTER 58

I escaped the dinner table and Ned by clearing the dishes and putting the leftovers into storage containers and organizing them inside our refrigerator. I put more distance by retreating to the living room with a bowl of pellets for Damien. I hid them in various spots around the room and let him out of his cage. He walked around hunting for food, chortling each time he found a pellet.

Eileen and Ned continued drinking wine at the table. About twenty minutes later, Eileen drifted into the living room. She gave me a droopy-eyed look. "I have a headache. I'm going to bed." Without waiting for a response, she disappeared around the corner toward her bedroom.

Before Damien had finished locating all the hidden seed pellets, Ned appeared with two martinis.

He settled beside me on the couch and placed the drinks on the table. "Why don't you put the bird in the cage and have a drink with me."

"He's happy hunting for his food."

"It's not good to have him walking around. You never know when he might shit on the carpet."

"He hasn't yet, and if he does, I'll clean it up."

"That's not really the same as a clean carpet, is it?"

"He hasn't done it, and I think it will be fine."

He picked up his drink and took a sip. "You're living with the love of my life. You have access to her every hour of the day and night. In some ways, you have access to her money, which is not insignificant. And—"

"I do not have access to her money."

"Please let me finish. From a manipulation perspective, you do. I think it's time for the gloves to come off between you and me. Here's your chance to give me a different story than what Kent told me."

"I'm Eileen's roommate. If she has any questions, she can ask me."

"I think we both know that Eileen is too trusting."

Damien peered behind the end table. *Delicious mango.*

"Maybe you should keep the bird in your room. He's really distracting."

"Eileen doesn't seem to mind. She likes him as much as I do."

"Eileen is too polite."

I was tempted to leave the martini untouched, but I was also tempted to drink it. I yielded to the latter temptation.

"I have nothing to tell you." I moved the stir stick around the glass slowly, as if sweeping the sides. "Like I said, if Eileen has any questions, she can ask. She's an adult woman. She doesn't need you to take care of her."

"We're a couple. Partners look out for each other."

"It sounds to me like you're trying to create a rift between us."

"How would I do that? Unless you have something to hide, something about your life that could hurt her, or impact her life in a negative way."

I began sipping my drink at a speed that wasn't wise. If he thought he was going to pressure me into telling him stories about myself or explaining a single thing about my life, he hadn't assessed me well at all.

"I'm not going to relax until I find out what you're up to," he said.

"I'm not up to anything, Ned. Eileen and I get along well, and we decided to share an apartment. That's it. There's no deep secret to find out, nothing to watch her back about. Everything is right on the surface."

That's it, Damien said. *That's it.*

"That is a lie."

I took a long, heady swallow of my drink. I placed the glass on the table, pulled out the stir stick, and ate both—he had only provided two—olives at once. I chewed carefully and returned the stick to the glass. "Thanks for the drink. I've had enough."

I stood and went to where Damien was perched on a small table, leaning sideways to check out his reflection in the dark TV screen. I held out my hand for him to climb onto my forearm. He did it willingly, and I carried him to the cage and placed him inside.

Dangerous woman, he said.

"Indeed," I whispered.

Without turning to face Ned, I sighed. "Headaches must be going around. I have one now too. I'm going to bed." I went into my room. I left the door cracked open because I was suddenly aware that I didn't want to leave Ned alone and out of earshot with Damien. I did not trust that man at all.

CHAPTER 59

I'd never felt so crowded in my life. Everyone was asking questions. Even the guy who I was so taken with I felt as if I had a physical addiction to his essence, was a little too curious.

I was a butterfly stuck to a board with a thin, sharp pin.

I was a cockatoo in a brass cage, who, even in an aviary, would feel confined.

As often as I combed through the memories of each thing I'd done the night I killed James, I couldn't identify a single mistake. My only mistake happened in the weeks before, when I exposed my obvious dislike of him, but that wasn't a crime. Fallon didn't like him either. Rada had a lot more reason to kill him than I had. Hopefully, I hadn't inadvertently put her under the spotlight.

I was certain no one had seen me who might identify me with either Rafe or James. I knew that when Tess told me not to kill James, she was joking. I knew that Diana's past with James wasn't passionate enough to drive her on a relentless hunt for his killer. I knew there wasn't a single hair or skin cell left behind in any of the hotel rooms. Even if I *had* been less than absolutely meticulous with my cleaning, my DNA was not in any database. Yet.

Of course, if one of my brothers eventually decided they wanted to find out about our family heritage, it could become a big problem. So far, they all insisted they had zero interest.

Still. There was a sense of claustrophobia even in my spacious, beautifully furnished apartment. It was the claustrophobia of too many people with just a little too much interest in me, a few too many questions, and a growing quantity of knowledge about my life.

Perhaps the best way to escape the claustrophobia was to leave New York. Or, more importantly, to make a plan for my future. I wanted more freedom. I wanted more money. I wanted a lot more of both, and they're so intertwined.

The problem was, I also wanted more Hunter.

A NOTE FROM CATHRYN

When I first started writing about Alexandra Mallory, I thought she would be a character threatened by a strange roommate in a stand-alone psychological thriller—The Woman In the Mirror. Within a few chapters of starting that novel, Alex took on a life of her own. Her voice came into my head in a way I had never experienced with other characters. By the time I finished writing that book, I knew she would have a few more stories ... and here we are, with the thirteenth book and no end in sight. Yet.

The response to this woman with clear sociopathic tendencies and deeply held opinions on everything from olives to the place of religion in the world has overwhelmed me at times. Readers have told me she scares them, they see a small pieces of themselves in her, and they've felt empowered by her. The greatest thrill for me is that I've experienced all of those reactions myself.

There are no words to express the gratitude I feel in knowing people enjoy reading my books and find a few hours of escape through the stories I tell. Knowing that you've enjoyed this character through so many books is humbling and an honor that I don't take lightly.

Thank you so much for reading. It means the world to me.

ABOUT THE AUTHOR

Cathryn is the author of over thirty psychological suspense novels, including the ALEXANDRA MALLORY series featuring a sociopath you can't help but love. Readers have called the series "addictive".

The things that torment us in real life—obsession and revenge, guilt and envy and longing—are endlessly fascinating in fiction and she never grows tired of writing stories about characters struggling to overcome the worst.

Cathryn also writes ghost stories because who knows what lies beyond our senses—The Haunted Ship Trilogy and the Madison Keith series of novellas.

When she's not writing, she's usually reading, walking on the beach, or playing golf, going way out of her way to avoid hitting her ball in the sand or the water. She lives on the Central California Coast with her husband and her cat, Cleopatra.

You can get in touch with her by email, find her social media links, or sign up for her monthly newsletter at cathryngrant.-com/contact. As a thank you for signing up, you'll receive a free short story about Alexandra Mallory.